CW01650092

Small, brown-haired and ordinary looking was how Student Nurse Cherry Langton thought of herself. So why on earth did the extraordinarily attractive new eye consultant Mr Ashley Treneager pluck her off the wards and demand her company?

Barbara Perkins began writing when her children were small as a way of combining her nursing training with an earlier ambition to be a writer. The children are grown up now but Barbara still writes Doctor-Nurse romances because, she says, hospitals are fascinating worlds of their own, and where else would you find all the ingredients of drama under one roof? Modern nursing information comes from friends still in the profession and from a future daughter-in-law who has usefully just completed RGN training. Barbara lives near the sea in Kent.

A NURSE'S PLACE

BY

BARBARA PERKINS

MILLS & BOON LIMITED
15–16 BROOK'S MEWS
LONDON W1A 1DR

All the characters in this book have no existence outside the imagination of the Author, and have no relation whatsoever to anyone bearing the same name or names. They are not even distantly inspired by any individual known or unknown to the Author, and all the incidents are pure invention.

The text of this publication or any part therefore may not be reproduced or transmitted in any form or by any means, electronic or mechanical, including photocopying, recording, storage in an information retrieval system, or otherwise, without the written permission of the publisher.

This book is sold subject to the condition that it shall not, by way of trade or otherwise, be lent, resold, hired out or otherwise circulated without the prior consent of the publisher in any form of binding or cover other than that in which it is published and without a similar condition including this condition being imposed on the subsequent purchaser.

First published in Great Britain 1985
by Mills & Boon Limited

© Barbara Perkins 1985

Australian copyright 1985
Philippine copyright 1985

ISBN 0 263 75271 2

Set in 9½ on 10 pt Linotron Times
03–1285–65,800

Photoset by Rowland Phototypesetting Limited
Bury St Edmunds, Suffolk
Made and printed in Great Britain by
Richard Clay (The Chaucer Press) Limited
Bungay, Suffolk

CHAPTER ONE

'NURSE LANGTON,' Sister said drily, 'I suppose you *are* still with us?'

'Yes, Sister—sorry, Sister,' Cherry said hastily. Looking round to see sympathetic smiles, she knew she must have been asked a question, and that Sister Potter's reproving glare was for her own dreamy gaze through the window.

'You've always assured me that you *do* want to be a nurse, Nurse Langton,' the tutor said sarcastically. 'Perhaps I should remind you that it requires listening to lectures as well as working on the wards!'

'Yes, Sister,' Cherry murmured again. She knew apprehensively that if Sister had read her ward reports, she would now make a meal out of a general public criticism of the way a first-year nurse should behave. It was a surprise as well as a relief when the tutor turned her attention back to the whole class, asking someone else to volunteer to describe the function of a group of muscles known as the Bundle of Hiss.

Cherry, trying to look alert, made an effort not to feel despairing. To judge by the number of hands which went up, everyone else seemed to be able to concentrate, even after a night duty. Northborough Royal Hospital made a habit of slotting in compulsory lectures from time to time, to keep theory up with practice. It was considered an honour to be accepted to train at the Royal anyway.

Stealing a glance outside under her lashes as her mind began to slip again, Cherry knew she could hardly have told Sister Potter that her attention had been distracted by watching an extraordinarily elegant man emerging from an extraordinarily elegant car out there in the car park. He was gone now, but she could remember very clearly what he had looked like. His height would have made him noticeable at any time, particularly when accentuated by a dark suit of obviously expensive cut, and even from a distance it was possible to see that he had a splendidly aquiline profile. What really completed the picture, though, was a white flash clearly visible at the centre front of his beautifully-cut black hair, looking just as if *other* people might go grey in patches or stripes or even all over, but the really smart way to approach middle age was to go pure white in just one place.

It was hardly surprising, after all that, to see that the car he was getting out of was a Rolls.

Her attention came back to the lecture with a jerk as everyone else began chanting the blood vessels that joined the heart. Northborough's teaching methods were scarcely modern, Cherry thought absently, but that suited her fine, because she actually did remember things better if she chanted them. Since she had taken the precaution this time of fixing a wide-open gaze on Sister's face before her thoughts had drifted, she didn't really need that warning hack on the ankle from Lisa sitting beside her.

'And that will do for this morning, nurses.' The tutor's hand was raised in admonition as everyone began to shuffle their feet. 'While I know you want to make straight for your beds, I *require* all of you to go out and take a quick walk round the grounds first. You need fresh air as much as you need sleep. After that, I would advise a milky drink, which you can either buy in the canteen or make for yourselves in the Night Nurses' Home. Good morning, nurses!'

'Good morning, Sister Potter,' they chorussed—sounding for all the world like an obedient junior school class, Cherry thought with amusement. She was pulled up short as the tutor paused beside her in the very process of sweeping out of the room.

'*You* look particularly tired, Nurse Langton,' she said admonitarily. 'Mind you get your fresh air, now!' Then she turned away and was gone.

'My goodness, sympathy!' Suzanne said, on a laugh. She was one of Cherry's particular friends, out of the group which had started together: twelve then, now down to nine. She peered at Cherry's face in amusement. 'You do look startled! What did you think she was going to say?'

'Something nasty about not attending!' Cherry stretched

wearily and smothered a yawn. She went on in a resigned tone, 'It's sure to be because of *something* I'm doing wrong, isn't it?'

There was a general chuckle. Buzz, one of the two male nurses in the group, said teasingly, 'Poor baby. But cheer up, we like it that way, it takes the heat off the rest of us!'

'You're a beast, Andrew Bascombe,' Cherry said without rancour, but giving him his full name as a sign of disapproval. He had become 'Buzz' during the group solidarity of their preliminary training, when they had been the newest people in the place and had felt it. Even now, half a year later, none of them ever called him anything else. 'For that, I won't go through all your test papers with you next time we have an exam!'

'No, please, mercy!' he clowned. In spite of everything else, Cherry actually was good at exams. She was apt to say mournfully that it was her only skill. 'Everything else' included being clumsy, untidy, and accident-prone, which was a gloomy thought because they weren't exactly ideal qualities in a nurse.

'How is it on Private Wing?' asked Suzanne now as she, Buzz and Lisa took Cherry out with them into the grounds for their compulsory walk. They agreed on one circuit of the main hospital block, and set off at a quick trot with their cloaks pulled around them against the sharpness of the autumn air.

'Yes, have you met any millionaires who want to sweep you off and take you away from all this?'

'What, me? Some hope,' said Cherry on a deliberate note of fatalism. 'I do know I'm not the glamorous type! The most flattering thing would be for Buzz to deny it, of course—'

'But I won't, because you'd know I was lying,' he retorted in brotherly tones. Cherry was used to him brotherly, and liked him that way. Buzz had drifted into being part of their particular foursome in the early days and nothing had changed. Suzanne, however, said in outraged tones,

'Nonsense, Cherry looks very sweet, you know she does!'

Cherry thought for a wistful moment that it would have been nicer to have someone say, 'Nonsense, Cherry's very smart'—or very elegant, or very graceful—but unfortunately none of those things were true. They were the sort of descriptions you might give to the man with the Rolls earlier this morning, but you wouldn't give them to someone small and brown-haired and ordinary-looking. The best she could hope for was 'sweet', which always made her think of something rather yukky like sugar mice.

'*I* was wondering how they dared let her loose on the Private Wing at all,' said Buzz, sounding as if he meant it. 'I thought no one got sent there until their second year at least. And Cherry of all people—'

'Oh, I'm not allowed near the actual patients! I'm there as a runner—and sluice-cleaner, tray-clearer, medicine-fetcher—but the sky would fall before they'd let me near any treatment!' Cherry answered him realistically, with a wry grimace.

'Actually, none of us going near the paying patients until we're second-years seems a bit much,' Suzanne commented, tucking her hand into Cherry's arm with a sympathetic squeeze. 'I'm not talking about your well-known tendency towards accidents, love, just general principles! I know we only have very few private beds, but they shouldn't really have special treatment, should they?'

'They don't, medically speaking,' said Cherry, but Buzz came out with,

'Well, if you can't see *that*—'

'Oh, go on, Buzz, you can't defend privilege!'

'Don't let's quarrel,' Cherry put in hastily, pacifically. Buzz could get touchy and think any criticism of wealth was aimed at his family, since his father was a prominent local builder and, this year, Northborough's Mayor. 'Mm, smell the air, everyone!' she exclaimed with bright enthusiasm. 'You can almost taste the moors, if you think about it—'

'Idiot,' said Lisa on a giggle, 'the moors are miles away, and what you're getting is chloroform or something—we're just passing the Path Lab drains! So much for romantic idealism!'

Luckily, though, the sight of the Path Lab put her in mind of a piece of gossip which lasted for the rest of their compulsory round and distracted everyone from being short-tempered over nothing just because of being overtired. On night duty, Cherry felt, one was permanently tired with no real let-up. People said it was because it was their first one and they would get used to it.

People were always saying they would get used to things about hospital life, Cherry decided with her spirits suddenly zooming downwards, as they parted with Buzz on the ground floor of the Night Nurses' Home where he had a room. The rest of them were right up at the top of the house. It was a large Victorian edifice in one corner of the grounds across which sprawled Northborough Royal and all its outlying departments. There was a Day Nurses' Home in a more modern block in another part of the grounds. After the first year, anyone who wanted to and could find digs was allowed to live out, though since it was cheaper to live in, not many people did.

'How *are* you getting on in Private Wing?' asked Suzanne, as they toiled up to what must once have been housemaids' rooms.

'Interesting having patients from different departments, I suppose, but in spite of that I don't like it much. You don't *see* people,' Cherry explained—though even as she spoke she found herself wondering if she'd see the man with the Rolls. He might easily be a private patient arriving for admission. Lisa, however, was answering across Suzanne.

'You could swop with me, and welcome! You see far too many people first night post-op in General Surgical, and most of them with drips and drains to be checked, too! Ouf, I think my tiredness is catching up on me . . . See you at supper, I mean breakfast!'

Her slender figure and curly red hair disappeared round the corner on a wave. Cherry opened her mouth to call a reminder that it was Lisa's turn to wake all three of them for tonight's duty, then shut it again as she remembered that some people might already be sleeping. She found Suzanne was giving her a motherly look.

'Don't worry, I'll see you're awake if Lisa forgets. Sister's right, you do look tired!'

'I know, if the lines under my eyes get any darker I'll turn into a panda. How do you manage to look so unruffled?'

'It's probably just the way my face is arranged.' It was also the fact that Suzanne's hair held to a smooth dark coil under her cap, unlike Cherry's which always escaped to curl riotously in the wrong directions. Although Suzanne's face was too narrow for beauty and perhaps a little too colourless, it was classically arranged and given character by a pair of fine deep blue eyes. Cherry envied her the eyes, which made her own brown ones seem nondescript, but she had liked her immediately and had never found any reason to change her mind. She grinned at her now ruefully and said, with sudden solemnity,

'Sue, do you really think I *will* make a nurse? It's what I've always wanted to do, but I seem to be so bad at it!'

'Nonsense. You came second in the Prelim Exams—and I bet the patients like you! And if you make mistakes, that *is* the way to learn.'

Suzanne's answer was prompt and loyal. All the same Cherry pulled a face.

'I do wonder sometimes if I'm going to be next in the "wasted ones"!'

'No, you're not! You've only got to concentrate a bit more! Now look, we lost three of our set early on, two for failing Prelim, and one after just a week on the wards when she decided she didn't like it—but the rest of us are *going* to make it!'

'I'll drink to that,' Cherry said on a yawn, and grinned at her friend's militant expression. 'Just at the moment, though, I'm going to have to lie down before I fall down!'

All the same, sleep didn't come at once when she was in her room and curled up under her duvet. She was aware of the whole hospital buzzing away like an anthill, across its large site which had once been on the edge of the town, but had now been overtaken and lapped round by suburbs. Farther out still there were the moors, in long stretches of wildness to free the spirit.

Southwards there was Northborough's ornate, slightly pretentious Victorian centre, full of massively complacent buildings dating from the wool trade days. These had now been joined by more modern and boxy office buildings stretching skyscraper fingers up into the sky. Streets of workmen's cottages had turned into estates of high-rise flats. Thanks to a couple of computer firms moving up to provide light industry, Northborough was still reasonably well off as a town. It was more mixed now, with a lot of Pakistanis coming in to do factory jobs or to run small shops, but its past was echoed in the old mill chimneys here and there, and by the big market square which still flourished with colourful stalls selling anything and everything.

Cherry had come to Northborough at twelve years old to live with a grandmother, her last remaining relative. Then when she was thirteen her grandmother had died and she had been sent to foster-parents. They were nice people, Aunt May and Uncle Joe, even if she had never managed to feel really close to them. They had waited until Cherry was through school and set on a career before they moved to Bournemouth to be near their own eldest daughter. Although Cherry was still in touch with them, she felt that she belonged in Northborough if she belonged anywhere. Besides, she had got into the Royal by then, as she had planned.

It seemed a long time since then, though it was only eight months. Nursing had always been Cherry's aim, but there was an enormous amount to learn once one was actually doing it. She was blessed with good health and a sunny nature and a willingness to work hard and, optimistically, she had imagined the years of training to be a steady progression towards her RGN. Northborough Royal might be slightly old-fashioned—even down to keeping the title of 'Matron' instead of the modern nomenclature—but it had a good reputation and didn't accept just anyone.

What Cherry hadn't visualised was the amount of time she would spend feeling rushed off her feet; the number of things which could be dropped, mislaid or tripped over; the formality of the hierarchy so that you had to know who you were allowed to speak to and who not; and the constant feeling that a junior nurse's place was in the *wrong* . . .

She woke up blearily to Suzanne's shaking her shoulder, and staggered down to evening breakfast. She was still on Private Wing when the evening's changes were read out.

'Think of me,' Lisa groaned. 'It's been the *other* darned consultant's op day . . .'

'Mr Hughes usually does a long list, too, doesn't he,' Suzanne siad sympathetically. She and Cherry had both done General Surgery on days—Cherry as her first ward, which she had found totally terrifying. Nowhere could seem more rushed and muddled than a surgical ward on an op day, until you were used to it and could sort out the rhyme and reason of beds being wheeled in and out and patients in varying stages of consciousness.

The bell went for the end of breakfast. Everyone was scrambling up with cloaks and bags to collect, caps to pin on even more firmly, and a stream of nurses was already emerging into the evening to make for the main hospital block or scatter in the direction of separately-housed departments, like Neuro-surgery in its shiny new wing, or ICU which was housed near the accident unit. Northborough Royal had grown in a seemingly random way so that its different blocks were not only architecturally varied, but often quite separate except for a snail-trail of tunnels built to join them up at ground level. These, useful for stretcher cases, were often not the shortest route so that the medical staff were used to doing a quick flit through the open air.

Cherry decided that one thing about being a floater—an unattached junior sent wherever a ward was short-staffed for the night—was that it had finally taught her her way about the hospital. She now knew where to find almost any ward, even if only through going to them by mistake. All the same, as she cut through one corner of Radiotherapy to reach the stairs up to Private Wing, she knew she wasn't sorry that night duty was coming to an end. The first six weeks, attached permanently to one ward, hadn't been so bad. This second six weeks was somehow both lonely and exhausting.

'Ah, Langton—good, it's you again,' the night senior greeted her, with a comforting goodwill, Cherry thought. Staff Nurse Cairns was a pleasant senior, young and blonde and pretty and sure enough of herself not to need to stand on her dignity. She had an engagement ring pinned in her top pocket, which might be why she was so good-tempered. 'Just get the dirty linen sacks shoved out for the porters first, will you?' she said. 'They *will* come round so early!' Then she disappeared into Sister's office to receive the day report which she would then pass on.

Everyone up here was senior besides Cherry. There was an agency staff nurse as a special, identifiable by her plain white belt, and three third-years in check dresses like Cherry's but with three stripes round their caps to her one. There were half a dozen patients in their single rooms and two were new since last night.

One was an eye patient, a Miss Bartholomew, admitted with query detached retina. The other was female too. The elegant man with the Rolls hadn't been a private patient, then . . .

Cherry suppressed a quiver of disappointment, and smiled at her own reactions. As if he would have noticed *her*, anyway! But she had somehow been curious to see what he looked like close up.

'Any questions?' the staff nurse enquired.

One of the third-years asked, 'Which consultant's Miss Bartholomew under?'

'Mr Treneager. And there's her bell now—Archer, will you take it? Everyone else, let's get on with the usual drill!'

Routine caught Cherry in its inexorable arms, and made her feel like Cinderella as she made hot drinks (but the third-years carried them in) and found a clean pillowcase for one patient (but a third-year went to change it) and started in on giving the sluice a good scrub while the third-years went from room to room settling the patients down for the night. She actually might just as well be a ward-maid. She accepted it philosophically. That was what it was like being a junior—unsung, unnamed, unspoken to, she thought with a grin. Definitely the lowest form of life!

Around midnight Staff Nurse Cairns caught her as she was passing the office, popping her head out of the half-closed door. 'Could you please bring a cup of coffee? Strong and black, no sugar!' She disappeared again and Cherry heard the murmur of voices. Hers not to wonder what male doctor was closeted in there at this hour of the night, though the voice was deep and very pleasant. Like dark honey, Cherry thought fancifully.

She pushed the door open with the cup of coffee a few moments later, and was so surprised she almost dropped it. She managed not to, but it was him—black hair with a white flash, superbly elegant dark suit . . .

He turned to glance at her, and idiotically she found herself thinking that although he wasn't handsome seen close up, he was somehow all the more striking for having a face which slanted a little instead of being evenly matched both sides . . . and his eyes were the darkest brown she had ever seen, deep pools in his thin face.

'Thank you,' he said pleasantly as she handed him the cup. Yes, his voice *was* like honey. Then, to Cherry's surprise, he looked deliberately at the label pinned to her uniform dress and added, 'Student Nurse Langton'.

'So you want us to go on keeping Miss Bartholomew on bed-rest, Mr Treneager,' the staff nurse was saying as Cherry backed away. She sounded as ultra-respectful as all nurses, even seniors, were supposed to be towards a consultant.

So *that* was who he was—the new head of the Eye Department. Obviously a very successful doctor too, with that beautiful Rolls-Royce and those impeccably-cut clothes . . . but polite enough to address a very junior nurse by name. Wonders would never cease!

Cherry decided with a grin that she must tell Lisa: there was a senior doctor in the place who *didn't* ignore the very junior staff to the point of walking through them. Anyway, Lisa was endlessly interested in the male hospital staff, of whom she claimed there were far too few, percentage-wise, in hospital life.

Cherry didn't know how Lisa had the energy to be so curious about everybody, particularly as night duty ground on—but she couldn't help thinking, with a quirk of amusement touching her lips, that the new senior doctor was just the sort to rouse *anyone's* interest. He only looked about thirty-five, in spite of the flash of white hair. Since she was the first for once with a bit of news, she really *must* remember to pass it on that this Mr Treneager looked striking if a trifle formidable . . .

She didn't remember, of course, with her increasing exhaustion catching her by the end of the night; and the following night she was 'floated' to General Medical instead of the Private Wing, so she forgot about surgeons altogether. And within a few days she was blearily reminded by the fact that Lisa had got the news from somewhere else, but Cherry was really too tired to care.

'He's an expert on micro-surgery, he's only thirty-three, and he's single,' Lisa enthused. 'And his first name's Ashley. He's young to have got the Royal's top eye job, isn't he? Sister Beaumont's the one with the advantage, of course, because she's on his ward. She's rather beautiful, too, in that hard sort of way, don't you think?'

'Advantage in what?'

'With the gorgeous Mr Ashley Treneager, of course—don't be dozy! Rumour has it,' Lisa said on a chuckle, 'that a fair number of Sisters and senior staff nurses have taken to wearing extra eye make-up since he's arrived. *And* that he's not averse to noticing the best-looking ones, too! And he's got that super silver Rolls. Just imagine going out with him in that! Dreams, lovely dreams . . .'

'Don't say that word, it makes me think of sleep!' Cherry begged. But, fortunately, night duty was almost over. One of these days she might even manage to feel alive again.

Suddenly it *was* over, and they could surface back into the light. They had the usual week's grace before going back to day duty. Everyone seemed to be scattering except Cherry. Lisa was going down to London for a cousin's twenty-first, and Suzanne's home was going to be thoroughly overcrowded for her elder sister's wedding. She urged Cherry to come and said room could be made for her, but Cherry gave her a firm refusal.

'I don't know what you two are flapping about, I'll be perfectly all right here on my own! I'll just move into the Day Nurses' Home and sleep!'

She didn't actually mind being on her own. Even after she'd caught up on sleep she could always find plenty to do wandering around Northborough, and she assured the others of that without the least resentment that they'd got homes to go to and she hadn't.

By the Saturday which fell in the middle of their week off she had revived completely, and went to wander round the market. The Saturday market was always crowded and she enjoyed the profusion of stalls. It was even more crowded than usual now because Christmas was approaching, and Cherry viewed that with surprise. Night duty, she thought ruefully, had muddled her, or she might have realised it was the beginning of December already.

She paused by a stall selling silver and enamelled earrings, and picked up one to inspect more closely, wondering whether to buy it for Suzanne. It was a long dangly one, perhaps not quite the right shape for her friend. The design was very pretty, and she was contemplating it with a small frown when a male voice right beside her said firmly,

'No, you've got the wrong shaped face for that. *Those* would suit you much better!'

The finger which was pointing to a pair of earrings farther up the display was long and well-shaped but very firmly masculine. The voice, which Cherry would have told herself she had forgotten, was immediately recognisable. Dark honey . . . She didn't even dare look round. He couldn't be talking to her, of course—

He was. You couldn't exactly miss Mr Ashley Treneager if he chose to lean forward into your line of sight. If he chose to take an interest in your choice of earrings you couldn't exactly ignore him, either. He gave her an amiable glance, pointed again at the small floral circles he had picked out, and raised an eyebrow at her.

'Try them on and look in that mirror, and you'll see what I mean. Don't look so stunned,' he added impatiently, 'I'm not a total stranger accosting you—I distinctly remember that we've met. In fact we work at the same hospital. Are you going to try the earrings on?'

'They—aren't actually for me—I was thinking of buying them for a friend—'

'Ah, well then, it depends what shape *her* face is, doesn't it?'

'I think I'll leave it—'

Cherry began to back away hastily from the stall. She was stunned that he should have a vague memory of seeing her in the hospital, but he obviously *didn't* remember that she was a very insignificant junior. Unfortunately her backing away didn't get her far, because she immediately fell over a child's push-chair. Mr Treneager fielded her neatly to stop her landing on the child.

It was more unnerving than ever to be caught by one long, strong arm, which then held on to her firmly instead of letting her go. It was almost as if he thought her an unsteady toddler herself, Cherry thought crossly, between embarrassment and annoyance. She could feel herself turning bright pink.

'Difficult to see where you're going in these crowds. Now then, if you've finished at this stall, what shall we go and look at next?'

The calm question brought Cherry's head jerking up so that she could peer up at him in surprise. The dark brown eyes were watching her with a disconcertingly amiable expression. 'I've only been in Northborough a few weeks,' he explained, drawing the words out in that beautiful voice which instantly made Cherry feel mesmerised, 'so you undoubtedly know more about the place than I do. I thought you might like to be obliging and show me round. Yes?'

Gazing up at him, Cherry was swept with consternation. It was all very well for him to stand there looking very tall and extraordinarily attractive, like Prince Charming turning up on Cinderella's doorstep, but by Northborough Royal's rules she ought not to dare to talk to him. If she didn't mention it, he'd only blame her, later. 'Look,' she said desperately, and trying to sound meek, 'I'm much too junior for you to speak to, Mr Treneager, as I'm sure you don't remember!'

'Nonsense, of course I remember. You're a first-year nurse—and looking rather healthier than you did last time I saw you, thank goodness—and, let me see, you were wearing a label that said Student Nurse C. Langton. It helps having a photographic memory,' he said silkily, as she jumped.

'Well, if you remember *that*, you'll realise that—that—'

'You're very helpfully trying to teach me manners? You know,' he said smoothly, as Cherry gulped, and with a small frown touching his eyes now, 'I'm well aware that Northborough Royal has its formal ways, but to go so far as to refuse to speak to me off duty, because of some hierarchical nonsense, does seem the outside of enough! Personally, I talk to whomsoever I feel like talking to, and shall go on doing so!'

There was really no answer to that, except the weak one that she was simply trying to behave properly, and there was no answer to his scowl, either. Expecting him to turn on his heel and walk away, Cherry was startled to find herself, still in the circle of his arm, being marched firmly amongst the dawdling shoppers. 'I saw somewhere suitable for drinking coffee,' his voice said above her head, 'so let's go and drink some, instead of discussing all this out here in the cold!'

Cherry was too hot to have noticed the cold, even though her breath hung in the air in front of her as she panted along beside his long-legged stride. She was flushed with annoyance and embarrassment and the doom-laden feeling which came back to remind her that she was never, somehow, going to do things right.

She sat opposite to him at a table for two in the Kardomah with a sense of wary resignation. She found herself telling him what he wanted to know about Northborough, too, and even explaining how long she had lived in the city, and why. *He* came originally from Cornwall, and said she should have known that, with Tre at the beginning of his name. Mostly, however, he was asking her questions, in that voice which sent shivers down her spine if she let herself be conscious of it. If she felt a little like a fly being questioned by a rather intimidating spider, she kept that feeling firmly to herself.

Besides, he really was much too attractive to be compared with a spider . . . looked at objectively, of course. In fact, the thing he most reminded her of was an eagle—with that proud profile, those quick, alert dark eyes, and that chiselled mouth which looked as if it could thin into angry bad temper . . .

It was thoroughly unreal sitting talking to him. Cherry decided to accept it as a dream. She told him about the symphony orchestra which gave concerts in the Civic Hall once a month through the winter and spring; about the local operatic group whose performances were in truth best avoided; and which clubs and restaurants had the best reputation, though Cherry couldn't guarantee them since she hadn't actually been into any of them. He seemed to want to know such things. And she told him about her beloved moors, too, just in case his tastes weren't entirely urban.

They didn't touch on anything to do with the hospital until they were outside again a whole hour later. Then he said abruptly, but with a smooth note of mockery in his voice,

'There you are, that was relatively painless, wasn't it? It is perfectly possible to treat me like a human being, if you try hard! What does your C stand for? I haven't asked you.'

'Cherry,' she told him.

'Hm, that's an old-fashioned name, isn't it? Or is it short for a more modern one, like Cheryl?'

'No, just Cherry—like the fruit.' And she wouldn't have dreamed of telling him that *his* name was old-fashioned, she thought broodingly, though she found herself also thinking that Ashley was rather a nice name.

'Small and sweet? Cherries. No, I'd have said *you* were small and sharp.' He seemed to like mocking her. 'Where are you going to now? I'm driving back to the hospital, to pick up someone for lunch. Shall I give you a lift?'

'No, you can't! I might be seen in your car. It's no use your scowling at me,' Cherry added recklessly, 'it *matters*! I'd get asked for all sorts of explanations, and have to pretend you knew my foster-parents or something. Not,' she added with a sudden wistfulness, 'that I wouldn't like a ride, because I've never actually been in a Rolls!'

'I'm certainly not going to offer to do a detour and drop you off secretively in some back street!' he retorted trenchantly. Then he seemed to soften, because he added carelessly, 'I'll take you for a drive some other time. Out to your beloved moors, perhaps. I won't fix a date now, but I shan't forget.'

'Why?' Cherry asked baldly.

'Why what?'

'Why are you offering to take me out for a drive? It doesn't make a lot of sense!'

'What an extraordinary girl you are! And very much given to looking gift horses in the mouth. All right—' he looked down at her enigmatically, 'there's really no sinister reason, first-year Student Nurse Langton. Merely, because it would amuse me. Will that satisfy you?'

Something about the tilt of his mouth suggested he meant *she* amused him. As a temporary measure, when he happened to be bored and have nothing else to do. That made sense to Cherry, even if it wasn't very flattering. He'd probably liked the fact that she admired his car, too: most men were proprietorial about their cars. 'Thank you,' she said meekly, 'that's very kind of you. And—er—thank you for the coffee. I think I'd better go now, Mr Treneager—'

'Where are you working?'

'Why?' Cherry asked again, suddenly jumpy.

'So that I'll know where to ignore you!'

He said it with a deliberate drama, to show that she was amusing him again. Cherry bit her lip, hard put to it not to give him a resentful stare. 'I don't know where I'm working at the moment,' she said neutrally. 'We've just come off night duty and haven't gone anywhere else yet.'

'Ah. So, I may even find you in *my* department. Why did that make you wince?' he asked suddenly with real disapproval. 'If you're squeamish about eyes, you'll certainly never make a good nurse!'

'Not, it wasn't that!' He was looking at her angrily, so she had to elaborate, however unwillingly. 'Working for you would make me nervous,' she blurted out, 'and when I'm nervous I get clumsy. I wish I didn't, but I do!'

'Don't be so spineless. If you don't want to be clumsy, learn to breathe more slowly and keep your movements even. It only takes the wit to stop and count to ten whenever you feel you're at risk.' His answer was prompt and caustic.

'*If* you were about to tell me you can't count to ten because you'd then be blamed for slowness, that's rubbish. You'll work faster anyway if you're steady!'

'Yes,' Cherry said on a gulp, and added, 'sir,' because his tone made it necessary.

'Sir is only required when we're on duty. Or were you sending me up for giving you advice?'

'No, I certainly wasn't!'

'And why,' he asked, scowling at her fearsomely, 'would working for me make you more nervous than working for anyone else?'

'I don't know,' Cherry said truthfully. Fairness, and the fact that the whole conversation was too unlikely to be real anyway, made her add, 'After all, I don't suppose you frown *all* the time while you're working, and I doubt if you're so—so *unexpected*, too—'

She wasn't aware that she was looking up at him in a considering fashion as she spoke. She only knew that his eyebrows began to go up—and then that flashing laughter came suddenly into his face, lightening it into a complete change. His eyes were dancing and his lips curved ruefully in a humour so infectious that Cherry felt her own heart lifting and her mouth beginning to smile. He said drily,

'I really must remember not to ask you direct questions! It gets me such appallingly straight answers. Well, since you won't ride with me, I must leave you. My lunch appointment is someone who might find me a flat. Since I'm already getting tired of camping out at the hospital I don't want to miss it. Goodbye for now, Cherry Langton!'

He turned away without waiting for her reply, and was striding off through the crowds. It was easy to watch him go, because he overtopped most of the Saturday shoppers. Cherry watched him until he turned a corner and went out of sight.

She shook herself rapidly to bring herself back to some sort of sense. She decided that Mr Ashley Treneager was a deliberate eccentric, probably to go with his height and unusual appearance. There was no other reason why he should have plucked one very ordinary and very junior nurse off the street and demanded her company.

He really *was* odd. Cherry grinned to herself, then bit her lip ruefully. He was, in some strange way, extraordinarily good company, too.

CHAPTER TWO

CHERRY decided there was no need to mention this morning's weird happening to her friends when they came back from holiday. She'd only get thoroughly teased, and Lisa would make too much of it, when there was nothing to make.

The list of ward changes went up, and Cherry saw with relief that she wasn't down to go to Eyes. Buzz was.

Cherry was to go to the children's wards, on the top floor of the main block. Running her finger down the list to find L. Wetherstone and S. Pardoe, she discovered that Lisa was being posted to the cancer-chemotherapy complex of wards, and Suzanne was going to Intensive Care. With Christmas coming up, Cherry decided she had the best of the draw.

The others came back next day, to have a lively and chatty reunion. Buzz immediately disabused her of any idea that she'd been lucky by reminding her that the Children's Department Sister had a reputation as a stickler.

'Oh . . . Oh well, I'll just have to be careful, won't I?'

'And Buzz is on Eyes.' Lisa had been uncharacteristically quiet but wearing what Cherry called her foxy look. She threw the comment in with such a wealth of meaning that the others turned to look at her. Her pretty pointed face was looking quite smug, and her eyes gleamed. 'I heard some *very* interesting news about our new eye surgeon while I was away! You know my cousin's a staff nurse at one of the London hospitals? Well, her boy-friend's a houseman at the hospital where our Mr Treneager was until recently—and *he* said there was quite a scandal to do with his private life not more than eighteen months ago!'

'If it's scandal you shouldn't repeat it!' Cherry said abruptly, and met Lisa's surprised eyes steadily. She knew guiltily that she more than half wanted to hear what Lisa had to say, but the protest had jerked out of her.

'I don't see why not, when it was common knowledge down there. Apparently he was married—and his wife fell out of a window, at a party. I mean, did she fall, or was she pushed—or did she jump, for that matter—'

'Cherry's right, you shouldn't repeat it,' Suzanne said firmly, giving Lisa a reproving look. 'Poor man, after all! I should think he'd simply hate to have it discussed, and wouldn't anybody?'

'I only thought it explained why he's come up here instead of staying in the fleshpots of London. He's much more of a London type, isn't he?' But Lisa had the grace to look shamefaced, particularly when Buzz too gave her a warning look.

'You ought to be careful not to be heard saying anything about it—particularly that *was she pushed* line you've just given us! That could be slander!'

'I don't mean anyone's suggesting *he* pushed her! It was just one of those parties where everyone was a bit high. I believe he wasn't even there.' There was no real harm in Lisa, and she was looking uncomfortable now as well as sounding defensive. 'I'm only telling *you* lot,' she said crossly. 'I just thought it was interesting, that's all. That he was married, and his wife died, and now he's turned up here—which looks like getting as far away from his past as possible!'

'I expect he came up here for the promotion,' Buzz said dampingly, 'unless he was a consultant already down there? Northborough isn't exactly the end of the earth!'

'He was a senior registrar,' Lisa said sulkily, and then, on a wail, 'Oh, *bother*—now you've made me feel guilty! You're all looking at me like Sister Tutor spouting, *A Nurse Must Always Be Discreet!*'

That made them all laugh, though a moment later Suzanne reiterated that Lisa should not pass the story on any further. Lisa agreed and made a display out of saying 'cut my throat and hope to die' with gestures—a sacrifice on her part, since she always did like to be first with any kind of gossip.

Cherry hadn't said anything further at all, since her first protest. She couldn't help feeling an instinctive sympathy, though, towards a man who had suffered that kind of shattering tragedy. Then a moment later she found herself thinking that a man with that eagle profile wouldn't take kindly to pity, either . . .

She had plenty to do getting back into the swing of day duty, on a new ward.

The Children's Department had two Sisters, a senior one and a junior one, and Cherry wasn't at first sure which of them was supposed to be the perfectionist. She soon found out: both.

Sister Temple, the senior, must be on her way towards retirement age. She had iron-grey hair, a lined face, and round glasses. She was very thin and her voice was deceptively mild. It was only after Cherry had re-made a cot three times, because Sister Temple didn't feel she had placed a plastic undersheet smoothly enough for the cot's inmate, that she realised just how icy that lady's grey eyes could turn, on finding that a junior nurse (who had just re-made a cot three times) could be late with a sick infant's mid-morning bottle.

Sister Grayson, on the other hand, looked like a princess out of a fairy-tale who happened to have strayed into a Sister's royal blue uniform and lacy cap. She had golden-blonde hair, a perfect profile, and very pale blue eyes, and she had a mania for tidiness. Her particular fetishes were the children's locker-tops, the position of the bed and cot wheels, and the condition of the sluice cupboards; and she particularly could *not* bear a nurse to have untidy hair even if a toddler had just been pulling it. Cherry discovered all that in the first two days—and also discovered that she liked Sister Temple better.

'Have you noticed that she may fuss, but it's *always* about something which might matter to the children?' she asked Peter Lee, as both of them tore downstairs at a nurse's fast non-running walk to have a shortened coffee-break. Peter was the other male student nurse out of her set. For once, two of them had washed up on the same ward.

'Yes, I think if I were a sick child I'd rather have her to look after me,' Peter said gravely. He was small and dark and plain, quite the opposite of Buzz who was fair and almost too good-looking. 'Maybe Sister Grayson comes into her own with the very seriously ill ones—she's very efficient, isn't she?'

'I haven't been sent to the cubicles yet, have you? I suppose, being first-years, they're bound to start us off on Convalescence and Recovery.' Cherry thought of the ward with its bright paint, patterned curtains and cheerful day-room full of toys. She also thought of the sluice and bottles which must be put away in line to the millimetre, and added drily, 'All I know is, I never *did* like Goldilocks, and my sympathy's still with the Three Bears! She keeps giving me the feeling she's just waiting to jump out at me . . . No, I mustn't *let* myself think that she unnerves me, and I must count to ten!'

She made the resolve absently, without knowing why it had popped into her head, or where her eyes were resting. A moment later, and with the tingle of an involuntary blush starting, she realised that she was gazing straight at a tall approaching figure some yards away down the corridor—a figure in the long white coat of a consultant on a hospital round, with another of those elegant dark suits beneath it; a figure topped by a thin aquiline face, black hair, and a white lock just at the centre front . . .

It was the first time she had done more than glimpse him in the distance since she had come on day duty. She could have sworn that those hooded dark eyes had been staring straight at her until just the moment she realised she was staring at him; though now he was casting one of his bad-tempered looks at the young, and very plain, female doctor who was walking along beside him, and who was probably one of his house surgeons. With a tremor, Cherry wasn't sure whether the bad temper was for her, for the temerity of having stared at him, or for something the other doctor was saying to him. One thing she did know, though, was that she and Peter must draw well to the side of the corridor to keep out of the way of the top brass as they—he—processed regally down the middle. That was the way things were done at the Royal.

Only two things could take precedence over a consultant: an emergency patient on a stretcher, and the cardiac resuscitation trolley with its team heading for a crisis. Cherry had had to dodge out of the way of the resuscitation trolley a couple of times, particularly when taking an illicit short cut through Casualty, so that she knew enough to get out of the way fast if she heard flying feet.

This time, as there was a sudden thud and flurry and a voice behind her saying sharply, 'Clear the way, please!' it was a stretcher patient, with a drip up and a nurse holding it high as the whole collection went by at speed. Cherry had grabbed Peter and dived left. It was a pity that Mr Ashley Treneager had moved to *his* right. Before she knew what she'd done, Cherry had cannoned into him . . . and had felt herself caught in strong, impatient hands, swept out of the way, and planted against the wall.

'Look where you're going, Nurse,' a deep voice said sarcastically—and unfairly—before Cherry could frame an apology. She was aware of a pair of very dark eyes staring down at her, with a critical but impersonal gaze which held no recognition whatsoever, but which seemed to sum up both her lack of inches, and her lack of status. Then he was past, and walking away.

Cherry, biting her lip and trying not to feel hot and bothered, accepted Peter's look of rueful sympathy as they joined up again. She was annoyed with herself for feeling hard done by, because these things happened. And she certainly hadn't expected him to say hallo to her, had she? In fact she greatly *preferred* it if he'd forgotten who she was again. So why on earth did she suddenly feel hurt?

The hospital was busy enough to keep her too occupied to think about tall forbidding consultants. Time went by at a run, and suddenly Christmas was almost upon them.

Cherry cradled a small child's head against her shoulder as she tipped a feeding cup gently, murmuring, 'That's right, Katy, drink it all up, there's a good girl.' Except for a slight dullness in the eyes, a touch of floppiness in the way she held her head, it would have been difficult to see that Katy was brain-damaged. She seemed to have an inbuilt weakness to infections, too, and had been admitted with pneumonia. She needed special looking after even now she was convalescent.

The ward was almost empty. Even Katy would be gone tomorrow, well enough for her parents to take her home. Only the most acute cases would be kept in over Christmas, which was the day after tomorrow.

Sister Temple came down the ward, gave Cherry a brief nod of approval, and moved on with her eyes making their usual watchful check. Surprisingly enough, Cherry had gone on finding Sister Temple reasonable to work for, because even if she was a martinet she was always fair. She thanked her stars silently that it was Sister Temple on duty this evening because Cherry was due off at half past five: if it had been Sister Grayson she would probably have set her to some long cleaning job at five twenty-five precisely.

Oddly, though—and in spite of Sister Grayson—so far Cherry had managed to keep her head on the children's wards. Perhaps it was her attempts to breathe steadily and count to ten before diving into anything. She had told herself wryly that if a consultant gave you advice you might as well follow it.

Lifting Katy back into bed, she spent a few moments encouraging the little girl to pick out her favourites from the decorations scattered around the ward, before leaving her and getting on with her duties. In common with the rest of the junior staff Cherry had spent a lot of time on the top of ladders during the past couple of weeks, putting up paper-chains and cardboard lanterns and strings of gold and silver shapes. Cherry took as much of a childlike delight in Christmas preparations as the children did, so even if the decorations gathered dust she thought they were worth it. They certainly made everything look more cheerful and human all over the hospital, which was suddenly sprouting decorations even in the most unlikely places.

'Nurse Langton—'

'Yes, Sister?' said Cherry, coming to an instant stop as Sister Temple appeared abruptly out of the linen cupboard.

'I was glad to see you taking the trouble to talk to Katherine—she needs mental stimulation. You're off in ten minutes, I believe? Very well then, just see that the kitchen's tidy and you may go.'

'Thank you, Sister.'

'You find it odd being on a ward that's so quiet, no doubt. So do I.' The older woman suddenly sounded extremely human, and even smiled—something which she didn't often do to the nurses, though she had been seen to laugh with the children. 'Don't worry, we shall be back to being rushed off our feet all too soon! How is the Christmas choir going?'

'Quite well I think, thank you, Sister. We've got our last rehearsal tonight,' Cherry added, volunteering the information.

It was Sister Temple who was responsible for her being in the Christmas choir. Cherry hadn't known that it was a tradition to have someone from every ward, so she had been startled when after only three days on the ward she had been told to volunteer. Sister Temple had said coolly, 'Nurse Langton, I've heard you humming nursery rhymes, so I know you have a voice. You will represent this department for the carol singing.' And that was that, because her tone had brooked no argument.

Cherry wouldn't have wanted to argue, because she enjoyed singing carols and welcomed the chance. Her voice wasn't outstanding, but it was sweet and true and could hold a tune, and once she had got over thinking that she was probably being sent off to sing to get rid of her, she appreciated the fact that she was given extra time off for rehearsals. Besides, it would be an honour to be one of the band who would tour round to every ward in the hospital on Christmas Eve, and again on Christmas Night, wearing their cloaks reversed to show their crimson linings and singing all the favourite carols, so that even those who had to be in hospital for Christmas could have a share in the season's magic.

'Good, I shall look forward to hearing you. I intend to stay on duty through Christmas, of course,' Sister Temple said. She turned away dismissively as she spoke, to go on with her linen-sorting, making it clear that her brief conversation with her junior was over.

The 'of course' seemed to hang in Cherry's head as she went off duty a few minutes later, making her wonder suddenly whether that would be her some day—staying on duty 'of course' because work was her whole life. Sister Temple wasn't married and had obviously given herself entirely to her profession. Had she ever had a choice . . . ?

Cherry shook herself, annoyed by the tiny shiver that went through her at the thought of being almost sixty and alone. No doubt Sister Temple found her life entirely satisfactory—and why not? Nursing *was* a very satisfying job. She only hoped she'd do it as well. Just now, anyway, it was laughable to be imagining herself as the Sister-in-Charge of any ward—and definitely over-optimistic!

The choir rehearsal wasn't until seven-thirty, so she had plenty of time to change out of uniform and have an early supper. Time, too, to wander into the nurses' sitting-room after supper to get some coffee from the coffee machine. Buzz was in there, obviously off duty like herself and sitting leafing through the day's paper, so Cherry ignored the group glued to the television at one end of the room, and went to sit companionably by him.

'Hi, stranger. Do you have a half-empty ward, like us? It really feels strange, doesn't it—even though you can see why they wouldn't do an ordinary take-in at this time of year.'

'Mm, we're only on emergencies. I gather we're supposed to go round any long-stay wards and be jolly, on Christmas Day itself, if we're working.'

'Oh good, it'll make a change from extra cleaning,' Cherry said drily. She was down to work all through Christmas morning—and would be back in the wards in the evening, of course, singing. 'I wonder,' she mused idly, 'whether it's actually more fun to be on nights at Christmas, or days?'

'Dunno. If you were on nights you'd want to stay up and not sleep, wouldn't you? That might make it hard for the next night! Besides, you'd miss such heights of socialisation as the charity Christmas lunch for the scanner appeal—and the ancillary staff's come-as-you-are Christmas rave-up

—and, of course, the first year nurses' special Christmas disco!'

It was true that parties had been sprouting everywhere, though in strict layers of seniority. 'Hey, Buzz, do you realise,' Cherry asked, suddenly struck with awe, 'when we've finished our present ward and then two weeks' study block, we'll be second-years?'

'Well, it has to come, doesn't it? Even for you,' he added teasingly, pulling a face at her. It made Cherry notice that he had been sitting there looking a bit down, and she asked,

'How is it on Eyes? Is—is it turning out to be a very difficult ward?'

'No, actually, it's hard work, but it's pretty interesting. You have to run a barometer on Sir's temper—Miss Ronay, who's his houseman, is absolutely terrified of him —but as long as you keep out from underfoot it's all right.'

Cherry had wondered whether Mr Ashley Treneager was a hard taskmaster . . . and whether he was given to cross-questioning junior nurses. Since Buzz didn't mention it, presumably not.

She had made herself accept, with philosophical humour, that she had been thinking about him too much just because he was a glamorous figure who had once deigned to notice her. She had accepted too that he wasn't likely to go on noticing her now that he had settled in. It would be very uncomfortable if he did. So that was that. All the same, she found herself asking Buzz casually,

'Is your consultant away for Christmas? I merely ask because our paediatrics Professor has swanned off to Switzerland to take his family skiing, and left his registrar to handle everything!'

'No, ours is still here, and I expect he means to work. You can't fault him on the hours he puts in, he's even around for emergencies. Oh, and d'you know who one of them was, in the middle of last night?' Buzz asked, looking a little grim about it. 'One of the Peace brothers, though not because of a fight, for once!'

'Oh really, which one?'

'Darren.'

'Oh, I was at school with him. Well, I was at school with all of them,' added Cherry in the interests of accuracy, 'but Darren was our year. Dave was older and the twins were younger.'

'You were at school with the *Peaces*? You're not going to say they were friends of yours? I'm surprised to hear they ever *went* to school!'

'They weren't in very often, and I don't know them at all well,' Cherry said with a grin for Buzz's lofty attitude. Since if there was trouble the Peaces were in it, and the more public and the more delinquent the better, she supposed she couldn't blame him. She added, 'What on earth is Darren doing in the eye ward?'

'Having one eye expertly stitched back in, after coming very close to losing it in a motorbike accident. He went over the handlebars into some railings—the spiky kind.' As Cherry winced, Buzz added with grudging admiration, 'He's dead lucky Mr Treneager *was* in, because I heard Sister Beaumont saying that no one else would possibly have had the skill, *or* the nerve, to reattach every tiny muscle and fibre so accurately that he'll probably have normal vision. And all that for a yob like Darren Peace—'

'Oh, come on, Darren's not so bad—more stupid. Keith and Wayne were always much worse than him, when we were at school anyway. Besides,' Cherry said reprovingly, 'I don't suppose Mr Treneager cared whether he's a yob or not, do you? And I don't think you should, either—he's just another patient to nurse. Hey, I'd better go, or I'll be late for choir practice and feel awful having to creep in at the back—see you!'

Cherry seized up her anorak and did a quick dash out into the dark to get to the hospital chapel, where the rehearsal was being held. She didn't really want to be late, particularly since the hospital Deputy Administrator who was acting as choirmaster and conductor had shown signs of wanting to give her a solo verse in one of the carols. It was probably only because she was small and at the front, but it would be fun if he did choose her.

She was thinking about that, but she was also thinking about Buzz, and wondering wryly whether nursing would ever cure him of that slightly superior attitude of his. Then she decided she was being unfair. It was probably that the Peaces (who were nothing if not clannish) had been in to see Darren, had recognised Buzz as the Mayor's son, and had made some sneering remark. They hated anyone who represented authority, so it was quite likely.

She could quite imagine that it would be difficult for Buzz to be faced with people like the Peaces. They were just the sort of people who would look on nursing as 'women's work' too—as had Buzz's father, Cherry knew from what her classmate had let fall once, about Mr Bascombe senior feeling that nursing 'wasn't quite a proper profession for a man'. She had admired Buzz for sticking to his guns about his choice of career, but she *could* see that it didn't help if, like Buzz, you were fair and so handsome that you could almost be called pretty. He was far from effeminate as a person, but that wouldn't stop tough types from airing their prejudices.

She had taken the shortest route, out of habit, and dived in through a side door in the main hospital building which would bring her out near the lifts, and thence upwards to the first floor chapel. It was another of those short cuts one wasn't supposed to take because it led through one corner of Administration, which had the Residents' Block above it. Since it was after office hours there shouldn't have been anyone about, and Cherry was a bit daunted to see that there were lights along the Admin corridor, and a burr of chatter as if something was going on down there. She pressed a hasty finger on the lift's bellpush and prayed it would come quickly.

It did: the heavy hum started off above almost immediately, and could be heard coming steadily down. That was just as well, because Cherry had suddenly caught sight of Matron, unmistakably she even in full evening dress, crossing the far end of the Administration corridor and disappearing round a corner. It was lucky she was going the other way, not this way . . .

The lift came to a halt and the doors purred open. Cherry was geared up to take a leap inside, and had even taken the first step—when she realised that someone was in the lift already, and wanting to come out. Not just *someone*, either. As she met a pair of very dark eyes—and a frown—Cherry's heart gave an odd jerk, before she remembered to step to one side and get out of Mr Treneager's way.

He too was in full evening dress—black tie, black jacket and trousers, with that look of indefinable elegance which seemed to characterise him in anything. Cherry was very abruptly aware that she was wearing jeans and a gigantic scarlet sweater which she'd bought at a jumble sale, and that her anorak, on top of that, must look thoroughly peculiar since it left a rim of scarlet sweater sticking out beneath it.

'And where are *you* going?'

She'd thought he wouldn't bother to notice her. Why should he, after all? That he did, and with a look of cold surprise and distaste, seemed quite unnecessary, and made her eyes fly to his face with resentment.

'Chapel—sir.'

'Chapel?'

He really didn't have to look as if it was the most unlikely thing she could have said; nor to examine her with a stare which travelled slowly down her clothes. 'For choir practice,' Cherry explained, firmly, but feeling a blush start as it suddenly occurred to her that any nurse taking one of these lifts *might* be heading for an assignation with a resident doctor. After all, this block was where they slept. 'The chapel's on the first floor just above here,' she babbled hastily, 'er—it was probably handy for the original wards, though it's a bit out of the way now—'

'Thank you for the potted history,' he said silkily. He still hadn't got out of her way. He was leaning negligently against the open lift doors, stopping them from closing again. That did at least mean the lift couldn't vanish off upwards while he was still grilling her. 'I really didn't know there *was* a chapel, but I'm sure it's something I might want to know some time. Oh, by the way, I *haven't* forgotten that you're going to show me the moors—the weather's just been against it!'

'I wasn't expecting—'

'Weren't you? I thought we'd made a date about it, even

if we hadn't said an actual time. You don't mean to say you're going to let me down, Cherry Langton?'

There was even less need for him to look at her in that mocking manner than there had been for him to frown at her earlier. Cherry met his eyes stare for stare, suddenly angry to be the butt of his amusement once more—and why *did* he find her so funny, anyway? Because she had jumped at his saying her name, when she would have expected him to have forgotten it? She opened her mouth to say something cool and dignified; but before she could frame any words he was going on, with his eyes glinting with laughter.

'You're looking at me like an angry kitten. Why's that? Do you know, I don't think I've ever come across a girl who was so determined not to talk to me?'

The corridor was empty, with no one to see and take an interest. 'Are you still living here?' Cherry asked politely, just to prove to him that he was wrong. 'I thought you had the hope of a flat, wasn't it any good?'

'That's better, even if it did sound a bit artificially social. Thank you, I did find a flat, but I'm still waiting to move in. It's in . . . let me see, Ebury Road. Would you say that was quite a respectable address?'

'Yes if you're the north end, less so at the south end.' Well, he had asked, hadn't he? 'I expect,' she went on decorously, 'that you're in the new development at the north end—'

'No, as a matter of fact. In a Victorian house in the middle, which has been converted into flats. It has a more interesting shape than the new ones. Am I holding you up?' he asked, in a sudden access of politeness. 'I'm supposed to be meeting someone here to go to—heaven help us—the Senior Staff Dinner. As if Christmas wasn't bad enough without adding a formal dinner-dance—'

'You can't say that! I mean about Christmas—' Cherry was beginning, in an automatic protest. Then she suddenly found herself wondering if it had bad memories for him. His wife . . . 'Of course lots of people say they hate it nowadays,' she said hastily, feeling awkward, and then felt worse as his eyes seemed to sharpen into intentness on her face.

'Now why are you suddenly looking like *that*, young

woman? Why—' his voice had hardened—'do I suddenly need your sympathy?'

'Anybody who doesn't like Christmas needs my sympathy,' she told him rapidly, and with what she hoped was a convincing air of innocence. Luckily at that moment the outside door swung open and they were no longer alone. A moment ago she wouldn't have wanted to be interrupted, even if he was amusing himself by mocking her. Now, in the face of his alert suspicion, she was only too glad to see him straighten up from his elegant leaning position and look across the small vestibule.

'Ah, Emily, there you are,' he said on a deep drawl—and then, coolly, to a point several inches above Cherry's head, 'The chapel is on the floor above this, Nurse, and I should imagine you can use this lift to get there!'

Cherry wanted to choke at the nerve of him, giving her back the information she had just given him in a bored tone as if she had been lost and asking him directions. She might have given him a searing look, with her back safely to the new arrival, if that arrival hadn't spoken in a sweet, but all-too-familiarly dulcet tone.

'Oh dear, it's Nurse Langton. You *should* have gone via the main hall, Nurse—and let alone being in the wrong place and bothering people, do you have to look so scruffy?'

'No, Sister—sorry, Sister,' Cherry muttered automatically. She didn't know whether Sister Grayson had the right to criticise what clothes she wore off duty or not, but she wasn't prepared to risk anything but a blank expression as she turned to face the senior nurse. It was somehow pleasing to see that Goldilocks looked rather less beautiful in an evening dress too covered in bows and flounces than she did in her trim uniform—but she still had a doll-like, porcelain purity and an enchanting slenderness which made Cherry feel conscious of being round-faced and still inclined to puppy fat.

'Well, you can use this lift now, but I think we must do something about the short cuts you juniors take,' Sister Grayson trilled with sweet disapproval. Then she quite distinctly dismissed Cherry from her consciousness, as she looked up at Mr Treneager and fluttered her eyelashes.

They deserved each other, Cherry found herself thinking savagely, as she shot past the consultant who was still holding the lift door open with one obliging arm. She was careful not to look up at him as she went. Had she really been feeling sorry for him a moment ago? Well, he was obviously heartwhole if he was already taking Sister Grayson out. And *wouldn't* she just be called Emily? In children's books Emilys were always good little girls with clean white socks who knew everything . . . who probably grew up to be picky Ward Sisters with sweet voices and stainless-steel hearts. If *that* was the way Mr Treneager's tastes ran, well, serve him right!

Luckily, her own temper almost always ended up by making her laugh. It did this time, as she found herself visualising a battle of wills between the tall consultant and the beautiful Sister Grayson which struck her as a fairly equal contest. Somehow, though, it wasn't until she had sung her way through several of the more soothing carols that she had thoroughly calmed down. It took until then for the music, and concentration on the conductor's baton, to take all her attention, and not leave anything left over for the memory of a smug, cat-and-cream expression on Sister Grayson's face.

She might have looked for traces of that expression the next day, but Sister Grayson was off for the whole of the Christmas period. There were mercifully few seriously-ill children in the cubicles which were used to nurse severe cases, so Christmas Eve nursing was mainly a matter of skating through the ward routines and then packing for the remaining children who were well enough to go home. Cherry had the afternoon off and then it was back into uniform to go round the wards with the choir.

She didn't think she would ever forget the stillness in each ward as they sang; nor the feeling of total absorption from their listeners as if pain, unease, fear were being banished for a short time. Cherry had the warming feeling of being part of the whole hospital as they moved round from ward to ward, in some places grouping themselves round a ward Christmas tree, in others being careful to keep clear of doorways where other staff were still having to hurry to and fro on emergency procedures. It was almost unbearably touching to sing to the coma patients in Suzanne's current ward, the long-stay section of Intensive Care. It was cheerful in Orthopaedics where, according to the staff nurse in charge, they had been having a party all day to celebrate somebody coming off neck traction. They sang in a corridor outside the isolation wards and hoped the sound would carry, and stuck to soothing rather than rousing carols when they were with the cardiacs. And in the eye ward, those patients who were bandaged turned towards the music and seemed to listen even more eagerly.

There were only a few of them: eyes were less often emergency procedures, Cherry supposed. She looked for Darren Peace but guessed he must be behind a set of curtains which were temporarily closed. She saw Buzz and, in the pause between two carols, gave him a quick grin and a wink.

It wasn't until a moment or two later, when they had begun the next carol, that she realised Mr Ashley Treneager was there too—something she saw with a sudden jerk of selfconsciousness which almost made her miss a note.

It shouldn't have been a surprise to see him on his own ward. It was, because there weren't many consultants about at this time in the evening so that, after a first surreptitious glance round, she had concluded that he wasn't here. She had felt relieved because they were due to do the carol which started with her solo verse—and now, halfway through it, she was suddenly feeling a dryness in her throat, sure that her voice was going to desert her before the end of her few lines. Oh, *why* did she have to notice him just then? And how long had he been standing there, like a disapproving ghost, in the doorway of Sister's office?

She finished her verse, managing it in the end without losing anything, and as the other voices surged up to join her she stole a glance from under her lashes to see if he was still standing there. He was, wearing a brooding expression which made his face look blank, and with the dark eyes hooded as he seemed to be staring down with remarkable interest at his feet. Sister Beaumont, the Ward Sister, was standing next to him—and Cherry decided that she could see Lisa's description of her as 'rather beautiful in a hard sort of way'. She was one of those pale-skinned, dark-haired, swan-necked people who looked more like ballet dancers than Ward Sisters. Snow White, streamlined and without the softness, perhaps . . . ?

Seeing Ward Sisters as fairy-tale characters seemed to be becoming a habit, she decided drily—and then suddenly wanted to giggle as she caught herself trying to decide whether Mr Treneager should be cast as the Demon King or the Big Bad Wolf. He certainly ought to be something larger than life—with that height, those remarkably dramatic looks.

The carol ended, the tableau broke up, one or two of the patients applauded—and Mr Treneager gave the choir one long thoughtful look and disappeared back into Sister's office. It was left to Sister Beaumont to say a polite 'thank you and Merry Christmas' on behalf of her ward; and to tell the patients who were begging for more that the choir would be round again tomorrow evening, to finish Christmas as well as heralding it.

There were only two more wards after that. Then, by tradition, they had to visit Matron, who gave them hot punch and mince pies. That lady was extremely gracious and even quite informal, but even though it was a remarkable honour to be drinking mulled wine in Matron's own living quarters, to Cherry the tour of the wards had been so special that this was no more than an anticlimax.

She felt rather lightheaded when they all split up—probably because the Deputy Administrator had insisted on giving her more punch, and she'd skipped supper rather than risk singing on an overfull stomach. She didn't know why he kept turning up beside her, and it was even more disconcerting when he took a dive at her and kissed her under a piece of mistletoe surprisingly hanging in Matron's hall. Cherry supposed, kindly, that she was the best he could do, but she tried not to flinch on the grounds that it wouldn't show a Christmas spirit—and besides, she had to sing for him again tomorrow night. Luckily she managed to lose him in the ruck of other people coming out, so there was no risk of his being kind enough to offer to escort her back to the Nurses' Home.

She found herself crossing the car park alone, and on impulse she did a small detour to take her to the part reserved for consultants. The silver Rolls was there, in splendid isolation—its owner was obviously the only consultant to be found in the hospital tonight. Thinking about the brooding look he had been wearing, and his apparent disapproval of Christmas altogether, Cherry decided in an excess of goodwill and charity that the least she could do was put a spell on his vehicle so that as soon as he next climbed into it he would cheer up. The idea made her giggle, but she stopped, waved her hands solemnly, then walked right round the car to make the magic set. It was a nutty thing to be doing in the car park in the dark at ten o'clock at night but, after all, there was no one to see—

She stepped round from the other side of the car just as a figure emerged from a nearby pool of shadow, so that she almost cannoned into it. Hands steadied her as a deep, dark-honey voice asked impatiently,

'What on *earth* are you doing?'

'I wish you wouldn't startle me like that!'

It suddenly seemed quite logical that he should be there, standing in front of her in person instead of haunting her thoughts; but Cherry's lightheadedness was abruptly gone. At least she thought it was. Matron's punch did seem to have the effect of loosening her tongue, though, because she found herself coming out with,

'I thought you were indoors, and I wish you wouldn't be so *sudden*!'

'Have you,' he asked ominously, 'by any chance had too much to drink?'

'No, and if I had it would only be because of Matron. And the time of year. Why didn't you enjoy our singing? Everyone else did, but *you* just stood and frowned!'

'I was frowning about other things. For instance, a post-operative patient who's running a fever—'

'Darren Peace? The motorbiker whose eye you mended yesterday?'

'No, a corneal graft I did this morning. Am I really explaining myself to *you*?' he asked on an explosive note, and sounding as if he couldn't quite believe it. Neither could Cherry: her own impertinence was suddenly sending her cold. Unfortunately the sane part of her mind didn't seem to be stopping her tongue, because she heard herself say chattily,

'Does it help having a photographic memory when you're operating? I was wondering, the other day—I should think it would, because you could set up a diagram in your head to follow, couldn't you?'

'Yes, and yes. This really is a most unlikely conversation.' He muttered it crossly, and before she could reply he added caustically, 'You really have had too much to drink, haven't you? That fair boy on my ward, who I *presume* is your boy-friend, must be off duty by now—why isn't he keeping more of an eye on you?'

'He isn't my boy-friend, we're just in the same set, we all go around in a gang. Besides, what has that got to do with it? And I *haven't* had much alcohol, honestly. Only a couple of glasses of mulled wine on an empty stomach. So if you were going to report me—'

'I wasn't. I probably should, but I presume you're not on duty. So you're just hungry, are you? Well then, since I missed supper too, you'd better come with me.'

'Come with you where?'

'Out to somewhere which stays open late enough to provide food. The canteen's closed except for pre-ordered meals—or hadn't you noticed? I suppose even the ancillary staff feel entitled to a holiday.' He didn't sound at all charitable about it. 'And I don't fancy the local takeaway—do you?'

Cherry was seized with a sudden longing to go with him. It hadn't exactly been an invitation, more an order, cross but casual, and if he wanted to be so eccentric as to command her company, what could she do? Was it really any worse than standing here in the dark of the car park, so close to him that his hand was still brushing her elbow where he had taken hold of it to steady her . . . ?

Sanity told her that it was, much worse, because if she

was seen in his car driving away from the hospital, speculation would be instant. And she *would* be seen, because they would drive out past the well-lit section by the night porter's lodge which was part of every short cut to everywhere. It wouldn't have occurred to *him* that anyone would speculate, because he didn't mean anything by it. She swallowed, and peered up at the man beside her, wishing his face wasn't too shadowed for her to see his expression—merely the outline of his head, the gleam of his eyes, and the white flash in his hair.

'That's really very nice of you—but I don't think I'll eat. I could do with getting thinner, actually—'

'Yes, you probably could,' he agreed, with a noticeable lack of politeness, 'but I should do it gradually if I were you. Tonight you need blotting paper.'

'Well—'

'What you're trying to say is, no doubt, that you can't be seen with me!'

'All right,' said Cherry, exasperated by his heavily sarcastic tone, 'I *was* trying to say that, only politely! I can see you don't realise how much we have it drilled into us that we've got to keep to our correct place! But—but after seeing the way Sister Grayson was last night, I should think it might have occurred to you that however little you may mean by it, *she* wouldn't stop short of killing me!'

She could have bitten her tongue out the moment she'd said it, appalled by the fact that she'd let it come out just because it had popped into her head at an unwary moment. She felt the man beside her stiffen, and waited for some searing comment. When he spoke, though, there was a tremor in his voice which she could almost have mistaken for laughter, even if there was a menacingly silky note in his drawl.

'Since I was only offering to feed you, is it actually Sister Grayson's concern? And do I detect a certain criticism in my choice of company? I have the strangest feeling there was disapproval in your voice just then!'

'I couldn't possibly criticise you, could I? It isn't my business. She's very pretty,' Cherry said rapidly, trying not to say it between her teeth, nor to add nastily, 'if you like that sort of thing'.

'Yes, isn't she? But she doesn't actually have any ruling on how I spend my time. Nor do any of the other attractive young women I ask out from time to time. I must remember to ask your advice about who I should take to the New Year's dance!'

'There's no need to—to cut me down to size—'

'That would be difficult, if not impossible,' he said drily, 'and besides, I'm sure your advice will be invaluable. I'm only trying to point out, Cherry Langton, that I'm a free agent, and I intend to stay that way. I'm far too old and cynical to do anything else. But, just in case it was bothering you, I should point out that I don't go round corrupting the unsophisticated. How old are you?'

'Nineteen.'

'Really? You look younger. But I can assure you, as far as I'm concerned, anyone under twenty is a child. My private life may not be without amusement,' he drawled, 'but I can assure you, *you* are perfectly safe.'

Cherry was opening her mouth to tell him that she knew that quite well—she wasn't that much of a fool—but a voice across the car park was suddenly calling his name, and as he swung round, a third-year nurse was there hurrying towards them. She said breathlessly,

'Mr Treneager, Sister asked me to try and catch you. There's an eye damage case come in to A and E, and she thought you'd want to know—'

'Yes, of course. Where is it—still in Casualty? I'll come.'

It was natural that he should forget Cherry instantly, and turn on his heel to move away fast. He wouldn't get his meal, then, either with or without her. The third-year nurse gave Cherry a mildly curious glance, and shot away after him. Cherry was left standing there, suddenly feeling cold, and a little flat, and junior, and useless.

Of course she'd known she was safe with him—how could he think she hadn't? She wasn't that stupid. She wasn't one of those striking, noticeable people; not even pretty like Lisa or attractive like Suzanne; she was just ordinary. There wasn't much you could do with a round face and brown hair and ordinary mud-coloured eyes, let alone a nose which had a tendency to be snub. She wasn't even a good nurse, though she was trying. She'd have needed to be very conceited to think he was interested in her as a *person*.

All the same, and even accepting all that—and feeling suddenly cold stone sober and very un-Christmassy—Cherry couldn't help knowing wistfully that she would have liked it to be different. Because even very ordinary people could be caught by dreams.

CHAPTER THREE

CHRISTMAS was suddenly over and the wards started to fill up again. Cherry, after giving herself a strict talking to, went back to being her usual philosophical self. She congratulated herself on the fact that she wasn't the sort of person to let dreams rule her life. Keeping up with the busy state of the children's wards without losing her cool was enough to keep her thoughts occupied anyway.

The New Year's dance came and went. It was the Royal's largest annual event and was supposed to be for everyone, though the more junior nurses rarely went, either avoiding it as being too formal, or staying away because they hadn't been there long enough to feel that much part of the hospital. Seniors traded off-duty times or drew lots to see who would stay on duty. Cherry's only contact with it was to admire the extremely varied clothing seen going out of the Nurses' Home on The Night—and to wonder why Sister Grayson seemed extra-snappy both before and after the dance. It was tempting to wonder whether she had, or hadn't, partnered a certain person. Cherry carefully didn't. She was being meticulous about what was her business, and what wasn't. Wondering about consultants certainly *wasn't* her business.

January had come in wet, but now it cleared to a bright, sparkling frostiness which suggested colder weather to come. Walking off duty on a Saturday afternoon, and contemplating the fact that because of a change-round of duties she had Saturday afternoon off as well as her usual day off of Sunday, Cherry wondered idly whether to go down to the market, or do her mending, or take advantage of the brighter weather to go somewhere by bus. Or were her feet too tired after scurrying round after sick and convalescent children for her to do anything but put them up, for the moment?

For now, they were taking her automatically round by

the pigeonholes to see if she had any post. Rather to her surprise, there were two missives for Langton, a postcard and a letter. The postcard turned out to be from a school friend who had emigrated to Australia and was wishing her a belated Happy Christmas. The letter was more of a mystery because it was unstamped, and bore her name in capitals, in black ink. Cherry tore it open and unfolded a single sheet of white paper.

A brief message was written in the middle of it, in the same black ink and penned in an elegant but firm hand.

'The weather forecast for the weekend is good. I intend to drive to the moors on Sunday afternoon, and if you would like to join me, will pick you up halfway along the Melcrum Road at 2.30 p.m. A.T.'

Cherry stared at it in disbelief. Her heart had given a thud of pure shock, before settling down to beat in an uneven tempo—but more than anything, she suddenly wanted to laugh. She could almost see the sardonic look he must have been wearing as he wrote the instructions, with their cloak-and-dagger overtones—picking her up halfway out of town, well away from the hospital!

The most sensible thing, of course, would be not to go. After all, he couldn't possibly know whether she was actually off duty.

On the other hand, there really wasn't any harm in showing him the best spots on the moors, surely? Given that he was a stranger, wasn't it only charitable of her to show him round? And besides—

Cherry was still telling herself that she could, sensibly, have been too busy to come as she stood beside the Melcrum Road the following afternoon. She was ten minutes early because that was when the bus had dropped her there. She was feeling strange and awkward and wondering whether Mr Ashley Treneager might have changed his mind, and not come . . .

She was still thinking that when the silver Rolls slid to a halt beside her at two twenty-nine precisely, and the near-side door was pushed open for her with the brief but friendly instruction, 'Hop in!'

He was looking casual in tobacco-coloured slacks and a

white fine-knitted sweater. Informality made him look younger, and brought out a devil-may-care quality in him. He looked as if he might have been a racing driver rather than a working surgeon. To stop herself staring, Cherry found herself looking everywhere but at him. A dark leather jacket was thrown carelessly across the back seat. There seemed to be an amazing array of dials on the dashboard. The seats were upholstered in a pale grey to go with the car's silver bodywork and felt almost like a soft suede, and the engine had an incredibly quiet purr. It was definitely the most expensive car Cherry had ever been in, and was so different from the fourth-hand old bangers which was the most any of her friends had so far achieved that she felt suddenly tongue-tied and wondered what on earth she was doing here.

'I'm glad you were on time. It would have spoiled all my careful spy-story planning if I'd had to cruise up and down the road waiting for you,' the deep voice said beside her, drily, and making her feel no less selfconscious. Before she could answer, however, he was going on, 'I'm glad you've come properly dressed, so that we can get out and tramp about if we want to. It would be a waste not to get some fresh air. I seem to have spent too much time this week closeted in Theatre! And to judge by your sensibly thick coat and brogues, *you* feel like some fresh air too!'

'Have you had a busy week?' Cherry asked politely. There seemed no point in telling him that the sensibly thick coat was the only winter one she possessed, so that she hadn't actually had much choice in what to wear. She glanced at him shyly, aware of feeling bundled-up in her thick tweed skirt and jumper, and wondering if he could *really* have sounded approving about the way she looked. But then she was sure he hadn't done more than glance at her, and why should he?

'Yes, pretty busy, but let's not talk shop. What do you think of the car, by the way—now you're in it?'

'It's—it's amazing. I mean, amazingly comfortable,' Cherry said hastily.

'Yes, isn't it? It's also bullet-proof—'

'Bullet-proof?'

'Yes, believe it or not.' He was sounding amused, so that she wasn't sure whether he was teasing, but he went on casually, 'It was given to me by an oil sheikh, after I'd operated on his nephew. No, it *wasn't* a question of ill-gotten gains from a private patient! The boy came in as an emergency after a street accident, and I didn't even know who he was until afterwards. It took some explaining before the uncle could accept that I didn't want a fee because I was simply doing my job under the National Health. The upshot was that he insisted on giving me the car instead. Apparently it could have caused a diplomatic incident if I'd refused that as well,' Ashley Treneager explained, sounding cynical about it, so that Cherry was suddenly unsure whether he had simply made the whole story up for her amusement. It was as if he had read her mind when he added drily, 'True, I promise you! Mind you, I suppose I *might* not have kept it if someone hadn't been rash enough to tell me I ought to sell it because it was far too unsuitably flashy to drive around in!'

'Goodness, did somebody dare?' Cherry asked involuntarily, and received a chuckle in response.

'Oh yes! Naturally, after that, I decided to keep it, and drive it, as ostentatiously as possible!'

'As anyone with any character might . . .'

'Particularly since in my profession, if you want to be successful you don't only need talent and application, you need to *look* successful. You might say things oughtn't to be that way in something like surgery, but it happens to be true.' He flung the words casually in the direction of her listening face, though there was a thread of seriousness underlying them which made her feel that however much he might put on a mask of cynicism, his work was something he would never take lightly. Then he added, with the dryness back in his voice, and with the merest touch of a drawl, 'Mind you, it also happens that I can afford to run this kind of car—so I'm not suggesting you should look on me as some kind of misunderstood saint!'

That was so unlikely that Cherry found herself choking on an involuntary giggle. Since he laughed with her, the atmosphere lightened and she found herself relaxing. However unlikely it was that she should be here in his company, she might as well accept it as a gift, and enjoy it.

The moors opened out in front of them as the last houses fell away and countryside took over. For Cherry, the rolling wildness never failed to hold a magic all its own—all browns and dull greens and gold, with the silver gleam of water here and there, and grey rocky outcrops in counterpoint. There was a frosty sparkle in the air which added to the winter beauty. It seemed natural to park and get out and walk through the sharp, crisp air which seemed to sing in her blood like wine, and she was seized with a kind of recklessness which made it easy to treat him as a companion rather than as someone senior and daunting.

If he drew her out to talk rather than talking much himself, it was done with an easiness which made chatting to him seem natural. It was natural too to walk in quietness sometimes, simply drawing strength and restfulness from the wide unending view and the distant horizon. They might have been any two people, here in the emptiness, where it was rare to see anyone else except perhaps in the distance walking a dog, and where the sense of space and continuity shrank human cares into smallness.

The early dark was beginning to creep in from the edges by the time they got back to the car. Pausing on a rise of ground before covering the last hundred yards back to where they had parked, Ashley Treneager stretched, and said on a sigh, 'This was a good idea.'

'The moors take the cobwebs away.'

'Fanciful, but true.' A pleasant note in his voice robbed the words of any crushing effect. 'I suppose it's too much to hope that there's somewhere around here which would provide us with tea?'

'There's a place in one of the villages which does teas in summer—but January's not exactly a likely time for trippers,' Cherry told him dubiously, 'so I shouldn't think . . . Oh, Ashley, look!'

A line of geese had suddenly strung themselves out across the yellow and orange of the sunset, for all the world like a Vernon Ward painting. They looked almost unreally decorative with the last rays of the sun gilding the edges of their wings, and Cherry was too absorbed in watching them to realise that she had used his first name unthinkingly and quite naturally. Somehow, during the afternoon, it hadn't come up to call him anything at all.

'Al-most too theatrical,' he drawled now, causing her to give him a glare of reproach. Then he reached out a quick hand to catch her as she stepped back, and stumbled over a tussock of grass. 'Careful, or you'll wrench an ankle—no? That's all right, then. Come on, if there isn't anywhere locally to provide it, we might as well go back to my flat for a cup of tea. And hot buttered toast suddenly appeals to me!'

It appealed to Cherry too, as soon as he mentioned it. He didn't wait for her agreement or disagreement either, but began to draw her towards the car with his arm still linked through hers. She knew that he wasn't even aware of it, but *she* was suddenly selfconscious all over again, her arm tingling where he held it so casually, her mind coming back to earth with a thump. Now was the moment to point out that he'd better put her down, as he had picked her up, on the Melcrum Road, a suitable distance from the hospital. Now was the moment, she thought with a touch of wistfulness, for Cinderella to stop pretending that she belonged here. It was time for her to go back to her proper place.

Suddenly she didn't want to, and particularly not if it meant seeing Ashley turn back into Mr Treneager, and make scathing remarks besides at her carefulness. While he must know how far above her he was in the hierarchy, he probably *didn't* know just how much gossip could arise from how little, in a hospital as dedicated to its old-fashioned attitudes as the Royal. Cherry decided recklessly that she wouldn't raise the subject. And she *would* go and have tea at his flat in Ebury Road. It was perfectly possible that no one would see her anyway; and she really didn't want to spoil the mood of the afternoon . . .

He didn't seem at all aware of the struggle going on in her head as he opened the car door for her, then went round to his own side to drive back along the moor road and purr gently into the outskirts of Northborough. The long fingers looked relaxed as they nursed the wheel, and he was humming softly to himself. It was a bare twenty minutes before they pulled up outside a tall Victorian house in

Ebury Road and he shut off the engine, and the lights which had been necessary in the swiftly falling dusk of the winter afternoon.

'Upstairs,' he said explanatorily, as he let them in through an imposing front door into a wide hall. 'I've got the first floor.'

To judge by a child's bicycle stowed in one corner of the hall, he had a family for neighbours. Somehow that made it all the more surprising that he should choose to live here, rather than in a modern luxury block, when there *were* one or two very smooth developments in Northborough. Cherry went ahead of him up the stairs and stood aside while he put his key to a highly-polished door with discreet brass fitments, opening off a landing whose most noticeable feature was a large stained-glass window. Ashley glanced at it as he saw her looking, and said in a tone of easy amusement, 'Magnificently hideous, isn't it? I think I could get quite fond of it!' Then he was ushering her through the open door into a small hall and immediately on into a large, well-proportioned sitting-room which managed at the same time to look both comfortable, and tidy.

The comfort came from deep leather armchairs which gleamed against the muted gold of a thick carpet. A music centre took up one alcove with books ranged on shelves above it, and a desk occupied a second alcove. A polished dining table and chairs stood at one end of the long room with a half-open door beyond giving a glimpse into a small modern kitchen. Velvet curtains in a paler gold hung beside two elegantly tall windows, and Ashley moved to draw them across and shut out the shadowy dark tree-shapes of a garden seen dimly from above.

'Put your coat down somewhere, and I'll put the kettle on,' he said over his shoulder, adding, 'Bathroom's second door along the hall if you want it. I hope your silence means you approve of my choice of flat, rather than otherwise?'

'Yes, of course,' Cherry said hastily, and wishing his teasingly-raised eyebrow didn't make her feel selfconscious for having looked round so curiously. In fact she had been wondering why the room felt slightly anonymous when its owner had the sort of powerful personality whose stamp she would have expected to feel. Luckily he turned away and made for the kitchen without seeking any further comment from her. Cherry slipped obediently out of her coat and stood hesitating for a moment wondering where to put it down, then laid it across the back of one of the chairs before going in search of the bathroom.

That was anonymous too, small and heavily modernised and extremely tidy with nothing at all lying about. The mirror showed her her own bright cheeks and a windblown tangle of curls which it took her several minutes, and some painful tugging with a comb, to tame. She was wryly aware that her reflection, bundled up as she was in woollens, looked as square and healthily sturdy as a fell pony when she would much rather have seen herself as a sleekly elegant racehorse. The image did at least make her smile. To save herself from starting to feel selfconscious again, as she made her way back to the sitting-room she concentrated on thinking about Ashley, and wondering whether the flat did in fact reflect his personality.

Specialising in micro-surgery as he did, he might well be a particularly tidy person. Certainly he wasn't the sort of man one could imagine living in a clutter. Perhaps everything here was too new to reflect him yet, anyway . . . though it was noticeable that the array of books in the shelves were the only really personal touch, and there were no pictures on the walls. Certainly no photographs on display. It was as if, even here where he lived, he kept his private self very private.

Music was playing softly as she re-entered the sitting-room, something tranquilly classical with a guitar in it somewhere, or perhaps a harpsichord. The smoked glass top of a low table had now sprouted a large silver teapot, a jug of milk, and two stout earthenware mugs which contrasted with the Georgian elegance of the teapot. Cherry hesitated, then crossed to the kitchen from which movements could be heard, and stood hesitating in the doorway.

'Can I help . . . ?'

The kitchen was starkly modern and full of worktops and stainless steel fitted neatly into a small space. The tall surgeon looked remarkably at home in it, with neatly cut bread within hand's reach one side of him and an eye-level grill the other, with a plate, knife, and butter ready laid out where he could reach them without moving. It was a little like a time-and-motion study of the most efficient way to make hot buttered toast and made Cherry hope with sudden wariness that he wouldn't accept her offer of help, because she would be sure to blunder into something. Luckily he glanced across at her and said pleasantly,

'It isn't the kind of kitchen which can hold two people, so you might as well stay out of reach. Besides, I've got my own system—What's *that* look for?'

'Nothing! Well, I was wondering if you were *born* well organised or if you just learned to be!'

'Anyone can learn to do anything if they try hard enough. But for that piece of sarcasm, you can take this toast in there and butter it while I make the rest. And don't drop it on the carpet!'

'I wasn't being sarcastic!'

'No? If I'm good at making toast in multiples, it comes from the practice of having hungry nieces and nephews,' his voice floated after her, as she retreated with the plate he had thrust in her hand. Cherry pricked up her ears, wanting to ask him about the nieces and nephews, but he was going on, 'I hope you don't mind the music, by the way. I put it on out of habit, but you can turn it off if you prefer.'

'No, I like it. What is it?'

'This? Vivaldi. If you'd like something else, go and look at the tapes in the rack on the back of the desk. I'm working on getting them into some sort of order, but don't be surprised if they seem to be thoroughly mixed up, because I haven't had time to get very far yet.'

The back of the desk, now Cherry looked at it, was taken up by cassette tapes arranged in stacks along a slotted shelf. There must have been at least a hundred of them, and she walked across to study the titles, curious to see his taste, and then intrigued to find that it was enormously varied. Classical concertos rubbed shoulders with nineteen-sixties rock music, and there was even a Police album. Cherry wondered when he had time to play them all, and whether he started the day with Beethoven or jazz—and because she was suddenly caught up in visualising him having breakfast, she found herself jumping guiltily when he came back into the room from the kitchen with a second plate of toast in his hand and said pleasantly, 'Found anything you want?'

'What's playing is fine, I was just looking. You obviously like music.'

'I'm gradually getting my theatre staff used to that idea—even if it's been an uphill struggle with the Senior Nursing Officer in charge of theatres!'

'You mean you have music *while* you're operating?'

'Yes. It's quite often done, you know. It helps concentration—mine, at any rate. It may not be "the way Northborough Royal's used to doing things", but since it quite possibly has a good subliminal effect on the patients too, there's no reason why Northborough Royal shouldn't be persuaded to change its ideas,' he said, with a militant gleam in his eyes. He added sardonically, 'If they didn't want to change, they should never have appointed me, now should they?'

'What sort of music do you play in Theatre?' Cherry asked curiously.

'Depends. On mood—on the type of operation—on the way I'm feeling that day! I don't go in for great sweeps of Wagner: more suitable for abdominal operations on a large scale,' he said with a grin, looking so amused that Cherry was suddenly sure he was teasing her again. 'And marching brass bands would probably be more suitable to orthopaedics—'

'Oh, you're joking!'

'No, I'm not, so stop looking at me as if you don't believe a word of it! You'd be surprised at the things surgeons do. We're an eccentric breed.' He gave her another mischievous glance, then added more seriously, 'But operating to music isn't really an eccentricity, it's just one more aid to a steady hand. And why not? Haven't you buttered that toast yet? Now what was the point of my giving it to you hot if you were going to—'

'Sorry,' Cherry said hastily, coming back to the table, but with her mind still on theatres. 'Oh, I *do* hope it catches on generally by the time I do theatre nursing—the music, I mean!'

'It probably won't. People are very diehard and to each his own method. Of course, you may end up in *my* theatre. But if you do, you'd certainly better concentrate on the surgical procedures rather than the music. And you needn't expect a disco atmosphere, either!'

He had picked up the teapot and was pouring the fragrant brown liquid into the mugs as he spoke. Cherry opened her mouth to tell him that that wasn't the point at all, she had merely thought the music might be a good aid against either fainting or dropping things. Since he would probably have been just as crushing about her fear of doing either, perhaps it was just as well that the telephone interrupted them. It was the modern kind with an insistent high-pitched bugling ring, and Ashley winced, frowning.

'Damn. If that's an emergency you'll have to have tea on your own and let yourself out afterwards . . . Though I'm not actually supposed to be on duty. Hallo? Treneager here.'

Though the telephone was on the desk and he had got up to answer it, Cherry couldn't help hearing that the tinny scratch which answered him definitely sounded female. There was a smoothness in his voice as he said, 'Yes, of course I remember you,' which suggested the same thing, and then he said, 'Just hold on a moment, would you?' and turned to Cherry with his hand over the receiver.

'Eat. I'll just take this in the other room.' Then he was unplugging the instrument from the wall and carrying it out into the hall, shutting the door behind him. Presumably he could plug the telephone back in in his bedroom and preferred to carry on talking there . . .

There was no reason for Cherry to feel suddenly cross and dispirited. He had every right to his phone calls. Besides, it ought to have been worse if he had gone on talking in front of her, making a date or whatever it was he was doing now, as if she was too unimportant for it to matter that she was there listening. Cherry tried to pull herself together and give herself a good scold. She was *not* going to fall into a dreamy state about Ashley Treneager just because he took her out for a walk with him. She wasn't going to acknowledge that he was attractive and fascinating and amazingly good company: she wasn't even going to fall into the trap of feeling a touch of harmless hero-worship. All the same, as she took a gulp of too-hot tea, she found herself wishing that the sparkle hadn't gone out of the afternoon quite so suddenly.

It was ten minutes before he came back, giving her plenty of time to remember that she was only here because he had commanded her company in a casual and arbitrary fashion. As he came back into the room she scrambled to her feet saying,

'I'd really better go, and stop taking up your afternoon—'

'If you were doing that I'd have told you so. Sit down and finish your tea, and I'll drive you back later.'

'I'll walk. It's hardly any distance—'

'It's also dark!'

'Northborough isn't exactly dangerous!' Cherry looked round for her coat, but it seemed to have vanished. He was regarding her with his eyebrows raised, apparently startled by her sudden fit of activity, and mildly amazed by it.

'You're not due back on duty, so why are you suddenly standing there buzzing like a—like an angry plum?' he asked, his lips twitching in amusement. 'No, I suppose plums *don't* buzz, but it's that purple thing you're wearing, which looks about three sizes too big—'

'It's extremely warm,' Cherry snapped, trying not to feel hurt at his description of her jumper, which had been a sale bargain even it was too big. Besides, she had been working on the theory that its size might make her look thinner. 'And I like this colour!'

'Hush, I didn't say it didn't suit you! It does. But you really don't have to go this minute, do you? If you do, I'll get your coat out of the cupboard for you—but is there really any rush?'

He was giving her a smile of such straightforward charm that to refuse would seem exaggerated and rude. Cherry subsided, feeling foolish. It didn't help when Ashley said negligently, 'That's better, I hate people who fidget,' and sat down himself right beside her, stretching out his long legs in front of him and reaching a hand for the untouched toast, now cool and slightly congealed. 'Another thing I hate,' he added, 'is people who *will* ring me up to ask me about the eye problems of their nearest and dearest, apparently on the grounds that having met me socially entitles them to a personal consultation!'

'Oh . . . Does that happen often?'

'Too often, and to most doctors. And,' he added with an air of gloom, 'I couldn't be as rude as I often am, since this one was a friend of my Ward Sister. Is it too much to ask that that should have made her know better?'

He sounded so martyred that Cherry lost her suspicion that he had merely been making an excuse for the phone call—though why should he bother, anyway? She couldn't help noting that he met his Ward Sister's friends socially, and therefore presumably her too. Sister Beaumont, she of the swan neck and cool beauty. To be fair, she probably made quite a good pair with her consultant. She did at least look nicer than Sister Grayson. According to Buzz she was quite pleasant to work for, anyway, and had even been known to laugh.

'What are you thinking, sitting there so silently?'

'Nothing,' Cherry said hastily, startled by the abrupt question. 'I mean—about doctors being asked for free consultations. I suppose people do always do that—when they wouldn't dream of asking a plumber to nip upstairs and fix a dripping tap!'

'Very true. I must remember that one next time someone tries to pin me down with an opinion on a patient I haven't even seen.' He sounded amused, and added, 'You're a funny child, aren't you? Half the afternoon you're splendidly restful company. Then all of a sudden you turn all jumpy again! I know we live in a free and easy world, and you're here alone with me in my flat, but I did tell you were perfectly safe with me!'

'I didn't think I wasn't! I didn't *say* I wasn't either—I said "*Northborough* isn't dangerous"!'

'That might have meant you thought *I* was.' He had suddenly gone into a challenging, teasing mood which made Cherry feel nettled and uncomfortable. She didn't like being described as a 'funny child' either, and would have been tempted to tell him so if he hadn't gone on, with a dry note in the deep voice and a stare from the dark eyes which combined challenge and resignation. 'I know just what you were saying—that I mustn't drive you back to the hospital for the usual reason. And I *have* discovered by now that the gossips like to have a field day over my every move. How idiotic people are, aren't they?'

'Yes,' Cherry said shortly. 'But—'

'But this is the world we have to live in. Since you know this particular part of it much better than I do, I think I'll make you my social arbiter. Who *may* I suitably be seen with, Cherry Langton?'

'I don't—'

'You disapproved of Emily Grayson, so I looked again and decided you were right. She looked so much better in uniform than out of it. There's a very striking staff nurse in Casualty who caught my eye the other day—but she may be another uniform girl. I don't think I ought to aspire to Assistant Matron level, do you? But, since I can't be expected to spend what little free time I have entirely alone, I really ought to know who's in the pool for me to choose from, so to speak!'

'If you're going to sound so patronising, I hope they all turn you down!' Cherry said crossly, outraged beyond politeness.

'Well said. I'm glad to see you stick up for your sex. But let's be realistic. If I ask, they won't,' he said, the black eyes gleaming with a cynicism which made her feel a sudden wave of dislike for him. She stared at him, and wondered suddenly if his mouth had always had that bitter twist. Surely, even with the accidental death of his wife behind him, he didn't have to see the world in such black terms?

She wasn't supposed to know about that, and a sudden fear that he would read it in her face made her get to her feet again, her face carefully blank. 'I think I *will* go now, if you don't mind,' she said with elaborate politeness. 'Thank you for driving me to the moors. And for tea—'

'Thank you for your company. And for not *quite* telling

me how much you disapprove of me,' he said silkily, the velvet tone in his voice very pronounced. He came to his feet with Cherry very carefully not looking at him, and said, 'I'll just get your coat, and then I'll walk you at least as far as the corner.'

'You don't have to. Northborough really isn't dangerous. It's not London and it isn't full of muggers. Not in this sort of area anyway,' Cherry amended. She felt as if she was talking for the sake of talking, and the easy relaxation of the early part of the afternoon seemed to have gone. He was a very moody person, she decided miserably.

He helped her into her coat, a process not made any easier by the fact that one sleeve of her jumper managed to get caught in the lining. It was as if her clumsiness jinx, which she was just managing to shake off on the wards, had suddenly come back to plague her. She felt flushed and stupid at having to be disentangled and was sure that his silent efficiency showed he was now bored with her company and glad to get rid of her. It was a pity that the afternoon had suddenly gone sour, making her feel glad to escape. It didn't help when he retained his sarcastic mood enough to say, as he walked her down the stairs,

'I meant it about your being my social arbiter. I'm obliged to go to some charity fund-raising dance that I can't get out of, though goodness knows why I should be expected to raise money for the National Health Service as well as working in it. Stop sulking and tell me who I should take!'

'Sister Beaumont,' said Cherry, off the top of her head, and trying not to sound snappish so as to avoid the charge of sulking. She *wasn't*, and he didn't have any right to suggest she was!

'Oh, don't you think her husband might mind? Or did you mean I should invite both of them and make up a party?'

'I didn't know she was married.'

'Yes—to a rather well-muscled sculptor, so I'd hate to try any conclusions with him. Besides, they're a very happy couple. Don't misjudge me enough to think I steal other people's wives!'

'I didn't. I really didn't know she was married. As well as not liking gossip, I never *know* any of it,' Cherry informed him, looking up—and up—and all at once feeling more cheerful, for absolutely no reason. Ashley was watching her with an unfathomable heavy-lidded stare through eyes which might only have been narrowed because he was having to look down at her, since he looked quite amiable. 'Thank you again for—'

'No, don't start thanking me again, and I'm going to walk you at least part of the way back. At least—no, damn, that sounds like my phone again! Wait there, will you?'

The distant fluting certainly came from upstairs, but as he made for it, Cherry let herself out, letting the door slam behind her and walking quickly off along the dark road. The air was misty now, with a chill in the darkness, and she huddled into her coat collar and speeded up. It wasn't far to the hospital, and the roads between here and there were all well lit, so she didn't know what he was fussing about. But it was nice of him to take so much trouble over her . . .

It had been the oddest afternoon, like something out of a dream. Tomorrow, or when she next ran into him in a hospital corridor, they would be on opposite sides of the social divide again, but this afternoon had been fun. Well, not exactly fun . . . more like a nugget to put away and keep; an unexpected and secret happening to treasure privately.

If he liked her at all, it was because he didn't have to put on any good manners for her, or any social behaviour, because she wasn't anyone important. He probably forgot her the minute she was out of sight. Somehow that didn't matter. What did matter was that she was hurrying through the streets feeling remarkably cheerful—and wanting to giggle suddenly at the memory of some of his comments.

She had better not remember what he had said about Sister Grayson when she next went on duty. *'You disapproved of Emily Grayson, so I looked again and decided you were right'*—goodness, Cherry thought on a bubble of laughter, even though she knew it wasn't true, just hearing it said was a splendid revenge for all the senior nurse's pickiness. And even if she shouldn't feel like that, she did; though undoubtedly she would be struck by a thunderbolt if only Sister Grayson knew!

CHAPTER FOUR

THERE was a package in Cherry's pigeonhole four days later. Her name and address were typed on it, so she had no idea what to expect when she tore open the large envelope and a pair of scarlet woollen gloves fell out. Luckily the note—on a single sheet of white paper, penned in black—stayed between her fingers, because she had time to see the initials A.T. as signature before she thrust it hastily back into the envelope and bent to pick up the gloves, while Suzanne was saying,

'Hey, that's lucky, you were saying you'd lost yours! Who's sent you some?'

'Auntie May,' Cherry said quickly, turning the envelope round so that its lack of stamp couldn't be seen. She felt a little guilty for the lie, but somehow there were things she didn't want to share even with Suzanne who was her closest friend. Besides, she could hardly say, 'I think they're from Mr Treneager' in an airy fashion, now could she?

Besides, ungratefully, she found herself slightly resentful that he hadn't returned her own gloves, if his flat was where she had left them. She felt even more inclined to be ungrateful when she escaped to her room and read his note. It said,

'You left your gloves in my car, and as they had a large hole in I thought you might like some new ones. I was buying some for my eldest niece in the market, so two pairs was no problem.'

It was extremely charitable of him. Unfortunately it also carried the memory of telling him about her own total lack of family and seemed to reduce her rather pointedly to the role of an amusing child, and a child furthermore who might be in need of a hand-out. He probably wasn't aware that it was the type of kindness to set Cherry's teeth on edge, and hadn't meant it that way, but she had to swallow a feeling of annoyance.

A stubborn streak in her made it necessary to work out a response which would pay him back without seeming rude. She considered things thoughtfully, and when she was off duty next day, went into town to a bookshop. The slim package which she posted to the flat in Ebury Road contained a paperback and a note in her rounded handwriting:

'Thank you for the gloves, and in exchange here is a paperback of Spike Milligan, since you said he amused you but you hadn't read any of his poems. Cherry.'

She didn't have time to wonder how he had taken it, because work suddenly took up all her thoughts with the skidding and overturning of a school bus which, to add to the horror, then hit another vehicle and caught fire. The children's ward cubicles for the seriously ill were all at once full, Sister Temple was never off duty, and Cherry's opinion of Sister Grayson rose as she saw at first hand how the older girl could act with calm efficiency in the face of horrific injuries. It was a bad time, and one which made Cherry feel as if she had grown up overnight as she was seconded to help with dangerously ill children instead of convalescent ones. And even those children who could be nursed past that stage would be in hospital for months, perhaps come back for years, for skin grafts to the burned areas.

The day the child who was her particular patient died was the worst day of all. There probably hadn't been a hope of saving him, but it still felt like a desperate failure. When at last she came off duty Cherry couldn't face the canteen or even the Nurses' Home. She didn't know where she was going as her legs took her walking through the streets like an automaton, and she wasn't aware that it had started to drizzle until the moisture soaking through her cloak began to make her shiver. It had only seemed natural to feel wetness on her cheeks even though the tears were still locked up inside her. She stumbled into a bus shelter when one appeared in front of her and stood there numbly, too taken up with anger and frustration to do more than pause automatically for shelter. She was only glad that there was no one else around so that she could lean tiredly against the concrete shelter and think her own bitter thoughts.

She didn't notice the car which swished to a halt because

she was staring at the ground, shut into her private world. She was woken by a voice saying, 'Cherry? Get in, and don't argue—there probably isn't a bus for another half an hour!'

The silver Rolls gleaming in the lamplight somehow didn't seem a surprise. Ashley Treneager's voice saying amiably, 'Are you going back to the hospital, or away from it?' didn't seem particularly surprising either as she obediently climbed in through the door he was leaning across to hold open for her. It didn't seem to matter, at this moment, whether anyone saw her with him or not, so she said briefly, 'Back,' and then, 'I'm off duty.'

'And getting extraordinarily wet, and looking extraordinarily cross about it. You'd better come back to the flat and get dry, if you don't want to catch pneumonia.'

'There's no need—'

'Oh yes, there is. I'm not going to dump you on a doorstep like a drowned rabbit.' There was a pause, and when Cherry didn't fill it he went on, 'You're not arguing as much as usual, but you *do* sound extremely hostile. Have I done something to offend you? Oh, and thank you for the book, though I wasn't sure that I liked the "in exchange" in your note. Did we need an exchange?'

'I don't really like being given things,' Cherry said very politely, but through stiff lips.

'Don't you? Why not?'

'Echoes of Social Security. It's probably a hang-up, but it's just the way I am.'

'O-oh. Well now,' he drawled, 'oddly enough, I thought we were friends. But the way you sound now, I'm surprised you didn't simply post the gloves back to me and demand your own—hole and all. Sorry about that, I'm afraid I threw them away. Anyway—' he pulled to a halt, and Cherry could feel him glance at her, even though she wasn't looking at him—'we're not going to quarrel over anything quite so trivial, are we? Get out and make a run for the door—you might as well not get any wetter!'

Cherry did as she was told, though she didn't know quite why: his challenging company was the last thing she felt fit to cope with. She went up the stairs with him too, and into the flat silently, suddenly too tired to resist anything. He said brusquely, 'Go and have a hot shower—and here, take this to put on afterwards,' handing her a towelling robe which he took out of a cupboard. 'We can put your cloak and dress in the tumble-dryer while you have some hot soup, since you've been foolish enough to get so thoroughly chilled! So bring them out to the kitchen with you when you've finished!'

She didn't have the energy to answer him. He probably thought she was being rude, sulky and childish. He was certainly wearing a very impersonal look when she came into the sitting-room a quarter of an hour later, the dark eyes very dark and almost blank. He said, with a cool impersonal note in the deep voice,

'Feeling any better? Here, give me those, and I'll fetch your soup. Sit down, I won't be a moment.'

'You're being very kind—'

'Not particularly.' He was back while she was still standing there holding the robe which was much too big for her wrapped around her and wondering numbly where to sit. She could hear the rumble of a tumble-dryer starting up in the kitchen behind him and he held a steaming mug in his hand. There was a touch of impatience in his eyes as he looked at her, but he was obviously reining it in as he said,

'It occurs to me that it isn't anything *I've* done at all. I'm quite a good listener if you want to tell me about it. What *is* the trouble—a quarrel with a boy-friend? That's the usual kind of heartbreak that sends young girls out tramping the streets in the rain—'

'No, it isn't anything like that. It's—I—'

'Wait a minute. You're on the children's ward. The school bus?' His eyes sharpened as he saw Cherry wince. 'You've been nursing those children, haven't you? Yes, I did hear about it.'

Suddenly it was unbearable not to blurt it out. 'Mine died—my special. He died this afternoon. I wasn't any *use*! You—you can tell me off if you like for being too involved, I can't help it, and if that means I'll never make a nurse then I never will!'

'It's the first death you've met?'

'No, but the others were—'

'Older? More obviously terminal?'

'You're going to say, "if you can't stand the heat keep out of the kitchen,"' Cherry spat at him, all the frustrated rage she felt coming out in anger towards him. 'Well, I c-can't —not—not feeling that I might j-just as well not have been there—not feeling that I *let him down*—'

'Why? Did you do something wrong?'

'No.' No, she hadn't: there had been no mistakes, no clumsinesses, nothing at all to blame herself for, in fact she had received quiet approval from her seniors for the way she had coped. 'There wasn't anything anyone could do,' she said on a wobble, and then, angrily, 'But he was only eight years old, and I wanted to *fight* for him, and I couldn't!'

'So you're tearing yourself to pieces because the world's cruel and an unfair place? Yes, I see. Well, you'll probably go on feeling like that. And on the day you've stopped feeling it at all—*then* you should give up. Certainly not now.'

The thoughtful look he was giving her seemed to look right inside her head, to all the flood of doubts which had gone with her on her walk. She *had* been thinking about giving up, thinking about it numbly but considering it all the same, because the ambition she had always had—to be a good nurse—had suddenly seemed empty. She obviously wasn't any use at it. Perhaps she never would be. She looked up at Ashley who was looming over her without touching her, and wondered why there was no scorn or mockery in his face. She wouldn't have thought he would suffer fools gladly . . . and she was being a fool, hysterical and over-emotional. Nurses were supposed to stay in control of their feelings.

'It doesn't always hurt as much as it does the first time,' he said, quite gently, just as she had been about to blurt out almost exactly that question. 'The first time you lose a patient who was particularly yours—the first time you're brought face to face with the—the arbitrary cruelty of fate . . . But we all do have to live with it. And I'm afraid you'll have to, along with the rest of us. There's a fine line between caring enough, and not letting it destroy you, and if this is the job you want to do, you're going to have to learn to walk it. Understood?'

'Yes, of course I understand. I—I just don't know if—'

'Can you imagine doing anything else?'

'No. It's what I've always wanted—I told you that!'

'Then you're stuck with it,' he said practically. 'I can give you a handkerchief for your tears, but I can't give you a cure for living. Sorry not to be more of a help, but there it is.'

Oddly, it *was* a help, as if the fact that even he had no answers made her own confusion bearable. Cherry, who hadn't even known that she had started to cry, rubbed her cheeks hastily with the handkerchief he had given her. A small part of her consciousness knew that if Ashley had sat down and put his arms round her and been comforting, it would have been wonderful—but it wouldn't have solved anything, and would have made her cry more thoroughly. It brought a flush of warmth to her cheeks to know that she had even thought of it, so that she couldn't look at him as she scrubbed her face with his handkerchief. The touch of his hand on her shoulder made her jump, but he was pushing her down gently into a chair, and firmly handing her the mug of soup.

'Now you're going to drink this, and we'll talk about it if you feel like talking about it—or we'll talk about other things if you don't. After all, as I said to you earlier, we *are* friends, aren't we? So let's share some time, and see if that makes the world look brighter and more bearable!'

It was extraordinary to realise afterwards that she had spent two hours sitting wrapped in his spare bathrobe just talking and listening and letting herself be gentled away from the pain of the last few days and the particular pain of today. Somehow it didn't seem strange to be comparing notes between a nurse's life and a doctor's—between the training and expectation and attitudes which made up the role each had to play. They stuck almost exclusively to shop, and it occurred to Cherry afterwards, though with a touch of wistfulness, that it had been clever of him to see that talk about hospitals was what she had needed most.

They only touched on the more personal side of their lives as she was leaving.

Ashley was sending her home in a taxi: he would have insisted on driving her except, he said with a frowning glance at his watch, that he was expecting an overseas phone call. He was firm that he was going to pay for the taxi, too. Since Cherry had very little money on her she wasn't about to stop him, but before she could open her mouth to say so he was informing her, caustically and pointedly, that it had nothing to do with Social Security. He added drily,

'Am I really supposed to apologise to you about the gloves? Of course, if the others had some kind of sentimental value—'

'No, they didn't. But gloves can be recycled,' Cherry told him. 'I could have cut the fingers off and turned them into mittens, couldn't I? And I can't abide waste!'

'Another of your hang-ups? Seriously, is it a real hang-up? And if so, why?'

'Pride, maybe?' She hesitated, glancing at him shyly and a little ruefully. There was no way he was likely to understand. 'I suppose,' she said carefully, 'that looking at it one way, my foster-parents were paid to bring me up. Not that they ever made me feel like that. But people sometimes think . . .' She stopped, and let out a chuckle. 'Oh, it's not your world, is it? I mean, it wouldn't tell you anything if I said "free school dinners", when you probably went to *Eton*!'

'I didn't, as it happens. I went to a Catholic public school. But I think I get the message. There's no need to overdo it, though, is there?'

'I don't. *Are* you a Catholic?' Cherry asked curiously, surprised in spite of herself, and then wishing her words hadn't made him frown.

'Not noticeably, or not nowadays, but I was certainly born and brought up that way.' He said it shortly, and turned his head as a hoot came from outside. 'That sounds like your taxi. Let's go down and see what he wants to charge for the trip and then I'll pay him in advance. Come along!'

Any more questions Cherry might have had died on her

lips as he turned and walked downstairs, leaving her to follow him. A moment later he had gone back indoors with a wave and she was almost at once being told about the cab driver's mother-in-law's symptoms because she was in uniform and had given the Nurses' Home address. It wasn't that she minded, but the man's chattiness got in the way of her thoughts, so that she had to switch herself off and simply listen to him.

He took her right up to the door of the Nurses' Home. As Cherry jumped out, another taxi came swishing in to pull up sharply in the small space which was left behind hers. To her surprise it was Buzz who got out and leaned over to pay the driver. Then he came in fast so that he and Cherry almost collided in the doorway.

'Hi. I thought you were on days off—Sue said you'd gone home. Buzz? Hey, it's *me*—Cherry!'

He had been about to march on straight by her, and as he turned back she could see why: he was obviously in a towering temper. 'Are you all right?' she asked quickly, and then—remembering Ashley's practical sympathy and how much it had helped her—'Do you want to talk about it?'

'Why—can you cure me of *parents*?' Buzz asked gratingly, and turned on his heel to make for the nurses' sitting room before she could answer. 'I need coffee. And a cigarette if the bloody machine's got any!'

'You don't smoke!'

'Well, maybe I'll start!' He was switching the lights on as Cherry followed him into the deserted room. The cigarette machine—which had always seemed an anomaly to Cherry on hospital premises—squatted in the corner next to the coffee machine. Buzz gave it a thump as he passed, but she was glad to see, when he dragged coins out of his pocket, it was only to put them in the coffee dispenser.

'Want some?' he growled, innate politeness apparently overcoming bad temper.

'All right. Have you quarrelled with your father again? Don't tell me if you don't want to!'

'Oh, it wasn't about nursing this time. It was about my friends.' Buzz was flushed, and his well-shaped mouth twisted bitterly. 'When I was at school, Kedi Singh was my best friend. Apparently it was all right then. A sign of how broadminded my bloody father was, I shouldn't wonder. *Now* it's apparently a question of, these aren't the sort of people it's best for me to know!'

'Horrible,' Cherry said pacifically, wrinkling up her nose.

'You can't actually get more respectable than the Sikh community! And why is it all right while we're at school, but not all right once we're out in the world? Don't worry, I don't expect you to answer that,' he said wryly, calming down suddenly, but with a tightness around his mouth showing how sick the whole thing made him. 'How can you be prejudiced against someone with three A levels and doing well at studying for accountancy and say "they're not like us"—*how?*'

'I honestly don't know. I've never seen why people have to live in little boxes.'

'Nothing much we can do about it though, is there? Nothing except walk out whenever my father's at his worst!' Buzz took a gulp of his coffee, looking bitter enough for it to be full of arsenic, adding on a sneer, 'And it isn't what he can afford to be heard saying in public, either, so that makes him a hypocrite too! He just makes me—' He broke off, seemed to pull himself together, and glanced at Cherry. 'Sorry to load it on you,' he said gruffly. 'You've had your own stuff to carry the last few days, haven't you? Has it been awful?'

'Yes. But I'm going to have to learn to live with things like that on duty, as we all are—though not too often, please God—and then cut them off when I come off duty. At least I don't have family troubles as well,' Cherry told him sympathetically.

'When it comes down to it I bet a lot of people would envy you,' Buzz grated. He threw her a glance of apology before she could open her mouth to protest, and added with a pretence of lightness, 'Oh, take no notice of me, and it'll pass! What can we talk about to cheer ourselves up? Who's Lisa in love with this week? Oh, and that's another thing—since I will do a "woman's job", my father has obvious doubts that I'm—ah—you know, *normal*!'

'You could always offer him a reference from that physio you've been going around with,' Cherry said sweetly—though more to distract him than anything else. And it worked, since he flushed abruptly and looked at her with suspicion.

'How did you hear about that?'

'Aha, I have my sources, let alone the fact that you were—um—*very* occupied with each other at the last disco! It's all right, you know, I'm only teasing,' she said, but glad to see that he was looking mollified.

'It's like living in a goldfish bowl around here,' he grumbled, but only half-heartedly. And then he added, quite solemnly, 'I wouldn't get mixed up with anyone seriously until I'd finished training, though. We can't afford to. Lisa's an idiot if she lets herself be distracted too much. Personally, I've got my sights on my RGN certificate, and on doing well on the way there. I intend to succeed, whatever anyone says!'

Cherry could see that he meant it. At that moment the Night Supervisor's voice spoke drily from the doorway.

'I'm glad to hear you say so, Mr Bascombe, but could you say it a little quieter? It's after eleven o'clock and not the weekend, so I think I'm entitled to suggest that you don't shout on the premises, don't you? I'm about to lock up, so if you should be going out again, please use the side door!'

The dry reproof hung in the air as she left again, leaving the two nurses to exchange sheepish looks. Cherry pulled a face and murmured comically, 'Why do they always know one's name when one's doing something *wrong*?' but Buzz had recovered himself quickly and gave her a stubborn look.

'Speak for yourself. I don't think there's any harm in being noticeable!'

'An advantage for you, then—since there are only about a quarter the number of male nurses in training as there are females. I'm just pointing out the plus side,' Cherry told him cheeringly, 'because it should make you rise to the top more easily, shouldn't it? Though when you become Matron, they really *will* have to go over to calling it

Chief Superintendent of Nurses or whatever the title's supposed to be!'

'There *are* more male Nursing Officers rising to the top,' Buzz retorted. He went on, 'Oh, by the way, did you hear that they've appointed a new Nursing Officer in charge of the teaching side? One with more modern ideas, too. The course is being reorganised and there's going to be a section on Management Training in the third year—'

'Help! That sounds more like office work than nursing!'

'No, it isn't, don't be silly. It's training in what to do when you're left in charge. Better to be taught properly than left to flounder, isn't it?'

Buzz was looking more cheerful, so Cherry felt she could follow her inclinations and leave him for the haven of her room. She said good night and went away upstairs. It had been a long, and strangely mixed, day.

The next day, with its tiny dread about going back to the ward, passed without incident. And the next. No more of the school bus children died, although two remained on the seriously-ill list, and Cherry was moved back to the convalescent children. After some thought, she had bought one of those cards with 'Thank You' printed on it and an attractive but restrained picture on the front, and posted it to Ashley's address, because she felt she *hadn't* thanked him. Two days later there was a note in her pigeonhole by way of answer with 'NO NEED!' printed in the middle in capitals and no signature. There was something almost comic about exchanging messages in this way—at least Cherry decided it was funny—and that was what made her spirits bubble up with an exceptional cheerfulness.

Because a late snowfall brought winter back again, it was difficult to realise that time had passed and suddenly there were only a couple of weeks left before Cherry was due to finish on the Paediatric Wing. She probably wouldn't have woken up to it even then if Peter hadn't reminded her, by asking her which children she had chosen to write up for the case histories they were supposed to hand in at the end of every ward, as part of their assessment.

'Oh, help, is it that time already? Who are you doing, so that we won't duplicate?' They had met in the doorway of the ward bathroom, both restraining active convalescent toddlers.

'I've done the kid with Hirschsprung's disease, and started writing up the pelvic fracture. D'you think I ought not to have done both abdominals, though, even if they're quite different?'

'I should avoid bones altogether,' a third-year put in helpfully, popping her head over the bathroom screens. 'You know you may get called in for questions by the doctors, if Sister manages to catch them to do it? Well, the Orthopaedic registrar's a beast about asking for details you couldn't possibly know at the end of your first year, so unless you're mad keen on the subject, I should play safe!'

'Thanks,' Peter said fervently. 'I wonder who to do instead, though?'

'Why don't you write up that little lass you've got there? She's one of the squints, isn't she? Yes, I thought so. Mr Treneager's registrar will be a *lot* easier on the questions. I know that because it's John Bland and he's engaged to one of my set,' she added with a grin, and then went on doubtfully, 'Of course you might get Treneager himself, I did hear he was taking an interest in the teaching side. Still, I gather *he's* not too bad either as long as he can see you're really trying!'

'Thanks,' Peter said again. The senior nurse gave him a smile before she disappeared again and said, 'Don't look so terrified, Lee, I'd say you've done quite well! In fact I don't think either of you will get a bad report, though you needn't quote me!'

'That's a relief,' Cherry said. It gave her a glow to know that she *had* improved, even if she was still told off (particularly by Sister Grayson) for looking untidy. She certainly did seem less prone to disasters—thanks to a certain person's advice, she told herself with an involuntary smile.

'You still haven't said which children you're going to do?' Peter's question cut across her thoughts, and she pulled herself together hastily.

'Betty's asthma for one, because I've got all the notes for that. And for a surgical I'll do—oh, Karl's intussusception,' Cherry told him, making her mind up on the spot. She *had* been thinking of writing up one of the children's eye cases, finding herself suddenly particularly interested in them, but after the senior nurse's words she decided abruptly not to. If she found herself being questioned by Ashley, she might forget everything she'd learned and written—and besides, he might think she'd made the choice on purpose expecting special treatment . . .

Not that she *would* expect anything at all, but the thought was always there. It was difficult enough to pass him in corridors and wonder if he noticed her as he strolled by at the consultant's regulation slow and measured walk. Then she was wheeling a ten-year-old down to Physiotherapy one morning when he appeared round a corner, and, disconcertingly when she hadn't expected him to acknowledge her, gave her a brief nod and said coolly, 'Good morning, Nurse,' as they passed. There wasn't anyone else around at that moment except a porter and a couple of ward-maids, and Cherry knew that it was idiotic of her to blush. She leaned hastily over her charge and hoped her hot cheeks weren't noticeable. It was just that seeing him at work was like having double vision; a world away from the man in whose flat she had sat, talking as if to a friend.

In fact it was only the registrars whom Sister managed to catch to ask her nurses questions on their case histories. Then there was the solemnity of their ward reports from Sister Temple herself, read out privately to each of them so that they could comment if they wished. Both Peter and Cherry were assessed as above average, which was a pleasant surprise for Cherry. Then, suddenly, they were leaving the Paediatric Wing for the last time at the end of duty.

'Do you realise what we've got now?' Lisa said blissfully, as the friends converged on Suzanne's room almost automatically as if needing a central point in a suddenly changed world. Duty hours might cause friendships to drift, but now that they were suddenly, almost awesomely, at the end of their first year, they moved back instinctively into a group.

'We have,' Lisa was going on, 'almost *six whole weeks* without having to set foot in a ward at all—'

'Don't make it sound like that, anyone would think you wanted to quit!'

'No, but I'm quite glad to be finished on cancer chemotherapy, and to know that I won't go back there at least until I'm trained. There's a good recovery rate, but it's still heavy. But what I meant was—do you realise that for once we've got *every evening off* for weeks stretching ahead?'

'We're supposed to be studying,' Suzanne pointed out mildly. 'For the two weeks of study block anyway, and then there's the three days pre-exam, and *then*—'

'Oh, don't let's think about that just yet! Unless you were going to say, *then* we've got our other three weeks of holiday entitlement before we have to do any work at all! *I* was just thinking,' Lisa said dreamily, 'of all the time it gives me to see Paul—'

'I thought he was called Richard, your porter or whatever he is!'

'He was a university student filling in as a porter, as it happens,' Lisa retorted to Buzz's lofty comment, and went on airily, 'Anyway, that's all over since I met Paul. He's the pharmacy student with the gorgeous curly hair, you must have seen him!'

'I don't go round noticing pharmacy students' hair—'

'Only physios?'

'Don't fight, children. Lisa, if I didn't know you took life more seriously than you pretend, I'd be ashamed of you. Buzz, don't be snooty.' Even when Suzanne was doing her schoolmistressy bit she managed to sound placid. 'Cherry, love, you're very quiet!'

'Oh, she's awestruck at surviving the whole first year. Do you realise that's what we've *done*?'

'Almost! We've still got the exam to add to our ward assessments! Cherry, you're not worried about that, are you? Not you, you can sail through written exams!'

'I was just thinking that I'll miss the children,' Cherry said lightly. It wasn't precisely true, even though she would miss them, after three months on the Paediatric Wing. It was just that while the others were talking it had dawned on her with a jolt that she would be thoroughly out of circulation for the next six weeks.

Study block would keep her out of the wards and corridors and wrapped up in the company of her own set, attending lectures and demonstrations and sharing all her time with the others. If anyone should—just by chance—decide to suggest a repeated walk on the moors, she wouldn't be able to get away . . . and after that there was holiday, when she was booked to spend a week visiting her foster-parents in Bournemouth and then the last ten days Youth Hostelling in Wales with Suzanne. The time suddenly seemed to yawn ahead of her.

'It's no use pining for a ward once you've left it, as my old granny used to say. Or would have said if she'd ever been near a hospital,' Lisa said flippantly. She didn't suggest that Cherry might pine for anything else. 'Cheer up—we'll be groaning about being back at work before we've had time to draw breath. You know how quickly holidays go!'

Cherry hoped so, even though she knew she was being idiotic. After all, there was no reason to suppose she would stay in someone's mind even if she *didn't* drop out of sight for six weeks.

CHAPTER FIVE

COMING back to the Northborough Royal was like seeing the hospital with entirely new eyes. Cherry paused at the main gate where the bus had dropped her and drew a deep breath, feeling like a voyager coming home.

Ironically, she had forgotten that any time after the first year trainee nurses could be sent thirty miles away on the other side of the moors to gain psychiatric experience at the mental hospital which came under the same Area Health Authority. Fate had decreed that Cherry should start her second year there, the first of her set to do so. It had been a three-month stint.

Pensmere, the mental hospital, was run on very modern lines and liked its nurses to wear their own clothes. Staff could even be seen sitting smoking with patients in the day-rooms. You could only tell which ones the staff were by the fact that they retained their badges and it was all part of a system to make the patients feel more relaxed. Cherry had wondered at first if she would ever get used to the informality. Now she was wondering how difficult it would be to get back into Northborough ways. Doctor-nurse conferences where even the most junior member was encouraged to speak out as part of the team wasn't a Northborough habit, and she would have to remember that . . .

During the second week she was at Pensmere a postcard had arrived for her, written in familiar tidy black handwriting, saying, 'Your disappearance made me wonder if you'd given up after all, but checking tells me you've gone to Psychiatric. Try to survive! A.T.' She had sent him one back, of course, to the flat in Ebury Road; and later she had sent him another one even though her first had produced no answer, telling herself that she was only sending it because it was a nice view of the moors from this side.

He hadn't responded, but then she had only dimly hoped he might. After a while she was too busy, with too much to learn, for any kind of homesickness; Pensmere was such a world of its own that anywhere else faded. When she had time to think at all, she could even decide philosophically that her enforced absence was probably a good thing. It gave her time to come to her senses instead of falling into an impossible state of attraction.

'Cherry! I've been looking out for you—I'm on a day off, isn't that a piece of luck?'

It was Suzanne, appearing in a nearby doorway as Cherry fitted her key into the lock of the room the Nurses' Home Supervisor had allocated her. Suzanne came forward to give her friend a hug, saying in a pleased voice, 'Oh, it's lovely to have you back! I'm in the room next door but one, so we'll be able to go back to helping each other to wake up in the mornings. Let's have a look at you—haven't you got thinner!'

'Yes, haven't I? It's having to do the patients' exercises with them. I'm not sure whether that came under befriending or positive reinforcement,' Cherry said on a chuckle, before she remembered that Suzanne wasn't up with the jargon which had been so much part of her life for the past months. She stepped back to look at her friend as they went into the room together, and was suddenly startled to see how pale she looked. Suzanne had never had much colour, but now she had an almost worn look. 'So are you thinner,' Cherry pointed out with concern, 'and *you* didn't need to be!'

'Am I? It's working in Theatre, probably—it always seems so hot. I've nearly finished my six weeks, thank goodness.' Suzanne pulled a face, obviously aware of her own tiredness, and plumped down on the end of the Cherry's bed with a sigh. 'We've been busy lately, not that Gynae Theatre ever isn't! Shall I help you unpack, or just be lazy and sit here and natter to you?'

'Natter,' Cherry said promptly. Her trunk had arrived and been put in her room, she was glad to see. She and Suzanne had kept in touch by telephone, but conversations had always been rushed and shortened by the coins running out, and they had never managed to match times off enough to meet up, even halfway between the two hospitals. 'Tell me about everything,' she invited. 'I thought you said you and Lisa were going to look for a flat, so how come you're still living in? Haven't you managed to find anything suitable, or did you change your minds?'

'Oh, Lisa still wants to, but I wanted to wait for you. There was some idea of making it a foursome, with Buzz too, to keep the costs down, you know? But Lisa and Buzz aren't speaking at the moment and I wasn't going to get landed on my own between the two of them before you got back!' Suzanne made an exasperated face, and tried to turn it into a grin. 'Never mind about all that! I can't get over how different you look—and I do like the short haircut, it makes you look really pretty!'

'That'll be the day,' Cherry retorted automatically—but in fact she was pleased with the short curls which clustered round her head and seemed to give her face more shape. 'I'd forgotten you hadn't seen it, I've had it like this for ages. I just got tired of trying to keep it tidy, so when one of the patients offered to cut it for me, I said okay, and sat down, and she did!'

'Honestly?'

'Yes, why not? It's the sort of thing you might find yourself doing there, even in the middle of a duty. There's no need to look so shocked—she was a professional hairdresser, and suffering from depression, not anything homicidal!'

'Goodness,' Suzanne said weakly, gazing at Cherry as if she couldn't quite believe her eyes, and then coming out with, 'You know, you *have* changed—quite apart from having a smashing figure now, you've sort of—blossomed. Psychiatric nursing must have suited you!'

'Not really. I certainly wouldn't want to change over to RMN. It terrified me at first, because you're plunged straight in and expected to take responsibility. But then you get used to it.' Cherry laughed, and added, 'I'll probably bore you all to death with stories about it, so maybe I'd better save trying to describe it until I've got a larger audience! I'd rather catch up with what's been going on here, anyway. *Why* aren't Lisa and Buzz speaking, for instance?'

'I'm not sure, because nobody's quite saying. I rather think they may have landed up together after a party—well, I've always thought those two had a spark for each other underneath the bickering!'

'Romance spoiling a beautiful friendship?'

'Something certainly did. And it would, wouldn't it—if it was just an impulse and neither of them really meant it? They haven't really got the right temperament for each other,' Suzanne said thoughtfully, 'she needs someone stronger, and he needs—oh, someone less flyaway! It's been too silly seeing them deliberately ignoring each other!'

'I'll try knocking their heads together,' Cherry said with flippancy. 'Where's Lisa working at the moment?'

'Oh, Eyes. She went there on the six-week changeover, which some of us had and you didn't. *I* just moved from Gynae Ward to Gynae Theatre, but all the people on specialisations changed. I'm not sure how you can learn a whole specialty in six weeks, but we seem to be expected to! Oh, you're going to Orthopaedics, by the way.'

'Am I? How's Lisa enjoying Eyes?' Cherry asked casually.

'Okay, I think. You know how she is, far too interested in passing on gossip to talk much about work. At the moment she's full of the fact that her consultant and his Ward Sister are supposed to be an item—'

'She's married!' Cherry said involuntarily.

'Who, the new one, Sister Lamb? How do you know?'

'I—I meant Sister Beaumont, isn't she there any more?'

'She left a couple of months ago. It's Sister Lamb now. Tall and very striking with auburn hair. Sisters' blue doesn't suit her very well, but she does look stunning out of uniform. I gather she worked with Mr Treneager before, in London. Lisa has it that they're secretly engaged.' Suzanne went on without apparently noticing how much Cherry was staring at her. 'You know that story Lisa found out before, about him being a widower? Well, I suppose they could have been waiting for a suitable time to pass before he got married again, or something like that? Anyway, that's the story, for what it's worth.'

'Oh. Well. It doesn't affect us much, does it?' Cherry said the words over her shoulder as she turned away to hang something up. Why should the news give her a pang, anyway? It really wasn't anything to do with her.

Except that it explained why he hadn't bothered to answer her postcard . . . because he didn't need an 'amusing child' to occupy his boredom now that his lady-friend had come up from London. He might at least have been honest, instead of putting on that teasing pretence about asking her advice as to who he should take out.

She switched the conversation quickly on to lighter matters, because she and Suzanne had plenty of personal news to catch up on—Cherry's brief acquisition of a boy-friend at Pensmere in the shape of a medical social worker, which hadn't really been much more than being flattered at attracting someone's attention; news of Suzanne's family; chat about what it was like being a second-year on the wards instead of a first-year. Cherry would soon find out how it felt to be one rung higher in Northborough Royal's hierarchy, since she was due back on duty in three days' time.

She spent that three days mainly out of the hospital catching up on old haunts, and buying summer clothes to fit her new figure. There hadn't been much to spend her pay on over at Pensmere, so she was feeling unusually rich, and since several of the shops were already stocking up their autumn clothes in June and holding summer sales, she could hunt out bargains. She went swimming in the Municipal Pool, and dragged the others out when they were off duty to go round the market with her, and in general gave herself a holiday without going anywhere—and convinced herself that she wasn't keeping away from the hospital grounds on purpose, and that she *wasn't* avoiding walking across the car park in order not to see a certain silver Rolls-Royce. She was over all that. It had been a pleasant and passing and unlikely friendship, but there had never been any reason for it to last.

It seemed strange to pin a second-year cap on to her short hair—the others must be used to their second stripe by now (and Buzz to his second chevron), but she wasn't, because she had been working out of uniform. The mauve belt was different too, a change from the pale blue one. Cherry's first shift was an afternoon one, and she walked over to Orthopaedics feeling faintly selfconscious and wondering what the rest of the staff on the ward were like. The ward was run by a male charge nurse, that much she did know. There were four actual orthopaedic wards and what she had to nurse would depend which one she was on.

She had her mind on that and not on her feet as she came round the corner, so she didn't see the overturned litter-basket which had spewed its contents across the path. Even then she might not have tripped if a backing lorry, hidden until then by the corner of the building, hadn't made her skid to a halt very suddenly with a sidestep which set her off balance. Her foot landed on something that rolled, and her legs shot out from under her. For one horrifying second she thought she was going to land right under the wheels of the lorry.

She didn't, by a couple of feet, but it had braked sharply anyway and the driver was running back to her with a panic-stricken expression on his face. He had just begun, 'Holy Mother, Nurse, I didn't hit you—' while Cherry was gasping reassuringly, 'I'm all right, I only slipped,' when several other people converged on them at speed, and turned out to be a passing porter, a ward-maid, and the young man who had been cutting the grass a hundred yards farther on. Cherry could feel herself flushing with embarrassment at causing so much fuss.

'I'm all right, really—' She was scrambling to her feet, with assistance. The most annoying thing was that she would either have to arrive at her new ward smeared with dust and dirt, or be late through going back to change—and she hadn't done anything clumsy for months! 'Truly, you *didn't* hit me,' she said to the young lorry-driver, who was looking white around the gills; and then a calm male Yorkshire voice joined in.

'No, he didn't, but I've said a hundred times that the rubbish lorries shouldn't be backing up just there. Yes, I know you have to collect all our old plaster, and don't quote the unions at me, there's a good lad, I'm not blaming you personally! And as for *that*, it's a disgrace.' The speaker cocked his head at the spilled litter. 'Someone clear it up, please! Nurse, you're all right, are you? Oh no, you're dripping blood, let's have a look.'

He couldn't have sounded more calm about it. Cherry, who hadn't realised she was bleeding, found her right hand being picked up and inspected and it was, sure enough, letting out a thin scarlet stream. 'Not too bad, but it'll need a stitch or two,' the Yorkshire voice said, 'you must have landed on some broken glass. I'm Charge Nurse Bairstow—you wouldn't be my new second-year on her way to Orthopaedics, I suppose?'

'Yes, I—I am—'

'Well, you got within twenty yards of us, Nurse, didn't you? I was looking out of the window, so I saw what happened,' he said, quite amiably. He was a very large charge nurse, not only tall but broad with it, and seemed, fortunately, good-tempered. 'I'll just take you in and put something over this and then I'll have to send you over to Casualty, won't I? Just my luck, now we'll be short-staffed again!'

'I'm sorry to cause so much trouble,' Cherry apologised, halfway between cursing her luck and feeling thankful that her new charge nurse seemed human enough to be sympathetic. 'I don't need to go to Casualty,' she added quickly as he began to lead her inside, into the two-storey building which housed the orthopaedic wards on the ground floor and part of the Chest Unit upstairs. 'I can just come straight on duty with a bandage on—'

'So you know more about what needs stitches than I do, do you? You'll do as you're told—and make sure you fill out a proper accident form too. If they forget, be sure to ask for one! Oh, Staff, there you are—take over adjusting that traction I was on, will you? And send me someone to walk Nurse over to Casualty while you're out there—an auxiliary will do, as long as it's a capable one!'

Cherry opened her mouth to deny that she needed walking by anyone, then shut it again as she realised she shouldn't argue with her charge nurse. A moment later

Cherry was on her way back across the hospital grounds in the company of a young auxiliary who seemed to think she might faint at any moment, by the protective way she hovered over her, and that made her feel more sheepish than ever. It didn't make her feel any better either when the Casualty Sister snapped, 'Now what have *you* done?' on seeing her, and clicked her tongue as she removed the dressing-towel draped across Cherry's oozing palm.

'You girls really must be more careful. How did you do it?'

'I fell on some broken glass, Sister.'

'Hm. Anti-tetanus and at least three stitches—but we'll see what the SSO says. What a nuisance, he's just left the department, I suppose I'll have to get him back. As you're a member of staff, the rules require that you have a senior doctor to stitch you up,' she added, glaring at Cherry as if this inconvenient regulation was entirely her fault. 'I just hope Mr O'Neill isn't already in theatre—'

'Can I be of any help, Sister?' a voice behind Cherry said—a very familiar voice which sent a tremor of recognition travelling down her spine. 'I couldn't help hearing what you said,' Ashley Treneager went on, coming audibly nearer while Cherry carefully didn't turn round. 'If *any* senior doctor will do, I happen to be here—'

'That would be very kind of you, Mr Treneager, if you're sure you're not too busy? Nurse here seems to have been rather careless—'

'Or unfortunate? Let me have a look. I've left your nurse putting atropine drops in my patient's eyes, by the way, so if you'll just send someone to clean this up, I'll get on with it.'

His shadow came between Cherry and the light, and even if she didn't look up, she was thoroughly aware of the dark suit under a white coat very close to her. In fact she felt riveted by the middle button of his shirt. Sister's footsteps went clicking away. Cherry, feeling extremely foolish with her hand stuck out in front of her like an offering, kept silent. The small treatment room which now held only the two of them suddenly seemed oppressive and she felt as if she was going hot and cold. Ashley's voice said abruptly,

'Don't faint, it's not that bad, and you should have the

sense to be sitting down! Here—and put your head between your knees!'

'I'm all right—'

'Do as you're told!' His hand on the back of her head pushed her firmly forward as the chair he had put her into cut into the backs of her knees. 'Stay down there until you're feeling better,' he commanded, and added mildly, 'Don't I even rate a hallo?'

'Hallo, Mr Treneager,' Cherry muttered obediently, a little muffled, and as she sat up again she managed a glance upwards. He was looking just the same . . . and watching her judicially out of those very dark eyes. He seemed to be satisfied that she was feeling better, because one corner of his mouth suddenly twitched with amusement and he murmured,

'We really must stop meeting like this . . .'

Since they hadn't met for months that seemed the outside of enough. Luckily for Cherry's inclination to give him back a sharp answer, a nurse came in at that moment with a kidney dish and swabs and began cleaning up her palm, and Ashley moved away to give her room. A few moments later he was back, drawing up a chair to sit down in front of her as the nurse moved a dressing trolley up beside him, then stood there ready to hand him anything he might require.

'How did you actually do it?' asked Ashley, reaching out a hand to lift hers for a careful inspection.

'I tripped and fell and landed on a broken bottle.'

'It's lucky you didn't go down harder. It doesn't seem to be more than superficial. Does this hurt? No? Or this? Oppose your thumb and little finger. Yes, that's all right, there obviously isn't any tendon damage. Nurse, it's all right, you can leave me to carry on with this, it sounds as if you've got another ambulance coming in. And shut the treatment room door behind you, will you, to show this one's in use?'

'Sister likes them left open if a doctor's not being chaperoned, sir,' the nurse objected. She got a glare for her pains.

'Well, *I* don't, and I scarcely need a chaperon when I'm treating one of our own nurses, do I? At least I don't *think* she's likely to sue me for malpractice or unbecoming conduct! And since I've done my share of accident work, I should imagine I can be trusted to put in a few stitches without help, shouldn't you?'

The door closed behind the Casualty nurse and an audible click which was almost as expressive as the retort she would probably like to have made, but couldn't, to a senior doctor. There was a pause while Cherry kept her face as blank as possible, then Ashley said,

'All right, I know it's a sensible rule in general, so you don't have to look so disapproving! *Or* tell me off for pulling rank on an inoffensive trainee nurse who's only doing what she's been told to do!'

'I wouldn't!' Cherry said rapidly, her head jerking up to give him a wide-eyed stare.

'Oh yes, you would, unless your character's changed entirely since I saw you last! When did you get back, by the way? I meant to send you another postcard, but I didn't get round to it, did I?'

'No. I got back a couple of days ago. Today *was* supposed to be my—ow!'

'Just sit still, I know it'll sting a bit, but it's just a mild local in a skin-wash. I don't want you jumping all over the place while I'm stitching, and spoiling my tidy handiwork. Today was supposed to be your what?'

'First day back on duty,' Cherry told him. It felt more than strange to sit here with her hand held firmly in his —and to have him talk to her as if there had been no break in their relationship. And, having told herself that she had completely got over the powerful pull of his attraction, it was exasperating to find that she wanted to study every line of his face in a moonstruck fashion. *That* wouldn't do at all . . . and besides, she found she had remembered with exactitude the dark saturnine colouring, the lift of his left eyebrow, the way the lines round his eyes deepened as he concentrated, and the cynical curve of his mouth. 'I mean, it *is* my first day back on duty,' she said rapidly, trying to sound detached and at ease and trying to crush the annoying fact that her pulse was suddenly strangely jumpy.

'Not now. You've just gained yourself an extra week off. Now, I think we can start—'

'*A week?*' she echoed.

'Naturally. You certainly can't go back on any ward until these stitches come out. Shut your mouth and sit still, and that isn't open to argument. You've had quite enough training to know that nursing staff aren't allowed on duty with unhealed wounds!'

Cherry subsided. She even gazed unseeingly at the long tapering hand in its sterile Casualty glove which was holding hers—until she realised that his other hand was hovering with a suture needle, and turned her head away quickly with the automatic knowledge that she was likely to wince less if she wasn't looking. Then she wondered in a confused fashion if that looked like distrust. She would have liked to see how dexterous he was with a needle anyway—if it hadn't been *her* skin he was stitching up. His deep voice instructed, 'Relax, Cherry, you're hardening your muscles too much,' and he even gave her hand a gentle shake to make her loosen up, then added, 'You're not needle-phobic, are you? Just remember that I spend a lot of my working life doing this, so there's no need to be scared.'

'I'm not. It's just difficult to relax when you know you've got to. That *was* the only reason I looked away, honestly!' After a pause Cherry added, 'It'd be difficult to be needle-phobic and nurse, wouldn't it? You'd get the shivers even *giving* an injection, wouldn't you, let alone having to do accident work and theatre?' She felt as if she was babbling, but went on, shyly, 'I hope I'll be able to watch you operate some time. If I land up on Eye Theatre. We're supposed to do specialist theatre in the second year, and then some more on general theatre in the third—'

'You'd think it'd be the other way round. So you're into your second year now, I see—the cap.' He nodded at it without taking his eyes off what he was doing. 'There you are, that's three, I think that should be enough . . . Oppose your thumb again, gently. Good. It should heal without scarring. You can look now—if you want to see that I really *can* apply neat stitches!'

'I wouldn't be likely to think you couldn't!' The stitches

were neat, as well as quickly done, and Cherry had an idiotic impulse to say they ought to be framed. She glanced at him cautiously, but he was still studying her palm, giving it a final inspection with thoughtful concentration. His eyelashes were as black as his hair and surprisingly thick. She jerked her eyes away from his face and wished she could stop wanting to stare at him—and memorise him from close quarters because she would only see him in the distance after the next few minutes. That suddenly seemed unbearably sad.

'I don't think it was deep enough for you to need an anti-tetanus jab,' he was saying thoughtfully, 'but we'll see what Sister has to say. It may be another thing on the staff accident rules—along with this form Nurse brought in, which you and I both have to fill up, I see. Description of accident . . . witnesses . . . Did you have any?'

'Yes,' Cherry said meekly.

'Then you'll have to take this when I've filled in my bit about treatment given, and get them to sign. Right, that's my part done.' His signature went down, and she saw that when he wasn't simply signing A.T., he used the usual doctors' illegible scrawl. 'Now,' he said amiably, putting his pen away, 'since I chased the nurse away, I'll have to dress the wound as well, won't I? Keep still, it only needs a light covering—there.'

'Thank you,' Cherry said almost inaudibly.

'Don't you dare look surprised that I can put a dressing on. It's a nurse's delusion that doctors are so helpless they have to be waited on.' His tone was teasing, and he almost seemed to be trying to cheer her up. 'Keep it dry and covered and report to—where, the nurses' sick bay?—in five days to let the RMO see how it's doing.'

'Thank you,' Cherry said again.

'And what are you looking so down about?' He had stripped off the surgical gloves, and a finger was suddenly under her chin, lifting her face so that she had to look at him. 'You're not pining to work, surely?' he asked cheerfully—and giving her one of those remarkably charming smiles of his, so that her heart gave an involuntary jerk.

'I was just wondering what I was going to do with another

spell off duty when I've just had one!'

'Oh dear, oh dear, short of ways of amusing yourself? All right, then, come round to the flat this evening and I'll lend you some books to read. Eight o'clock? I'll give you something to eat as well—and yes, I *had* noticed that you've got remarkably thin. Not just because you're not wearing so many layers of winter woollies, either—your face has hollowed out.'

He had let go of her chin now and was getting to his feet. His casual invitation had taken Cherry's breath away: it was the last thing she had been expecting. It was also given in the tones of an indulgent uncle. As he moved across to drop the plastic casualty gloves into a bin the look he gave her took in her shock and a sardonic gleam came into his eyes. 'The door,' he said pointedly, 'is still shut. Sister and all her minions *may* of course be ranged on the other side there waiting to burst in and see exactly what I'm doing to you, but—'

'Don't be r-ridiculous!' Cherry muttered, on a choke.

'Well, you do seem to be looking unduly alarmed! What's the matter? Don't tell me—you're working for another Sister I've been taking out recently?'

'I—I doubt it—' A vision of Charge Nurse Bairstow, large and male and phlegmatically Yorkshire, swam into Cherry's consciousness and made her want to giggle. Another memory, though, made her sober just as quickly. She was also bitterly aware that all the growing-up she thought she had done over the past few months went for nothing as soon as she saw Ashley again. There was danger in accepting any invitation from him—though she certainly couldn't let him see that. 'It's very kind of you,' she managed with careful politeness, 'but—'

'Hm. You look like someone who wants to wait in for a phone call.' He was frowning, briefly. 'My advice on that is, don't!'

'Well, I—'

'We'll leave it open. I'll be at home. If you feel like sharing my free evening, you can also share my omelette. I can't say fairer than that, can I?' He was frowning again, and hesitated, then said, in a tone which was rather carefully casual. 'At the risk of offending your dignity, it does strike me that since you haven't got any family you haven't got anyone to look out for you. So—'

'I have a lot of friends who spend their time looking out for me!'

'Oh, dear.'

'In fact to hear them talk sometimes you'd think I was a simple-minded child!' Cherry went on, suddenly smouldering, and sparked into ingratitude. It was on the tip of her tongue, too, to say that she was sure he had plenty of other people to worry about, particularly if he was about to get engaged as rumour said—and if he had a free evening, would rather spend it with Sister Lamb than concern himself with waifs and strays. Luckily she resisted the impulse, because the gleam of humour with which he was regarding her might be annoying, but was at least better than the anger her rudeness would probably have brought forth. She remembered abruptly that they were in Casualty; that he had just stitched up her hand; and that someone might come in at any moment.

'I *should* know better than to give advice to the young,' he murmured—and gave her a grin which was downright mischievous, but which then sobered into such a friendly smile that her heart suddenly felt as if it was turning right over. 'No, don't bite! I told you before that I'm accustomed to nieces—my sister's brood—so I've had some practice.'

'You've never said how old they are,' she pointed out.

'The eldest's seventeen—why? No, never mind, we can talk about it later—if you decide to come.'

His ears must have been sharper than Cherry's, because the opening door showed someone must have been approaching. He said coolly, 'Ah, good, Sister, I've just finished. I've signed the form, so I'll leave everything else to you. Nurse.' There was an impersonal nod for Cherry on the last word, then he was across the room and walking past her while Sister thanked him for filling in for the SSO and assured him that Nurse was most grateful to him for taking the extra trouble. As Nurse was—when she wasn't feeling a mixture of annoyance and confusion all mixed up with a resentful wish to be the sort of person who was taken seriously.

She knew she would be wiser not to go this evening. On the other hand, she knew that she *would* go—and told herself, very firmly, that seeing Ashley at close quarters would provide a very good antidote against dreaming about him. Particularly if he was in one of his irritating moods. Besides, it would be ungrateful not to accept . . .

If she *was* going to go, there was no reason at all why she shouldn't try out the prettiest of her new summer dresses. It was pale yellow with a pattern of tiny darker yellow flowers, and cinched in nicely at the waist to show off her new slimmer figure. Studying herself with critical eyes, Cherry decided that she still had too many curves—but at least she wasn't as puppy-fat-ish as she used to be, and high-heeled sandals would make her taller too. She brushed her short curls with extra care and wondered, with a touch of defiance, whether to borrow some of Lisa's make-up—except that that lady might want to know why, so for safety's sake it would be better not to tap at her door to see if she was on an early and therefore off duty. Besides, Cherry realised ruefully, it would be difficult to apply make-up skilfully without the proper use of her right hand, so she might as well forget it!

She didn't want to analyse why she was taking so much trouble, telling herself only that she was dressing to please herself, and dressing up for once made a nice change from jeans anyway. She walked decorously down the stairs at a quarter past seven, then realised that the habit of ward punctuality was so ingrained in her that she was going to be early if she set off now.

She hesitated, then wandered across to study the notice-board so as not to look as if she was hanging about. A quick glance had shown her that there was no one criss-crossing the hall that she knew, but she stared at the notices with great concentration, even though none of them was particularly interesting. There was a senior staff lecture billed for tonight, she noticed—and was reminded of Buzz when she saw that its title was 'Techniques of Modern Management'. No, it apparently wasn't on tonight after all, since someone had written 'Postponed' across the bottom in red. Then someone spoke behind her in an attractively husky voice with the faintest Scottish tinge to it.

'Oh no, look, they've cancelled it—isn't that annoying? Now why do they have to tell us they want as many Ward Sisters as possible to go, if they're just going to change it?'

'All right for some—at least you were off duty anyway! *I've* had to get up early when I wasn't due in the Night Office until ten!'

Cherry moved hastily out of the way, since she could feel her seniors peering over her shoulder. One of them, a Night Supervisor she knew by sight, gave her a pleasant if unrecognising smile as she dodged out of the way, but the other was someone Cherry hadn't seen before. She was presumably a Ward Sister, but she didn't look at all like one at this moment, since she was dressed in a brilliant emerald green shift over white silk trousers and her hair, a striking auburn, tumbled loose past her shoulders in a mass of gleaming waves. Her eyes tilted at the corners like a cat's and were the classic green to go with her auburn hair, so that the bright emerald colour she was wearing seemed to reflect them. She murmured a husky, 'Thanks,' to Cherry without looking at her and moved forward gracefully to gaze at the notice board again, leaning her slender height forward a little as if in search of information.

'They don't even say *when* it's postponed to—isn't that irritating?'

'Never mind, Annis,' the Night Supervisor said philosophically, and with a touch of amusement in her voice. 'I'm sure you'll find plenty else to do.'

'Oh, I shall! In fact,' the husky voice said clearly, 'since I'm free after all I may as well go round and see Ashley. I've been threatening him with a salad plant out of my window-box, and now's as good a time as any to persuade him to be less conservative in his eating habits!'

Cherry froze. She had been glancing at her watch and wondering whether to set off walking slowly: now, with a sick feeling, she was glad she hadn't left. Perhaps she should have guessed, after Suzanne's description, that the strikingly glamorous redhead was Sister Lamb . . . because that, certainly, was who it must be. His free evening was easily explained, if *she* had been going to a lecture. Released from that, naturally she was going straight round to see him. Naturally . . .

Cherry was halfway up the stairs before she had even thought about going back to her room. Sister Annis Lamb's outline seemed to be imprinted on her eyeballs—tall, slender, dashingly smart, and with all that beautiful hair. And an enchantingly husky voice to go with it. How embarrassing it would have been to land up on Ashley's doorstep at the same time.

It would have been even worse, she thought suddenly, bitterly, to find Ashley perfectly tranquil about having the two of them there together. And that was what would probably have happened. He would have introduced Cherry as a young protégée of his, probably—and then they could *both* have treated her like surrogate parents, or an adoptive aunt and uncle. They'd probably have discussed her after she had gone, too. After all, Sister Lamb might well be as kind-hearted as she was beautiful, for all Cherry could know. If she knew Ashley that well, she was probably accustomed to his avuncular attitude towards waifs!

Abruptly Cherry was retracing her steps. She had passed a pay phone at the last turn of the stairs, just inside the glass doors on to the corridor. She wouldn't be rude enough simply not to turn up: she would ring and make polite excuses. Her mind seemed to be working with unexpected clarity as she dialled Directory Enquiries, discovered Ashley's number which wasn't, fortunately, ex-directory, and then dialled the digits she had been given. A double purr and a click and then he was answering.

'Hallo, it's Cherry. I hope you won't mind, when it was so nice of you to invite me—' Her voice sounded light, and polite. 'A friend's parents want me to go and stay for a few days, since I can't be on duty. They're always asking me and it seems a good chance to go. They suggested this evening and I don't like to put them off, so would you think me awfully rude if I didn't come round?'

'Not if you've got a better offer,' Ashley's voice said, a dry note underlying the deep tones.

'It's perfectly genuine! Mr and Mrs Pardoe—my friend Suzanne's parents—kind of treat me like one of their own—'

'She's a nurse here with you, is she?'

'Yes. Why, do you want to check? I can't imagine what you think I might be up to,' said Cherry, carefully putting a laugh into her voice and hoping she sounded sophisticated rather than annoyed. 'The Pardoes live at Hallowfield; Mr Pardoe's a teacher; they've got two sons and two daughters; and the thing I'll most likely find myself doing at this time of year is umpiring a cricket match!'

'Just don't try bowling, or you'll split your stitches. Oh, can you hold on a minute? Someone seems to be ringing my doorbell.'

That was quick, Cherry thought grimly. 'I won't keep you,' she said on the same polite note, 'and thank you *very* much again for asking me!' Then she rang off, and stood stock still for a minute with her bottom lip caught between her teeth as she caught sight of her own reflection in the mirror above the phone.

Plain brown eyes instead of sparkling green ones . . . What on earth had she thought she was doing being pleased with her appearance earlier this evening? The most anyone would ever think of her was that she was, perhaps, endearing in the same way that a commonplace sparrow was endearing. Even the pretty yellow dress suddenly seemed very ordinary. Well then, it suited her, didn't it?

She blinked, gulped, forced herself to smile, and went on upwards to her room. Oh—*bother* it, and bother her unruly heart, which had to beat faster for quite the wrong person, and with no real encouragement at all! She made herself laugh at last, if wryly, by deciding that tall, dark and fascinating consultants ought to carry a government health warning, to remind the unwary to keep well out of their way.

She would definitely have to keep out of the way for the next few days or be caught out in a lie. It wasn't a total lie, because the Pardoes always *were* inviting her, with or without Suzanne: Mrs Pardoe had repeated the invitation only the other day on the phone to her daughter. Cherry contemplated the fact thoughtfully.

She waited until Suzanne would have come off shift, then went and tapped at her door. At first she thought her friend must be working late, but then she heard a faint 'Come in' and put her head round the door. Then she was inside quickly and kneeling beside the bed, because Suzanne was stretched out with her face almost as white as the pillow behind her head and dark shadows lining her eyes.

'Sue? What's the matter—you look dreadful!'

'Tired, that's all!' Suzanne managed a smile, though it was the merest flicker of one. 'I couldn't even face supper—'

'Well, I'm going to get you a cup of tea at least—*and* with lots of sugar in! You are an idiot, why didn't you knock on my door? I wonder if I'd better get—'

'*No*. Honestly, I really am only tired! But the tea would be lovely! Hey, what's the bandage for?'

'Tell you when I come back . . .' Cherry was off to the corridor kitchen at speed, and checked it quickly to see what snack supplies there were. Moments later she was back with a pot of tea and a plate full of crackers and cheese, which she made a mental note to replace for whoever had been their original owner.

'Here—and this time it's my turn to scold, because you know how many times you've made me eat even when I was flaked! A nurse's health is as important as her patients', unquote!'

'Bully,' Suzanne said weakly, but already there was a little more life in her face. By the time she had drunk some of the tea a tinge of colour was coming back into her cheeks too and she seemed to be coming to herself, almost as if sitting up and making the effort to chat was an additional cure. She ate something at Cherry's urging, but after a while waved away the plate being offered for the umpteenth time.

'No, I can't eat any more—and you can stop watching me as if I was one of your anorexics or something on a high dependency ward! I'm not, and just you wait until *you've* stood through two hysterectomies, two D and C's, and a long abdo-perineal resection and repair!'

'Sounds heavy. Another cup of tea?'

'No, thanks. My blood sugar must be well restored after the way you sweetened the last two!' There was a teasing smile behind the tiredness in her eyes, and she certainly was looking more like her usual self. 'What I'm going to do now is make good my suggestion by going and ringing Mummy to say you'll come and stay!'

The suggestion *had* come from Suzanne, very promptly, when Cherry had abandoned the idea of asking. 'Are you sure?' she queried now, dubiously. 'I still think you ought to report off sick—hey, maybe they'd give you a few days off and we could both go!'

'No way, I told you, I'm not going to risk missing any more when I've only got a week left to do. You know what they're like, they'll make me do the whole of Gynae Theatre again if I go above the allowed time off! I *don't* think I'll choose to be a theatre nurse when we get given our staff nurse options,' said Suzanne, pulling a wry face. 'Look, I'll tell Mum you'll go over on the bus tomorrow morning, okay? And don't you dare tell her you think I'm overtired or anything, because I'm not having her flapping about me when she's got Keith in the middle of his O levels! Promise?'

'Perhaps I shouldn't go—'

'Nonsense, she'd kill me if I hadn't suggested it, you know perfectly well! You'll be a help anyway because you can amuse Martin and stop him pestering Keith when he should be studying. That's final!' Suzanne added lightly, 'And I'm all right, so don't fuss, chuck!'

'You sound like my new charge nurse,' Cherry told her on a giggle, 'I can just imagine him calling people "chuck". He looks as if he'll be okay to work for, anyway—if I ever finally get there, of course!'

It was nice to find Mrs Pardoe instantly reinforcing the idea of having Cherry to stay for a few days. The Pardoes were a friendly family and had never made her feel anything less than thoroughly welcome.

Besides, it would keep her out of Ashley's way.

It was ironic, then, that he should be the first person she saw when she came back.

CHAPTER SIX

HE was standing near the entrance to the canteen when Cherry crossed the courtyard on a short cut through to the Nurses' Home, and his Ward Sister was with him, talking to him. They had probably been having lunch together. Sister Lamb was in uniform this time, and while it was true that the royal blue, and the need to put her beautiful hair tidily up under her cap, didn't really suit her, that was small comfort when she was smiling up at the dark head bent close to hers, and apparently absorbing his full attention.

Their open togetherness did seem to bear out the rumours. Cherry was just deciding grimly that at least Ashley wouldn't see her walking by when he was so thoroughly occupied—and that, in a way, was a pity because with her weekend bag slung on her shoulder she was plainly coming back from somewhere—when he glanced up and noticed her. She ducked her head quickly and walked on, annoyed to have been caught staring. Though perhaps he hadn't noticed.

'How's the hand, Nurse?' his voice said coolly just behind her, and as she jumped, he was suddenly there, catching her up with his long-legged stride.

'It's—fine, thanks—'

'Good. You must be almost due to have the stitches out. There's no need to stop dead because I speak to you: you're walking in the right direction for my ophthalmology clinic.' He fell into step beside her as she started to move again. It occurred to Cherry out of her confusion that there was no reason why he shouldn't be seen speaking to *her*, either. He might be expected to know who she was after Casualty, so her selfconsciousness was idiotic. She glanced up at him to see him watching her, and he asked, 'Did your friend's parents come back with you?'

'No, why should they?'

'Since she's been warded for the past three days, it seems

likely that they might have driven over to visit her. If, of course, that's where you were.' The last sentence was said very drily, on a suddenly cold, sardonic note. 'Such a pity to be caught out in a pointless lie, isn't it? You shouldn't have gone into such detail, or I might not have remembered the name. But it does explain why you gave me such an exceptionally guilty look as you scuttled by just now!'

'I d—'

'Please! You're about to say it isn't my business, and that's perfectly true. It's even Matron's, rather than mine, if you end up doing something so foolish that it's a waste of all the time and trouble spent on training you. *I'm* merely objecting to the unnecessary dishonesty! Oh, I can see my house surgeon waiting for me, so if you'll excuse me?'

He was walking away, turning off where their paths would in any case have diverged. Cherry was left gasping. How could anyone turn into an icily implacable judge and jury in a few sentences, and for no good reason? And *what* had he said about Sue? She found out a second later as her name was called and Lisa came hurrying to join her.

'Hi, stranger, and what were you doing hobnobbing with the mighty? What did old Lord-High-Everything-Else Treneager want with you?'

'It was him that stitched up my hand in Casualty. He asked me how it was. Lisa, what's happened to Sue?'

'She passed out cold in theatre, poor love. I haven't seen her because there's a No Visitors ban and they're testing for glandular fever, so I hear. Poor love, she *has* been looking peaky for ages. Look, let's get together tonight and buy her some flowers from the kiosk and see if they'll let us take them in, shall we?'

'Sure—but I don't expect they'll let us, if they think it's glandular fever—'

'Pooh, no one knows how you catch it anyway, and besides, if she's buggy we'd certainly have caught what she's got already. Worth trying!'

'Why haven't they got on to Sue's parents?' Cherry asked. 'They haven't, because I was just staying there.'

'They don't have to if she says not—we're legal adults. I'd guess she refused to have them worried at least until they've got a proper diagnosis. It's a shame, because if it *is* GF she'll have to be off for ages, and probably go down a set. Look, I'll have to shift, I'm supposed to be taking these ophthalmology notes over to the Clinic—see you tonight!'

She sped off in the direction Ashley Treneager had taken, leaving Cherry biting her lip in concern. Her first thought had been to ring the Pardoes, and she still felt as if she ought—but perhaps it would be better to wait and see what Suzanne wanted done. And, underneath her concern, she was feeling a delayed-action burn of resentful fury over Ashley's stinging comments.

How *dared* he jump to conclusions, and then make those conclusions perfectly clear? He had no right to criticise, and no right to comment anyway whatever on she'd been doing—particularly when, as it happened, it had all been perfectly innocent!

If concern for Suzanne hadn't been uppermost she would have fulminated longer. As it was, with a deliberate curl of the lip she decided that Ashley had done her a service by making it very easy to forget him. She certainly wasn't going to waste her time repining over anyone who could be so downright nasty, and that was that.

She had to attend the RMO's clinic at Sick Bay to let him see her hand. It had healed so well that he took the stitches out then and there and told her she could go back to work in twenty-four hours. Then there were the flowers to buy for Suzanne, and delivering them, along with the tin of home-made biscuits Mrs Pardoe had sent via Cherry. Suzanne was in one of the single cubicle wards set aside for sick staff, and the girls weren't allowed to visit, in spite of Lisa's persuasions to the staff nurse on duty; but the senior nurse did pop into Suzanne's cubicle with messages while they waited and came back out again with messages in return. It was thanks and don't worry and, specifically to Cherry, *don't* ring the parents.

'We could have sent the flowers from Buzz as well,' Cherry suggested as they went down the stairs, deciding to have another try at peacemaking, since Lisa and Buzz still appeared to be avoiding each other.

'Huh.'

'It's no good just saying "huh"—and now I'm thoroughly back, I should warn you, I'm not going to have any patience with people having feuds all round me!'

'You *have* got bossy!' remarked Lisa, staring at her with apparently genuine surprise.

'I never was a worm, but if I was I'm turning! Sorry,' said Cherry, suddenly rueful, 'it's probably the effect of Pensmere! Seriously, though—you haven't really quarrelled quite so disastrously, have you?'

'We-ell . . .' Lisa looked defiant for a moment, then suddenly laughed, giving her red curls a toss. 'He didn't have to be so bloody rude. The thing was, in a mad moment I tried to seduce him—'

'Lisa!'

'There's no need to look so prim; it happens! He was extremely snooty, and said I went round grabbing people unselectively, so—Well, anyway, we both ended up being pretty nasty. Actually, though,' Lisa said thoughtfully, even if without any apparent penitence, 'I have to admit he's not all that wrong about me. I *do* make a play for people and then get tired of them quickly and move on.'

'We've all noticed,' Cherry told her drily.

'I can't help it, and how can you tell who you're going to like if you don't experiment?'

'Honestly, Lisa—!' Cherry let out an exasperated sigh, though it came out as half a laugh. 'You really will get your come-uppance one day,' she warned, though not without affection.

'Probably, but meantime—Oh, we're young, we have to live on an intense level because of the job, and life's short! But Buzz *was* wrong when he said I didn't give a damn about nursing but just saw the hospital as a playground, because I *do* care, and I do work as well as play!' Lisa was looking defiant again; but before Cherry could decide with a sinking feeling that her two friends obviously weren't going to make up their argument she added, 'Oh, what the hell, I expect he was only angry! All right, I'll start speaking again if he will—because—well, it's an awful waste to lose real *friends*, isn't it?'

'Can I tell him you said that?'

'Okay, little peacemaker: but if he's rude, just remember that *I* made the first move, and thump him!'

She changed the subject then, and as she went on to chatter about the eye ward, Cherry couldn't help feeling a bitter echo on her own behalf about losing friends. There was a time when Ashley had said, 'We're friends, aren't we?' . . . But they obviously weren't. Probably never had been, except in her imagination. It was better to feel angry about it than hurt: better for her dignity, at any rate.

At least she could go back to work, with Orthopaedics to claim her attention. This time she got there safely, too. Charge Nurse Bairstow greeted her ruminatively, giving her a placid gaze through his rimless spectacles and saying, 'Ah, we've got you back, have we?' There were three other second-years on duty and he set one of them to show her the ropes. To start with she was assigned to a mixed male and female ward containing mainly elderly patients with total hip replacements and lower body fractures, though she gathered she would be moved around. Most of the patients were totally immobilised and a high proportion of them, being elderly, were also deaf; so that she got used to scurrying around answering bells, fetching bedpans, and raising her voice to make sure she was understood. After the first few days she stopped being surprised that the orthopaedic wards were assigned so many extra auxiliaries, too: with the amount of lifting which had to be done, there always had to be two staff available even to put someone on a bedpan.

'We've got patients from three consultants,' she wrote in a scribbled note to Suzanne, 'so we always seem to be tripping over doctors, even if when you want one, he's always from the wrong firm! Lisa says I'm talking in a permanent shout because of my deaf old ladies and my muscles are already beginning to bulge from the lifting! It's okay, though. I wish they'd let us visit you—how are you feeling? And would you like any more books? See you soon, I hope, and stay cheerful! Love, Cherry.' She could have said that Orthopaedics seemed a remarkably cheerful place considering the amount of pain and immobilisation contained within it. The ward was enjoyable and interesting and she had no business to be feeling miserable underneath. She had even, by passing on the peace overtures, managed to make a wary reconciliation between Lisa and Buzz.

But not between herself and Ashley. And—quite extraordinarily—*he* had tried.

It was her birthday—her twentieth—and amongst the cards from her friends there had been an unexpected extra one. Inside, along with printed birthday wishes, was the laconic statement, 'I owe you an apology. Will you ring me? A.T.'

Cherry hadn't rung him; she had decided there was no point in it. It just wasn't important. She was too busy.

It was two days later, when she was coming off duty, that she ran into him. She was making a detour to the porter's lodge at the gate in order to post a letter for a patient, and her route took her across the car park. It was a fine, light summer evening, so she ought to have seen him, but because she was walking along with her head down she didn't. He must have been crossing to his car, because he was suddenly there in front of her, directly in her way.

'Good evening, Cherry.' He said it gravely as she jerked to a halt. She had to do that or walk round him, and because her instinctive stiffening had made her pause, she couldn't simply side-step and go on, as she should have done.

'Good evening, Mr Treneager.'

'Still angry? I *have* apologised—'

'Thank you for your card,' Cherry said stiffly, and with a good attempt at indifference. 'I don't know how you knew it was my birthday—'

'You once told me when it was.'

'Then it was kind of you to remember. If you'll excuse me, I—'

'You're making a very fine show of bearing a grudge.' He spoke with remarkable patience, when she would have expected him to be looking sardonic by now. There wasn't even a hint of mockery in his face. 'I'm sorry about that,' he said, 'and sorry you wouldn't ring me. Look, I won't keep you, but—if you ever need someone to talk to, you know where I am, all right?'

'Am I likely to—' Cherry broke off; if there was one thing she hadn't meant to do, it was make a retort. 'Thank you,' she said politely, and perfectly well aware that it came out frostily. Somehow, she couldn't help it.

'That was all I wanted to say. Good night.'

He stepped to one side, so she had to move on—surprised, confused, and then by the time she had gone three steps, abruptly angry again. She wanted to swing round and tell him that he had had no right to judge her morals in the first place—since that was what he had obviously been doing—and, it appeared, he *still* thought she had been up to something which would require advice or sympathy. Some apology! She could feel her cheeks flush with resentment, and hurt—and some even more painful emotion which she didn't want to identify. But by now, her legs were carrying her swiftly away from him, and she told herself that she didn't care in the least what he thought of her.

She posted her letter and went into the canteen, and when she saw Sister Lamb there, eating supper with some of her contemporaries, she made herself wonder without any feeling at all when the rumoured engagement was likely to be announced. Maybe once they were married she would have several children and *that* would give Ashley an outlet for all his splendidly paternalistic feelings—and somebody to boss about!

Lisa was moved from Eyes on a ward changeover, so at least she wasn't chattering on about the one subject Cherry preferred to leave alone. Lisa had taken Suzanne's place on the Gynae Wards and was full of information on blocked Fallopian tubes, salpingectomies, ovarian cysts and fibroids. The house surgeon on Gynae was a Pakistani and wore beautiful saris under her white coat, and that occupied Lisa's conversation too, inspiring her to wonder whether a sari would be easy to drape if she got herself some material in the market, and whether it would be a good thing to wear to parties or whether it would look all wrong on a European. Cherry told her to ask Buzz because he had Sikh friends; then wondered if the suggestion was tactless; then forgot it. Buzz had been moved to the Neuro-surgical

Wing, and because it seemed to operate on different shifts from everywhere else, they rarely saw him. Cherry set herself to learn as much about orthopaedics as possible to keep up her recent good ward record. Charge Nurse Bairstow with his placid Yorkshire manner seemed happy to be informative—even if, in spite of his easygoing air, he could be a hard taskmaster when he chose. He didn't seem to mind a degree of informality, though, which was just as well when Cherry forgot she wasn't still at Pensmere and offered an unsolicited opinion in the middle of a ward report.

'Don't you think Mr Blamore's frightened rather than senile? He always seems quite lucid to me—'

'It's a bit of both, Nurse. The shock of his fall could exaggerate early senility, and they often get paranoid with it, you know. I'll grant you he comes and goes: he's had one previous minor stroke, remember, with accompanying oxygen starvation. Any other remarks?'

'Um—no, Charge Nurse—sorry, Charge Nurse.'

'It's all right, I don't mind intelligent comments. That's probably why they tend to send *me* people straight after Pensmere,' he said drily, but with quite an amiable look across the top of his glasses. 'I'll tell you what I'll have you do—make me out a report on this patient's patterns of behaviour, previous illnesses, and treatments—it'll be a good exercise for you. Come in the office at the end of Report and I'll go through his X-rays with you, so you can see the pin-and-plate they've done on him at the moment.'

'Mr Hamel's in the ward, Pat,' the staff nurse murmured at that moment. It was interesting to note that informality stretched as far as the second-in-command calling her senior by his first name—not usually a Northborough habit on duty.

'Is he, now? Just pop off and make sure that pretty young auxiliary's in a safe place, then, will you? One of these days, doctor or no doctor, I'm going to have a word with Mr Cliff Hamel!' Charge Nurse Bairstow ruminated, but on a note grim enough to make him sound almost as fierce as Sister Temple at her worst. He continued to Cherry in more normal tones, 'Come on, then, let's get this report finished.

Mrs Potts—fracture healing nicely, attention to pressure points as usual, please, and out of bed in a chair after bedmaking. Don't forget to give her her rubber ring to sit on. Mr Lacey—the traction's down today and he'll need turning regularly. That's the lot, but don't forget the extra fluids for Three and the blood-pressure checks for Nine!'

Cherry, following him obediently into the office as instructed, saw Mr Cliff Hamel down the other end of the ward being deflected towards his proper duties with his patient, and bit back a small grin. He was a willowy young man with curly hair and big brown eyes and was the type to be very pleased with himself. She had already been told that there was a general warning out on this particular house surgeon. Conceit, for some, went hand in hand with graduation—and Charge Nurse Bairstow obviously didn't approve of him at all.

She was given a lesson on how to read X-rays, with particular reference to the pin-and-plate inserted in Mr Blamore's fractured femur, while the staff nurse flitted to and fro in the background getting the medicines trolley ready for its round. The charge nurse obligingly showed her another patient's films too to illustrate the more usual fracture—of the neck of the femur—and then asked, amiably, how many wards she'd actually done in her second year. He didn't seem to mind that this was only her second. The staff nurse, who had moved up briefly to listen, put in,

'Oh, you're that group, are you? You must be in the same set as—'

'Ruth, get the drugs trolley going round for me, will you? I don't like to leave the four-hourlys over time when they're hurting.' When the charge nurse decided to send everyone back to work, he did it very firmly. 'Go on, Nurse, you too, I've given you enough of my time for this morning. I'll expect that report written up by the end of the week, too!'

It was odd that a moment later he had changed his mind again and shut the office door behind Cherry with his staff nurse still inside—but that was hardly her business.

It was a small point, but it came back to her later with sickening clarity. By then there had been other points to add to it.

The next one passed without her really noticing it. Another member of Cherry's set was working on the Chest Unit on the floor above Orthopaedics, so they often found themselves walking on and off duty together. She asked how Suzanne was, and when Cherry said they still hadn't been allowed to see her, commented that the poor girl was being kept in isolation for an awful long time—it must be three weeks by now. But at least her parents had been over to see her at last.

'Have they? Oh, I wish they'd got in touch with me . . . When was it? I wonder why Mrs Pardoe didn't drop me a note? I'd like to have seen them!'

'It was two or three days ago. I saw them in the distance, disappearing into Matron's Office. Poor Sue, I expect they were being told she'd have to move down a set after missing so much. Glandular fever does takes ages, anyway, doesn't it?'

Then Cherry popped up to the staff wards to leave a note for Suzanne, as she made a habit of doing, and was told she'd gone home. 'They decided to let her out quite suddenly, and her father came over to fetch her.' The staff nurse added, 'Are you Langton? Well, Suzanne left a message for you, then—to tell you she'd write. I shouldn't phone her parents if I were you—they're probably pretty busy getting her settled in at home.' There was something odd in the girl's eyes; but perhaps it was just that she was busy which made her sound so snappish.

Cherry sought Lisa out, and found her subdued. 'Yes, I heard on the ward that Sue's gone home—I was going to come and talk to you about it. Now, why does it make me feel cold inside when a Ward Sister's suddenly nice to me? And—and she shut one of the seniors up pretty smartish too, at least they stopped talking when they saw me coming!'

'Did they? Lisa—what else is the matter?'

Lisa gulped. 'I didn't say anything before, 'cos you lot are always accusing me of rumour-mongering, and anyway I just didn't want to think about it. But—'

'But *what*?'

'You know they've kept on saying "glandular fever"

whenever we've asked? Well, if it's only that, why have they been calling all the top pundits in to see Sue? And —and especially Prof. Chemotherapy?'

'I don't know.' Cherry had a cold feeling in the pit of her stomach. 'How—how can we find out? Can you think of anyone to ask—?'

'Not when they all shut up like clams when they see us coming—because they know we're friends of hers!'

'*I've* just been told not to ring her parents . . . But—but it would look perfectly normal if I did ring, just casually to ask how she is. Not—not that I'd expect them to say anything!'

They went to the phone together, Cherry trying to shut off a cold dread, and wondering if the Pardoes would think it was an impertinence for her to phone. But she knew them very well, after all . . . and a friendly call couldn't seem anything but natural. When she got through, it was a young voice which answered, and she recognised Martin, Sue's ten-year-old brother.

'Hallo, it's Cherry. I was just ringing to say that I'm sorry I missed your parents when they came over, and—and I hope they got my thank-you letter, and I've just heard that Sue's gone home, so I thought I'd ring up and say hi—'

'I'll just get Mum for you. Hey, I came top in English yesterday, aren't I great?' Martin told her with his usual bounce, and put the receiver to dangle before Cherry could say anything else. A moment later, after a few scratchy distant noises, he was back.

'Mum's making bread so she can't come to the phone. She said to give you her love, though. Sue's asleep at the moment. Hey, did you know she's decided not to nurse any more because she's sick of it? She's going to Switzerland to stay with Auntie Esther, lucky beast. Oh, I've got to go now—'bye!'

Cherry could almost have sworn someone took him away from the phone, but the receiver had gone down and there was nothing but a buzz. Martin had sounded cheerful enough—but then he wouldn't have been told anything, would he? And Suzanne giving up nursing 'because she was sick of it'? Suzanne who, like Cherry, had *always* wanted to be a nurse?

Relaying the conversation to Lisa didn't make either of them feel any better. Neither did the knowledge that the grapevine, at senior level, had obviously got hold of *something* and was playing it down.

'Why don't they think we ought to know?' asked Lisa, with a flash of anger. 'Oh, I just wish there was someone I could ask—who'd tell us the truth!'

Cherry could suddenly think of someone. It wasn't just Ward Sisters who were suddenly nice to people—there was a certain consultant, too . . . and if information was passed on anywhere, it would be at consultant level. Besides, hadn't Ashley said—with an odd deliberateness—'If you ever need someone to talk to, you know where I am?'

She didn't share her idea with Lisa, but simply said, numbly, that they'd both of them have to keep an ear to the ground. If something terrible was happening to Sue, it seemed important to know about it, whether they were supposed to know about it or not. It was certainly more important than pride or injured feelings or any vow Cherry might have made. She was suddenly very sure, anyway, that Ashley *did* know something about Suzanne's condition; and had expected that she would eventually hear about it, too. And would need—comfort . . . ?

It was later in the evening before she could find an excuse to part from Lisa so as to telephone him. At first attempt there was no reply. He was probably out for the whole evening, but she couldn't bring herself to leave it. In the end, as late as ten o'clock, the receiver was lifted to her ring and a familiar deep voice said, 'Treneager here.'

'It's Cherry.' She always seemed to be saying that, and it sounded stupid. 'Please could I come and talk to you?' she asked baldly. 'Now? At least, if you haven't got anyone else there—'

'No, I'm alone. Where are you?'

'The Nurses' Home. I—I can be there in ten minutes. *Please?*'

'I'll expect you,' he said calmly. It was only after she had put the phone down that she realised he might have said,

'Go away,' or, 'Not if you're going to be rude to me again,' or any one of a hundred things. But by then she was already running back to her room to snatch a light jacket out of the cupboard and making for the stairs.

CHAPTER SEVEN

ASHLEY opened the door in a blue short-sleeved shirt and a pair of fawn slacks, and his hair was slightly wet, as if he'd recently come out of the shower and had only roughly towelled it dry. It made the white streak somehow more pronounced, looking more as if it had been bleached by mistake than grown that way. He seemed even taller than usual, which was stupid considering he was only wearing flat toe-sandals. Cherry, whose mind seemed to have gone numb now that she was actually here, found herself noticing everything in acute detail: a small scar near his hairline which she hadn't observed before; a swarthiness around his chin showing how often he must have to shave; a light dusting of silky black curls in the open vee of his shirt. The dark eyes rested on her thoughtfully as he stood aside to let her in.

'Were you trying to get hold of me before? I've been helping the couple downstairs tidy the garden. Coffee? Or tea so as not to keep you awake?'

'Nothing, thank you.' There was just one lamp on in the sitting-room and he had left the curtains drawn back so that the last late dusk filtered in to the corners of the room. Cherry stood still in the middle of the floor feeling disorientated until he reached out a hand to touch her arm and give her a little push towards the settee.

'Sit down, then. What did you want to talk to me about?'

'Suzanne. Suzanne Pardoe.' Cherry said the words carefully, and tried to stop her fingers pleating her cotton skirt, arranging it tidily instead as she sat down. The name hung in the air, sounding extraordinarily blunt. Then all at once her eyes were fixed on his face, almost accusingly. 'You knew I would, didn't you?'

'You told me she was a friend of yours.' He had sat down opposite her, his legs stretched out. His face, half-shadowed, looked singularly inexpressive. 'What did you want to ask me about her?'

'*Please!*' The words were suddenly easier to find. 'No one will tell us what's the matter with her. But people *know*. My staff nurse started to say something and then shut up, and the same happened to Lisa, and all we're told is that she's gone home and isn't coming back. Please, if the grapevine knows and isn't saying it must be something bad, isn't it? And she's my *friend*!'

'Calm down.' The words were said quietly. 'You think I know, and ought to tell you? Something Suzanne probably doesn't know herself?'

'Oh, I'll bet she knows! Sue? She's bright, and sensitive, and she's nursed for more than a year, and—Is it true the—the Chemotherapy Professor's been seeing her? Well, she'll know it's *him*!'

'And weigh up the likelihoods? Quite honestly, Cherry, I don't know what she's been told. But yes, I do know the diagnosis. And I know that her parents know. Tell me, are you going to be seeing Suzanne?'

'I—I don't know. Probably not. Her brother says she's going to Switzerland. I rang . . . Her mother couldn't come to the phone. Wouldn't, I think. I don't blame her, if—But Ashley, please, how can I cope if I'm left in the dark?' There was a desperate appeal in Cherry's voice. 'You know it's going to get to me eventually,' she said, almost angrily, 'and I'd—I'd rather hear it from you! Don't you see—I'm going to get a letter from Sue one of these days, all b-bright and cheerful and not saying anything much so as not to worry me, and—'

'And you want to know enough to write her a bright and cheerful letter back? Yes, that's fair enough. You don't gossip but you want to know how to handle it when the gossips get to you. It's inevitable that it *will* go round, however hard the authorities try to stifle it. Hospitals.' He said the word ruefully. 'All right, Cherry, I'll tell you the diagnosis, though I certainly shouldn't. Suzanne has Coravel's Syndrome. Do you know—?'

'Yes.' She did know: it was fairly uncommon, but they had had a lecture on it, and she was trying all at once to remember the facts she had written down. It was the one which particularly hit people under thirty-five; it was progressive, with remissions; the recovery rate was . . . 'There are different degrees, aren't there?' she asked quickly. 'What type has Sue—?'

'It seems to have caught her rather hard. You might think it was a case of cobblers' children—how do you go down with a disease like that in a hospital, without it being noticed?—but it does seem to have been a rapid onset. These things happen. They've been trying to explain that to her father, but I'm afraid he's angry enough not to want her treated here. Maybe that's better for Suzanne, from the psychological point of view, anyway.'

'That's why Switzerland?'

'You'd heard that? Apparently she has an aunt who's married to a Swiss. There's certainly a good clinic there. Whether it's that particular one he has in mind or another I'm not sure.'

'She has a good prognosis, hasn't she? Hasn't she?'

He hesitation said much more than she wanted to know. By the time he said, 'Yes, of course,' she was cutting across him with a flood of words. 'She *has* to have a good prognosis! She's young, and she isn't usually ill, and she's got her whole life in front of her—Ashley? They do say she's going to get better, don't they?'

By way of answer he leaned over and took hold of her hands—maybe only to stop her gripping them against each other so tightly. 'She may,' he said steadily, 'who can tell? How many hundreds of times have you read about spontaneous remissions making nonsense out of prognoses? And you're right, she *is* young, with plenty ahead of her to hope for. If they decide to send her for holistic therapy, there've been some amazing results.'

'*You* believe in that?'

'Why not? The medical profession's learning to take notice, wouldn't you say?'

'But . . . the word is . . .'

'Do you *want* me to tell you?' He moved abruptly, and was sitting beside her, one arm going round her shoulders while his other hand still held hers. 'I wouldn't,' he said wryly, his voice a deep rumble, 'but I don't doubt the word's gone round along with the rest of the facts of the case. Suzanne's—not very well at all. But what *you* can do is hang on to hope. Do you understand me?'

'It—it *couldn't* happen so quickly—' There was a deep shaking inside Cherry as she tried to take his words in. 'Not very well at all'—that hospital euphemism for very, very ill.

'Sometimes it does.' He was answering her, even if his voice seemed to be coming at her through cotton wool. 'Sometimes, for some people, for no reason at all. But I meant what I said. *Hope*. Believe she's got a chance. Is Suzanne anything like you?

'Much, much nicer!'

'And as stubborn, perhaps, though I imagine few people are! Positive thinking's her best bet. And yes, I do believe in it, so let's hope she's got a lot of fight in her!'

'Oh, Ashley, it's not *fair*! *Sue!* She's the—the n-nicest person I know . . .'

Both his arms went round her as the tears came pouring down her cheeks. Cherry forgot she had ever been angry with him, ever tried to hate him: all she knew was that he was there to hold on to. He cradled her quietly through her storm of tears without making any attempt to stop them, and it didn't feel strange to bury her burning face against his chest as she shook with hiccuping sobs. When at last she had fought herself to calm she could feel his fingers smoothing her curls gently.

'I'm—I'm s-sorry—'

'Don't be.' He shifted a little without letting her out of the crook of his arm. 'D'you want another handkerchief to replace that very wet one?'

'No, I've stopped. For now.' She said the last two words bitterly, and made an effort to sit up. 'I've *got* to stop, haven't I? It—it doesn't do Sue any good!'

'Or any harm.'

'She w-wanted so much to be a nurse. Like me.'

'You'll just have to go ahead and do it for both of you. You're strong enough to cope.'

'I'm n-not behaving like it right now, am I?' Cherry asked, lifting her face to look up at him forlornly.

'This? You think it's wrong to cry for a friend? Don't be silly, you know better than that. Better this than letting bitterness twist you up inside. Believe me, little one, I know.' He said the last words from somewhere away inside himself. Cherry remembered suddenly how much he must know what loss was like; but while she was still wondering tentatively whether to show she was aware of that, he had caught himself up and was speaking again. 'You'll manage,' he said firmly, looking down at her. There was even the glint of a smile in his eyes. 'There's something in you that goes in for facing life head-on, isn't there? You'll never be a giver-upper!'

'I—I shouldn't have thought you were, either!'

'Oh, when life's unfairness rises up and hits me, *I* just get appallingly bad-tempered! Don't take *me* as a rôle model, whatever you do!'

'It isn't bad temper that makes you try for miracles when you're putting someone together after a bad accident—'

'That's part of my job.' He cut across her protest, which had been a half-shy attempt to offer back some of the comfort he had been giving her, and shifted again, turning a little so that he could study her. 'Do you think you've recovered enough to be offered a hot drink? Because that's what I think we both ought to have, right now.'

'You mean, hot sweet tea for shock? I'm sorry,' Cherry said quickly, and wishing she had been able to suppress her involuntary shiver.

'Try to avoid bitterness, I said. What do you think I ought to have been offering you—whisky?'

'I don't actually like it. I don't suppose I'll ever take to the bottle.' She had tried for flippancy, but it came out with a quaver in it, and she swallowed hard. 'I'm sorry,' she said again, 'I've got to stop thinking . . . I just wish . . .'

'Go and wash your face,' Ashley said gently, but he gave her a hug as he let her go; and for a brief moment she felt his lips brush her forehead. Then he was standing up and pulling her to her feet and giving her a little push in the direction of the bathroom, so that she had to walk away obediently, feeling suddenly bereft of his warmth.

She ought to go back to the hospital instead of taking up

any more of his time. She knew she ought to say so: as she splashed her reddened eyes with cold water reason came ebbing back. It had been nice enough of him to put up with her storming in demanding answers—and it had been ridiculous of her, just now, to want to offer him back some of the consolation he had been giving her. He had Sister Annis Lamb to help him get over his past. She knew that, in some numb centre of herself, even if it didn't seem to matter just now.

'Milky coffee,' he said amiably as she came back into the sitting-room, 'and it's what you've got, so you'd better like it. Sugar's on the table, so you can take it or not, as you choose!'

He took his place beside her again as she went to sit on the settee, though this time he didn't touch her. She had thought he would avoid any subject which might touch on Suzanne, but he didn't: he talked to her instead, quietly and reasonably, about holistic medicine, and the theory and practice of treating the whole person instead of any specific disease. Although he hadn't any personal experience of it he seemed to know quite a lot about the theories involved. It was interesting enough to take Cherry's attention away from brooding on specifics—as perhaps he intended. It occurred to her that if he hadn't chosen to be a surgeon he would have made a good teacher . . . but that did bring her back to specifics, making her give a tiny shiver.

'Cold?'

'No . . . I was thinking about the Pardoes. Mr Pardoe teaches science.'

'I don't suppose that stops him keeping an open mind.' Ashley hesitated, then added, 'At the moment I believe he's too angry to want to have contact with anyone from the hospital. Don't be hurt by that, will you?'

'No, I won't, I can understand.'

'Good girl.' He hesitated again. 'I've answered your questions because I could see you needed to know. You said "we" when you first came in—so don't be offended if I ask you how much do you intend to discuss it?'

'Not more than I can help. I'm certainly not going to go round saying—I'm not going to let anyone say it in front of me, either! Even if, if it doesn't help, *I'm* going in for positive thinking,' said Cherry, with an attempt at bravery. She frowned down at her hands, then looked up to find him watching her steadily. 'I think I'll have to tell Lisa that I've found out the diagnosis, though. And Buzz, before he hears it somewhere else. We were always a kind of foursome, you see. But Lisa won't talk if I tell her not to: she may have a reputation as a gossip, but she sticks to her word if she's promised. After all, she's never breathed a word about—'

'About you', she had been going to say, unwarily, if realisation hadn't suddenly stopped her. Luckily the lighting was too dim for Ashley to see, if she had flushed. He ignored her abrupt pause, and asked,

'And—Buzz, whoever that unlikely name belongs too?'

'His real name's Andrew,' Cherry said absently. 'Buzz is sensible, even if he *is* moody sometimes. I'd rather tell him, because he might be hurt if he thought I hadn't. Is that all right?'

'I'll trust your judgment,' he said, and added, 'You're a private person yourself, so I can imagine you'd respect Suzanne's privacy. Don't give me that wide-eyed stare: I know very well how rigid *you* are about causing gossip, don't I?'

'Only because people say such stupid things.' Cherry knew she *had* flushed this time, and tried to make something light out of it. 'It may be all right if you're at the top, but drawing attention to yourself gets you picked on if you're at the bottom! Besides, I—I've probably got a secretive streak: it goes with liking knights' moves in chess!'

'What do *you* know about chess?'

'I used to play in school tournaments. I played some games with one of my psychiatric patients, too—not that he didn't always win, but then he was a professor of something. He did say I wasn't half bad, though,' Cherry confessed gleefully. It was a surprise to find that she was able to smile, and gave her a pang of guilt for a moment, but Ashley was answering.

'I'll take you up on that some time. You do have unexpected talents, don't you?'

'I don't see why it's unexpected. Lots of people play

chess. I think,' she said carefully, and against a longing to stay here, 'I ought to go now. I—I'm sorry about—'

'Don't you dare!'

'Well, am I allowed to say thank you?'

'No. I told you to come. I'm glad you did.' He was looking up at her because she had got to her feet—and in spite of everything, her heart was suddenly, wistfully turning over at the kind set of his mouth. 'It's nice to know that you still trust me—instead of continually putting me in my place!'

'I—I don't do that—'

'Oh yes, you do. It's probably very good for me.' He glanced at his watch and stood up, uncoiling to his full height so close to her that she could feel his warmth again. It gave her another wistful pang, catching at her bruised emotions with a painful longing which she tried to crush because it was so out of place. 'It's late enough for me to walk you most of the way back without being noticed,' he said firmly, 'and be a good child and don't argue! You're not in any state to run into stray drunks or whatever. Besides, you're looking so owl-eyed that I suspect you're almost out on your feet. Come along!'

It was true she was tired, the exhaustion of her tears catching up on her, and in a way that was a relief because at least she would sleep. She knew Ashley had thought of that too when they paused a hundred yards from the hospital gates and he hesitated, then said, 'I don't think you need anything to settle you, do you? Will you be all right?'

'Yes, thank you. I *will* say thank you!' Cherry gave him one stubborn upward glance, but the street was so dark just here that she could only see starlight catching his eyes and the white flash in his hair. 'Good night, Ashley.'

'Goodnight, Cherry. Take care.'

She was perfectly well aware that he stood where he was watching her until she had reached the lights of the porter's lodge. In any other circumstances that might either have annoyed her, or warmed her: tonight it only added to the mixture of guilt and pain she felt inside her. Pain for Suzanne; and guilt because she had no business to be feeling anything but that. She certainly had no business to be feeling an aching longing to turn and run back to him.

During the next few days the news she had been given about Suzanne came back to her in waves, catching her painfully at unexpected moments so that it was like carrying a sharp sliver of metal around under her skin. She told Lisa, but without the worst of the prognosis. She sought Buzz out and found that he had heard something already and had wondered if she knew, but hadn't wanted to raise any hares by asking her. They all three of them agreed that they weren't going to add to the whispers which were filtering around and, before the rumours could spread any further, organised a card to be sent to Suzanne from the whole set with a cheerful message and everyone's signature. It wasn't easy to write, 'Sorry you've decided to give up, but have fun, and we all miss you!' but that was what they decided on. It wasn't easy to get Suzanne's promised letter at last, either—as bright and cheerful as Cherry had known it would be.

'By the time you get this I'll be in the Swiss mountains,' she wrote. 'Lucky, aren't I? Don't tell me off for quitting —theatre work showed me I didn't really want to nurse after all. I'm going to think up all sorts of other plans instead. I'm too lazy to write more than one letter, so this is to all three of you, and please thank everyone else for the card too. I'll send you a p.p.c. with an address on so that you can write and tell me all the news—if you've got time in between doing case histories! Be good, children, and *don't fight*, and I'm trusting you to keep each other in order! No time for more now, lots of love, Sue.'

Reading it made Cherry gulp hard so as not to cry again—especially the 'Lucky, aren't I?' But she wasn't going to think like that—not now, and not ever. And she would write a thoroughly amusing letter back, when she got the promised address.

Meantime, there was work to be done. Cherry was aware that Charge Nurse Bairstow had looked at her thoughtfully once or twice, and knew that she mustn't bring her troubles on duty with her: she set herself to become an exemplary orthopaedic nurse.

She also set herself to avoiding Mr Cliff Hamel, who for

no reason at all seemed to have decided to single her out for his current attentions. Midsummer was several weeks past now, but maybe he was suffering from midsummer madness. Cherry was certainly in no mood for him, in fact, in the end, she gave him a sharper set-down than she could ever have imagined herself daring to give to a member of the medical staff. He was leaning right over her on the excuse of consulting a patient's notes and his hands were definitely straying when she snapped,

'*If* you can't diagnose a deep vein thrombosis, Mr Hamel, shall I send for the registrar and ask him? And will you please keep your hands to yourself?'

'You must be suffering from PMT, Nurse—I've always gathered it makes women hysterical. Diagnosis isn't a second-year nurse's job,' he added nastily, and stalked away. He was a great deal too conceited to admit that any female might not want him, Cherry decided as she saw him deliberately trying to look amused, and then turning on the charm at deaf old Mrs Richards who hadn't even the least idea who he was, let alone being able to hear the questions he was trying to ask her.

He'd had the nerve to complain about her, she discovered later in the day when she was called into Charge Nurse Bairstow's office. He greeted her quite casually at first and apparently only wanted to talk about the rota change amongst the third and second years. It was only after he had dealt with that that he said, quite amiably,

'Just as a matter of form, Nurse—if Mr Hamel makes a nuisance of himself, come to me rather than speaking to him, will you? Not that I blame you, but it covers you in case of complaints!'

'Yes, Charge Nurse—sorry, Charge Nurse. If he said I was rude to him I was. Have I got to apologise to him?'

'Good heavens, no! I stick by my nurses, and sent him off with a flea in his ear. Privately, and between you and me, he's a pain, and as thick as two short planks. If you repeat that I'll deny it, though nobody will believe you.' He grinned at her, placidly. He was a good nurse, and a pleasant senior to work for.

Cherry had already been moved from hip replacements

and fractures to spinal column injuries, where there were more young people even if still a proportion of the old (and deaf) and at least half the ward seemed to be on skin traction, so that there was a constant need to take extra care over ropes and pulleys and sandbags. She couldn't help hoping that she would never, herself, end up on neck traction, because it looked almost as agonisingly uncomfortable as the cervical injuries which made it necessary. She said as much to Buzz, who seemed now to be on more liveable-with shifts so that they met up more often—as now, with both of them waiting to collect baskets of medical stock from Pharmacy.

'Oh, and, by the way, why did they change their minds and send one of our patients over to Neuro yesterday?' she asked him. 'The query laminectomy—?'

'They decided it looked more like an abnormal spinal formation than a slipped disc. I noticed it was your writing on the admission form.' Buzz glanced at her. 'Any address for Suzanne yet?' he asked with careful casualness.

'No, I expect she's still getting settled. Maybe she's decided to make it a letter rather than a card, so that she can type it like she did the last one,' Cherry said with determined brightness, and opened her mouth to go on so that a pause shouldn't develop between them. However, at that moment Buzz said, in muted tones,

'We seem to be getting a lot of high-level attention. I hope it's not for something I don't know about on my Eye Ward report—and *you* haven't been there yet, so it can't be you! Unless—you haven't had one of your disasters lately, have you, and cannoned into him in a corridor or something?'

'If it's Mr Treneager, he knows me from stitching me up in Casualty. The best thing to do with consultants is to say "Good morning, sir" if they look at you, isn't it?' Cherry said blandly, and turned to glance round to see if Ashley was coming. She knew he *would* look at her: she had been aware of his searching glance before, and knew it was his way of seeing if she was all right. Somehow she had stopped blushing, too. Perhaps it was because of certain admissions she had made to herself—admissions which didn't stop her heart giving an automatic squeeze whenever she saw him, but which had brought a wry resignation. Sure enough he was there, a few yards away with John Bland, his registrar—though before she could give him a polite acknowledging smile her ward name was called so that she had to turn away quickly to collect her Pharmacy basket.

'Wow, *you're* not the frightened rabbit you used to be, are you?' commented Buzz with surprised approval in his voice. By the time Cherry turned round again Ashley was walking away. She met Buzz's eyes and framed a light-hearted reply.

'Older and wiser. Anyway, haven't you found that things got less formal as soon as we left the first year? Suddenly they start treating us like human beings. Must go—see you!'

Older and wiser she certainly felt after everything which had happened recently. Or just older. It wasn't wise to have felt a twist in her stomach at the sight of Sister Lamb—out of uniform and restored to her full beauty—getting into Ashley's car and laughing at something he was saying to her. It wasn't wise to have fallen in love with a kind, temperamental man who saw her as a child. Twenty, Cherry thought wryly, was an awful lot older than *he* thought it was.

She knew, though, that she wouldn't avoid him. She could at least have the friendship he offered her. For now; for as long as it lasted. She might even learn not to cry for the moon or long for a man who always had been out of reach.

There was always the absorption of doing the job she'd chosen to do, anyway. Besides, she was feeling stubbornly—and perhaps sentimentally—that she and Lisa and Buzz were going to make it not just for themselves, but for Suzanne too. And because *that* was a subject she was rigidly determined not to allow to slip away from optimism, she had decided to live in the present, and take each day as it came.

She also resolved, suddenly, not to go on waiting for an address from Suzanne, but to write her a really funny letter full of Cherry-ish observations on ward life and send it to

Hallowfield with 'Please Forward' written on it. At least, she'd wait another week and no longer. With luck, whatever treatment Sue was having might have made her feel better enough to have a chuckle over a few mad anecdotes.

The letter never got written. It was just under a week later when Buzz came up to Cherry's room where she was just finishing an afternoon off, and handed her a folded local newspaper, mutely. It was folded to the page showing Births and Deaths and Engagements, and he pointed without saying a word. As soon as she read the darkly-printed name the page blurred, but she blinked hard and made herself focus and read.

'*Pardoe*: At Bad Hessen, Switzerland, after a short illness, Suzanne, beloved younger daughter of James and Margaret and sister of Mary, Keith and Martin. Funeral private, no flowers by request. Donations to . . .'

'Weeks!' Buzz burst out. 'It can't be more than that since she went out there!' His voice was harsh, and he was shaking, as if anger was the only way he knew how to cope. He pointed a finger at Cherry, almost accusingly. 'How's *that* for all that stuff you were reading out to me the other day, about cures, and positive thinking—all that *rubbish*—'

'Shut up! Just—just shut *up*!' She was shouting back at him. 'Just because it was too late and too much for Sue, I'm not going to stop believing,' she said fiercely, 'I'm *not*! And don't you ever say that again—not ever! We don't even know what sort of clinic she was being treated at, and anyway . . . Oh, I w-was just going to write to her . . .'

He came and put his arms round her then, tightly, as much for his own sake as for hers, she could tell. Although there was a heavy, solid lump in her throat her eyes were dry. They clung together like children until he broke away and turned his back and scrabbled for a handkerchief. Cherry wanted to touch him, but she could see from the stiffness of his shoulders that he didn't want that. He blew his nose hard and when he eventually turned back to her his expression was steady, if bleak.

'Thought I'd better come and tell you. You don't look at the local rag much, and anyway it's only just out. Look, try and catch Lisa, will you? Or I will—depends who sees her first. Look, are you all right?'

'Sure. I—I'd better get ready, I'm almost due on duty.'

'You could ask for time off if you need to. I'm sure they'd give it to you. You've gone as white as a sheet.'

'You're pretty white yourself. No, I'd—I'd rather get on and nurse. We're one short this evening anyway and—and —well, there are a lot of patients—'

He nodded, understanding what she meant. Life went on. It had to. For them; for a whole hospital full of people; and anyway, to be involved in the healing process might even help . . .

'I . . . I think I'll go and do some studying,' he said. 'Look, sorry about—sorry for telling you so suddenly. And for yelling. It—it was a shock—'

Less for Cherry than for him, perhaps, since she'd never shared the knowledge of how serious Suzanne's condition was. It had still hit her with a force whose numbness hadn't worn off yet, and she knew how difficult it was going to be to believe it even when the numbness went. 'It's okay,' she said quickly, and managed to smile at him. 'What's the odd shout between you and me anyway, we'll probably be doing it right up to finals and beyond! Can I—can I keep the paper?'

'Sure.'

'Thanks. I'll . . . maybe see you later, when I come off shift.'

He nodded, though Cherry thought she probably wouldn't see him: Buzz wasn't very good at other people's emotions and tended to shy away from them. It was quite something that he had come to tell her, and she was grateful for that. She was grateful too that he had left her the paper, as if seeing it in print gave her the strength to acknowledge that it was real. Not that it was going to hurt any the less for that.

But life went on. She gave a steady gaze at her pale reflection in the mirror, and patted her cheeks to put some colour into them. Then she pinned on her cap and went downstairs to go on duty.

CHAPTER EIGHT

'CHECK,' Cherry said triumphantly.

'Are you sure you want to do that?'

'Yes, I am. I think. Anyway, I've done it now. Or are you just trying to distract me because you don't want to lose your bishop?' she asked, removing it as he moved his king away from her attacking knight. It wasn't the first time she and Ashley had played chess, so that she had lost the advantage of playing a type of game he wouldn't expect. 'I hope you're concentrating,' she said firmly, 'because if I thought you were deliberately playing less well to give me an advantage, I—'

'I wouldn't dream of it. Check—and mate.'

'Oh, damn. I'd forgotten your queen was just there. That'll teach me,' Cherry said ruefully, and smiled at him.

It was quite possible to treat him as a friend if she kept her mind on it. She could play it as a game. One she was better at than chess, she knew wryly, and sometimes painfully, making herself smile at the knowledge that she was a subtler player at some things than he could ever be aware of.

'Do you want to play again?' he enquired, glinting a mocking glance at her, and with his hand hovering over the board to reorganise the pieces.

'Little as I like to refuse a challenge, you did say you'd got a book which would show me what a heart bypass looks like.'

'Oh yes, I'll find it for you.' He swept the chess pieces up and returned them to their box. He was always tidy: she remembered noticing his tidiness the first time she came to the flat. He always looked tidy too, even when, as now, he had simply pulled on a sweater against the cool evening air, and was otherwise dressed in his casual mode of pale slacks, bare feet and sandals. He was one of the few men, she decided, who didn't look odd in sandals . . . and one she couldn't imagine dressed in jeans, she thought. Somehow they wouldn't go with the profile. He had turned back from the bookshelves with a book in his hand and she was abruptly aware that he was looking at her quizzically.

'What's that smile about? Something's funny?'

'The way I got defeated,' Cherry said quickly, lightly, 'straight after accusing you of trying to let me win! Oh, by the way . . .' She looked up at him gravely, 'I did have a letter back from the Pardoes. In answer to the one I wrote them about Sue.'

'Good, I'm glad. You prefer to mention her, don't you?'

'Not all the time, but I'd hate never to talk about her again. I once read something—about how awful it is when people avoid someone's name, as if they'd never existed. I can see now what they meant.' She reached out to take the book he was handing her to show that she didn't want to pursue the subject now, and let it fall open where his finger had marked the place. 'Oh, thanks—*that* looks nice and clear!'

'You can take it and photocopy the diagram, if you want to. As you can see, they've clipped off the aorta there—and gone round there—'

'Can I really borrow it? Thanks. It'll certainly come in useful if I ever have to draw it out!' She looked up at him, adding, 'Why have *you* got a book on hearts, though?'

'Probably because I never like to part with a book once I've got it, which is why I'm always having to put up more shelves. Besides, it doesn't do to be completely over-specialised. It's not the cardiac ward you've been moved to, is it?'

'No, Intensive Care. We've got all sorts. It was bound to be a medical ward after Ortho and Ortho Theatre,' Cherry said absently, 'and after Ortho Theatre I'm not sorry to get away from the sound of sawing bones . . . It really *would* be better if at least one of the Ortho surgeons took to music in theatre, like you!'

She had pulled a wry face—and then wondered whether he, as a surgeon, would be critical of her for not preferring theatre work, of any variety. She found it less to her liking than the wards, though it had certainly been interesting. Ashley, however, didn't make any critical comment, but said merely,

'No, I gathered the habit hadn't spread. It isn't actually designed to drown unpleasant noises, anyway! Oh, by the way, my name's in that book—just in case one of your friends picks it up!'

'I can always say I found it in the library, and then dutifully return it to you.'

'You don't even trust your friends not to gossip? Or you just don't talk to them?'

'No.' She knew he was teasing her, and found herself saying, with a touch of sharpness, 'Why, do you talk to your—'

'Don't stop like that, or I'll think you're concluding I haven't got any friends!'

She had been on the point of saying, 'your fiancée'—or whatever Sister Lamb was—because some demon inside her wanted to know whether she was discussed, as some young nurse he had decided to keep an eye on, and as an explanation as to why he didn't always spend his free evenings with the beautiful Sister. The grapevine had settled down to accepting them as a couple because Ashley was never seen to take out anyone else. Aware that the pause was lengthening, Cherry decided hastily to let it go. She couldn't afford to let him suspect her of jealousy. 'I don't tell my friends anything they don't need to know,' she said airily, 'we usually have other things to talk about anyway! I must say, it's nice not to come off duty totally flaked! Theatre work really does keep you on your feet, doesn't it!'

'Not me, because I operate sitting down. In general yes, it does. It doesn't seem to have done you any harm, though,' Ashley said cheerfully, regarding her, and then, 'Is that a new dress?'

'No, I've had it ages.' It was the yellow one again—the one she'd put on the night she *didn't* come and see him—though this time she'd found a matching sweater to pull on over it. It was odd to come off duty to a prearranged date with Ashley, even if she was getting used to it. This was the third time now. It was almost turning into a regular arrangement.

She knew it was part of his kindness, and that he was still keeping an eye on her after Suzanne. All the same, she wasn't going to refuse.

'If you don't want any more chess, I'll play you at draughts,' he said lazily, and opened the checkered board out again. 'But I warn you, I'm a very good player, and I shan't *let* you win at that either!' He sounded for all the world as if he needed to be amused rather than feeling he must amuse her—and perhaps he did, she thought with a sudden stir of resentment, because after all she wasn't exactly scintillating company. The last twice, they'd talked about all sorts of things—shop, Cornwall, the reorganised teaching course the new Nursing Officer (Tutorial) was bringing into force, and the fact that Ashley preferred listening to the radio to watching television, which was why the television set was banished to his bedroom. Tonight, somehow, it seemed harder to talk.

She still wondered what Sister Lamb made of his setting aside an evening every ten days for Cherry—and she still didn't want to ask.

It came up though, involuntarily, later. He asked casually, 'How's your friend Andrew doing?'

'You mean because I said he took it badly about Sue? He seems to be all right now, thank you. He was flapping about his last ward assessment—though goodness knows why, he usually gets good ones—and now he's gone to Paediatrics on the last ward change.' Cherry glanced at him, wondering whether he knew that Sister Grayson had been promoted to Night Super and, at the same time, announced her engagement to one of the senior registrars. 'It's difficult to know what Buzz will make of Kids,' she said, following her own line of thought, and with a tiny smile, 'but it *should* keep him busy enough to stop him fretting over details!'

'Hm. He's worked in my department, hasn't he? I don't know how good he was. Can't have been outstandingly bad, because he certainly didn't come to my notice. What,' Ashley asked absently, inspecting the draughts laid out on the board in front of him, 'does he make of your disappearing every so often for the evening and not saying where you're going? Or was that one of the . . . "details"?'

'It's reasonably good for people not to know where other people are occasionally,' Cherry said—deciding abruptly that there was no harm in letting him assume she was particularly attached to Buzz. As she was, in a way—as a friend—but if Ashley thought it was more, there was a safety factor in that. All the same she found herself caught by the irony of it, and next minute found herself asking, in almost exactly his tone, 'What does your—'

'You've broken off on that word again. My *what*?'

'I was wondering what to call her. All right, your—your fiancée? What does she make of—'

'If I'm engaged, I certainly think someone should have informed me of it.' His head had come up, and he was regarding her carefully. 'So? Who?'

'It's just what everyone's saying! That if she's not already, she's about to be! It's no use looking at me as if I'm delving into your private life unasked,' Cherry told him with sudden reckless asperity, 'You know perfectly well who I mean! Sister Lamb!'

'Annis. If you're so well informed I'm sure you know her first name. And her likes and dislikes. Her shoe size?'

'There's no need to be so thoroughly sarcastic! If you're seen taking all sorts of people out, and then only one, people are going to jump to conclusions, aren't they? Particularly when—'

'When?'

'When it's common knowledge that she's known you for ages. And refers to you as Ashley and brings you salad plants!'

His eyebrows went up at that, but since she knew perfectly well that she'd overstepped the mark already, Cherry tried not to care. 'I suppose the flat isn't bugged?' he queried sardonically, looking elaborately round at his sitting-room. 'Your sources seem to be amazing—for a girl who claims never to know any gossip! Or to pass any on!'

'Well, that I don't! No one's ever said anything about—'

'About what?' he asked silkily, into her betraying pause. Because he was waiting, she felt she had to answer.

'All right. I really *don't* mean to pry, and I don't mean to rake up the past for you either, but I was going to say, no one's ever mentioned anything about your wife! And—and it was something just a few of us heard ages ago, but we decided you'd rather it wasn't talked about, so we didn't!'

'I—see.' He was frowning: he really did look extraordinarily forbidding when he frowned. Cherry began to feel two inches high. 'I didn't know Annis had discussed that,' he said thoughtfully, and with a look of distaste, so that Cherry felt obliged to be fair.

'It wasn't her, it was just chance, because—someone—happened to meet a doctor from your old hospital. Sister Lamb has a very pretty voice, hasn't she?' she added irrelevantly, and for no reason except that the comment popped into her head.

'Yes, she has. I'm glad to think you approve—at least partially—of my choice, this time!'

'You're still being sarcastic.' Cherry looked at him from under her lashes, caught between regret for upsetting him, and resentment at his manner. His conception of friendship didn't seem to include her knowing anything important about him—and his wife's death must be over two years ago by now, after all. 'I'm sorry for—for annoying you,' she said on a sigh, and with a hesitation in it because 'hurting you' would have seemed more reasonable, if he hadn't been looking cynical rather than hurt.

'I'd be glad to know exactly what you heard.'

'Just that your wife fell out of a window and was killed. I'm sorry,' Cherry said again, knowing that it had sounded far too blunt, but there was suddenly a flash of genuine surprise behind the intent look in his eyes.

'Killed? No, she wasn't. She broke her pelvis. And subsequently found a battery of divorce lawyers to complain that I hadn't been there to stop her falling out of the window,' he said—very drily. 'I thought there was rather a lot of sympathy in your face just now. Unnecessary, I can assure you. Besides, Elizabeth had quite enough fuss and sympathy from her loving parents!'

'You—you can't say *that*!'

'Why not? She recovered completely, accepted her parents' viewpoint that I was entirely to blame, and went back to America with them. It was a whole year after that before she did kill herself by driving head-on into a wall—in the company of the man who was tipped to become her next husband. So it's rather a different story, isn't it?'

Cherry wished he wouldn't look so sardonic about it. After all, he must have cared . . . once, at any rate, however much he liked to look as if he didn't. It was even worse when he added with heavy sarcasm, 'Is there anything else you'd like to know to satisfy your curiosity? From the look on your face—'

'I *wasn't* just being curious, and I'm simply trying to understand!'

'Flattering to think you find it hard to understand why anyone should leave me.' He said that in a nasty enough tone to make the comment almost unbearable. 'But don't set your ideals too high—I made a very bad husband!'

'Why?' Cherry asked baldly, without stopping to consider how rash she was being.

'Why? Why what? Oh, why did I make a bad husband? You really do believe in asking, don't you? All right, then: I started out by marrying the wrong person. Ambitious young surgeons shouldn't marry socialite beauties. Elizabeth was very young and—as she had a right to be—frivolous. And used to being spoiled. I set her down in a society she wasn't used to, and expected her to get on with it.'

'She wasn't medical, then?'

'No. If she knew anything about doctors at all, it was to imagine that anyone with enough money to do so—as I had, thanks to a legacy—would automatically set up in private practice. It was a nasty shock to find out that I preferred to spend more of my time working in a state hospital than going to parties, or cultivating the "right people". She couldn't understand why I had to be on call at weekends, or why I had to study for my Fellowship even when I *was* at home. And then go on working just as hard after I'd got it. Looked at from her point of view, it *was* unreasonable!'

'I don't see that—'

'Don't you?'

'No,' Cherry said stubbornly, but eyeing him warily and wondering why she was daring to argue with him. 'You seem to be blaming yourself for everything. And that doesn't help, does it? Besides, although I'm sorry I asked, and it's—it's very sad, surely the point is now that it's —over?'

'What sophisticated ideas! A quick divorce, and on to the next?'

'No! And you *know* that wasn't what I meant! I'm sorry if it sounded like that, but you did say—that she was dead—'

'Yes. Though there was a time, of course, when I was legally divorced, yet not divorced. Or had you forgotten I'm a Catholic?'

Cherry had, and the comment gave her pause. Was that the reason why he was still so bitter—his religious background making a broken marriage that much harder to accept? What she knew of him made her sure that he *had* loved his wife, however he cared to make it sound. The dead girl must have bruised more than his pride. She was painfully aware of wanting to offer comfort; but a glance at him, to find him staring at her with his eyes very black, and very sardonic, ought to have been enough to keep her quiet. Her heart gave a heavy thump, but she found herself muttering,

'You said you weren't a good one . . .'

'I'm not. That doesn't stop old habits dying hard. Now, don't you think we've had enough of this?'

'Yes, if you say so. But just because it didn't work once, it doesn't mean you'd be a bad husband another time!'

'You're extraordinarily persistent. That's what you meant by "over", is it? We're back to Annis again? To whom you seem to have decided to marry me off? Doesn't *she* have any say in the matter?'

'Presumably! But,' Cherry retorted, nettled by his sarcastic tone as well as by the reference to Annis Lamb whom she had for that moment completely forgotten, 'it's not *me* who's marrying you off to her anyway, it's . . . Oh, for goodness' sake, all I did in the beginning was ask you a civil question!'

'Let's go back to the question, then. And I'll answer: Annis is over twenty-one and free to choose the company she keeps. Even disreputable company like mine. I've told you before not to see me as a misunderstood saint: I'm not one, and I don't behave like one, either,' said Ashley, very sardonically. 'All the same—and while I'm sure she'd be touched by your protective instincts—I don't really think she needs you to ask me what my intentions are!'

'Of all the unreasonable—' Cherry could feel herself crimsoning, and her sentence broke off on a choke. 'I *wasn't*!'

'Oh, weren't you? Weren't you just going to tell me, in your comforting little way, that it wouldn't be at all the same this time, since she's twenty-seven years old and a Nursing Sister and highly suitable? Perhaps you're right and I'd better consider it. Do tell me, now that you've finished tidying up my private life to your satisfaction, what are you going to turn to next, Nurse Langton?'

It was on the tip of Cherry's tongue to blurt out that if Sister Lamb knew how horrible he could be and still wanted to put up with him she was welcome to him. He didn't have to look down his nose at her in a way that made her feel positively shrivelled, and she felt as if the evening had fallen apart with a reverberating crash. She swallowed hard, and got to her feet. 'I'm sorry for—for interfering,' she said with dignity, 'and I certainly didn't mean to. But if—'

'Are you going somewhere?'

'If you're going to *pull rank* on me, then I might as well go, mightn't I?' Suddenly, and in spite of the hurt inside her, she was giving him back glare for glare. 'You're perfectly capable of making any comments you like about *my* life, but I can quite see that it doesn't do to make it a two-way traffic! I didn't mean to make you lose your temper, but since I have, I apologise!'

'Oh, sit down, child, and stop looking like the picture of injured dignity! You won't let me get away with anything, will you?' To her absolute astonishment there was suddenly a flash of rueful laughter in his face, and he reached out to catch hold of her hand to stop her moving away. 'Cherry, I did warn you that I'm bad-tempered—besides, I'm sure it's another thing the grapevine says about me! And anyway—' his mouth twisted in self-mockery—'what *do* you expect, when you go digging into my past with a scalpel? Though I suppose you're too young to know . . .'

There it was again: 'too young'. Cherry could feel the warmth of his fingers holding on to hers so casually, and felt the familiar twist of longing inside her. He was exasperating—and particularly in the way he could change moods in a flash—and it would all be much easier if she could only dislike the worse side of him, instead of being stuck with loving him. She looked down at him with a carefully blank face, and said lightly, 'I'm sorry I mucked up the evening. Actually, I think it *is* time I went now!'

'Oh dear, are you *that* offended?'

'No. I *could* say, I know how nasty you can be when you try, but I won't, since I can see that I brought it on myself this time!' She said it with deliberate impertinence because she knew it was what he might expect, and managed to give him a grin, with a touch of apology in it. 'It's just that it's half-past ten, and although I've got the morning off tomorrow I've got a paper to write on aseptic techniques, so . . .'

'Have you? I've got a good book on that somewhere, too, if you want it—no? Better if you use the standard nursing manuals, probably.' He came to his feet, letting go of her hand to rub his absently through his hair. It left him looking slightly.rumpled, unusual for him. 'Yes, if it's half-past ten I suppose you *had* better go. And you may be off tomorrow, but I'm operating. I've got an extra list to do before I go on holiday at the end of the week.'

'Are you? I didn't know!'

'Yes, I meant to mention it. Three weeks off—enforced holiday absence. I'll probably go to London and look in on other people's operations.' He said that with a touch of his self-mockery again as he walked to the door with her, as if knowing that she might accuse him of being a workaholic. 'Shall I walk with you back to the hospital, or are you going to say no again? Or drive you? It's not raining, but the wind's getting chill.'

'I've got a jacket, and it's too early for stray drunks.'

'Determined girl! All right, I can see your point. But I suppose you do realise,' he added with casual mildness, 'that you've grown far too decorative to go wandering round the streets in the dark on your own? Or will you ruffle up at me for telling you so?'

If he had said it in any other tone, Cherry would have been pleased—and flattered—but the avuncular note was there so clearly in his voice that it took away the compliment. Against a sudden ache which made her rebel against *that* kind of approval, she said flippantly, 'I'm an acquired taste, and ten minutes' walk isn't time for anyone to acquire it! Um—won't you go to Cornwall to see your sister's family while you're away?'

'Yes, I may. Changing the subject? Or just reminding me to worry about other people rather than you?' he asked, a great deal too sapiently. As Cherry's eyes jerked to his face she saw that he was smiling at her, but looking thoughtful, too. 'I didn't miss your statement that I feel free to comment on your life,' he remarked mildly, but watching her. 'And the "acquired taste" seemed to carry some meaning, too . . . If I'm taking up too much of your time, you're perfectly free to say so!'

'No,' she said quickly—and then because the monosyllable sounded blunt enough to be a giveaway, she managed a laugh. 'Not unless you're trying to get rid of me!'

'That wasn't what I meant. I enjoy your company or I wouldn't ask for it. It's not all one way. I'm a family-minded man without a family anywhere at hand, and you're—'

'Family-less?'

'As prickly as a porcupine,' he retorted. There was still a great deal too much intentness in the dark eyes. 'I'm merely wondering if Andrew—*what* is it you call that young man?'

'Buzz. I've also been out with at least half a dozen other people,' Cherry said airily, exaggerating wildly. Suddenly Lisa's comment came into her head. 'As a friend of mine says, we're young, we have to live on an intense level because of the job, and life's short! I really had better go now instead of standing here suffering from clergy disease, so good night, and have a nice holiday!'

'*Clergy* disease?'

'Standing on the doorstep and not going. I'm off. Good night, Ashley!'

She escaped, running down the stairs to let herself out of the outer door, taking the memory of his sudden frown with her. If she hadn't distracted him with 'clergy disease' he would have said something disapproving, she knew. Probably something scathing, or a warning . . . but she had taken care not to give him the chance. Well, it didn't matter if he thought she was as light-minded about love affairs as Lisa was, because that was exactly the impression she had tried to give him. Anything was better than letting him guess how she really felt.

His bitter sarcasm about his failed marriage still scathed along her nerves. She really *shouldn't* have asked him about it—although her Pensmere training popped unwarily into her head to tell her, stubbornly, that it was probably good for him to talk about it. Then she gave a wry grin at the thought of herself setting up as Ashley's therapist: some nonsense! It didn't stop her confused and clumsy longing to be able to comfort him . . .

It really wasn't fair. Cherry hugged the book she had remembered to pick up as she hurried through the streets, and decided bitterly that the late summer chill was entirely suitable to her mood. She couldn't even take any consolation from the thought that he *didn't* seem to be planning to marry Annis Lamb, when it would probably be very good for him if he did. If she tried hard enough she ought to be able to think that, instead of feeling stabs of jealousy, and being stupid enough to wrap her arms round a book just because it was his. She was also dwelling wistfully on the fact that he was going away for a few weeks, so she wouldn't even see him.

There was always work, and a new ward to get used to. The Intensive Care Department was made up of a set of small six-bedded wards opening off a long corridor, with a large number of high dependency patients requiring constant monitoring. Several of them were attached to machines to help with the monitoring so that it had to become habit to watch for blips on a screen. The third-year nurse who first took Cherry round had defined flippantly, 'With high dependencies you watch them all the time to see if they're still breathing, and with low dependencies you just check every five minutes!' but her casual manner didn't disguise the efficiency with which the ward was run: it simply seemed to be the department's attitude for coping with the fact that these were all very seriously ill patients. The Sister in Charge was young, bright, cool, and impatient with anyone who wasn't able to work at the speed she set for herself and everyone else. Cherry regarded her warily and decided she was going to miss Charge Nurse Bairstow's placid good humour.

The run-through she had been given of the type of patients she would be nursing had been taken at high speed, and apparently without drawing breath. 'We've got post-renal failures—cardiac arrests on their third or fourth—accident head injuries—a couple of collapse-after-internal-haemorrhage—you'll have to learn them as you go round, Nurse. Relatives are allowed in any time, they usually know enough to get out of the way in an emergency. All the crash therapy trolleys are here in the corridor laid up and ready, and woe betide anyone who takes one away without seeing there's a spare. High dependency beds are always on the left as you go into a ward—and since that means we move people round, always check to see who you're treating! Crash call number to get a doctor here fast is seven: if you have to ask central control to bleep the registrar you ask for Dr Majid. Right? You can start bedmaking in Ward Four, that's the end one.'

It was all new, and rapid, with a lot to assimilate; though by the time Cherry had been on the department for three days she had grown used to notching up her work-rate to a higher level and being constantly aware of her surroundings. And by the time Ashley went away it certainly made an antidote to her thoughts about him, because when she was on duty she didn't have time for them.

There were cures off duty too, such as going to a party with a haematology assistant who surprisingly asked her out. Cherry had a feeling that he had really wanted to ask Lisa but picked on her as second best, but she went, and tried to be sociable. It was drinks and dancing in the Junior Doctors' Common Room, and since she hadn't penetrated into that fastness before, she was quite interested to see what it was like. Cliff Hamel was there, wrapped round a blonde third-year, and rather pointedly ignored her. Since it was quite a small party Cherry was relieved when he vanished halfway through the evening looking amorous.

She must have managed to be quite a successful partner, because the haematologist—who was small and fair and looked, Lisa had once said rudely, like a frightened rabbit—suggested another date. That was charitable of him, Cherry decided, considering that she had firmly refused to stay at the party after midnight on the grounds that her feet wouldn't stand for any more dancing, and didn't agree to go anywhere else with him either. As they were leaving she had the dubious pleasure, too, of catching the eye of a rather drunk junior anaesthetist who gazed at her soulfully and asked, 'Hallo, beautiful, where have you been all my life?' He had seen Cherry almost every day while she was on Orthopaedic Theatre—but since at the time she had been muffled up to the eyes in theatre clothes, she supposed it was fair not to have been recognised, and forbore to point it out.

'It's about time you started being appreciated,' Lisa told her, when she relayed the latter experience on a giggle. 'Listen . . .'

'I'm listening,' Cherry prompted, wondering why her jazzy friend was suddenly looking grave.

'I—suppose it's all right for us to be going out, and everything? You know—after Sue—'

'Yes, it is,' Cherry said firmly. She would never pretend that she didn't miss Suzanne, but it was something she just had to get used to. 'I wouldn't have wanted to in the first couple of weeks, but—She certainly wouldn't have expected us not to, would she?'

'Then I'm going to arrange all sorts of foursome dates and drag you in, so as to make sure you don't go back into your shell again! Either that,' Lisa said with sudden gloom, 'or I'm going to stop going out myself. I'm getting kind of—bored with changing about. Why can't we meet someone we *actually* fall in love with?'

Speak for yourself, Cherry thought silently, caught out instantly in wondering where Ashley was now. London? Cornwall? Doing what? She pulled herself out of her thoughts swiftly before Lisa could notice her abrupt quietness—and decided not to mention that Lisa was *always* claiming to be in love. If she was growing out of her endlessly changing passions, perhaps it was all to the good.

And it was time *she* grew out of her unchanging one. She bit her teeth on the resolve: she *would* grow out of it. And if that meant going out to all sorts of parties with Lisa and her friends, so be it. It might give her the strength to say politely that she was busy, when—if—Ashley rang her . . .

'Hey, shall we think about living out again?' Lisa was asking. 'Just you and me—we could probably find a flat—'

'No, I don't think so. It's—it's cheaper living in, and—Oh, let's leave it until after we do night duty at the end of the year, and think about it then, shall we?' Second-year night duty was something Cherry didn't look forward to, remembering her exhaustion in the first, and she was glad it was postponed to make the final spell of their second year. 'You wouldn't want to have to keep waking me up,' she temporised, making it an excuse she knew Lisa would accept—but knowing that wasn't why, at all, she was refusing the suggestion.

So much for her resolve, when her instinctive reaction had been to think that Ashley *couldn't* ring her, if Lisa might answer the phone.

All the same, she did go out in a foursome with Lisa when that lady arranged one—and even found she had garnered a further offer of a date from her evening partner, a young male physiotherapist. It was when they were coming back from a second foursome date, after an evening spent off hospital premises for once, at a town disco, that she discovered Ashley had returned, by seeing his car across the car park. She even thought she could see his shadowy form in it, but looked away quickly so that the others wouldn't see her staring. Her distraction made her unable to dodge away when her partner caught hold of her to give her a smacking kiss—not that she really objected to that, since it was merely a friendly one—but for some reason she rather hoped Ashley hadn't been in his car to see their noisy return.

She didn't ask herself why it should matter; nor even why her heart sank a little as the lights on the Rolls suddenly sprang to life and it moved out to sweep past them as they all walked across the car park arm in arm, with the boys insisting on escorting them back to the Nurses' Home. After all, *he* was unlikely to care who she was with—if he had noticed her at all, of course. And he hadn't bothered to send her a postcard while he was away . . . though why on earth should she have expected him to, and to a Nurses' Home where a good half of the staff would know his handwriting?

Stepping up her social life suddenly didn't seem such a good idea. It didn't help anything, anyway: it merely made her get up tired when she needed to be alert for duty on IC. Then Buzz, having one of his prim fits, took it into his head to tell her that she shouldn't take up with Lisa's rackety crowd, when they were having lunch together in the canteen. Since Cherry was sitting where she had a clear view of Ashley and Annis Lamb sitting together at another table in animated conversation—and since he hadn't even noticed her when he came in—she wasn't in the best of moods, so she snapped,

'Why? Because I'm the plain one, who should concentrate on work?'

'You'd be wiser if you did! I always thought you had some sense! After all—'

'We've got our RGN to get? Yes, I know. Anyway, *you* don't sit in every night! I know that, because I tapped on your door the other evening to see if you wanted any of my paediatric notes, and you certainly weren't in then.'

'That's different,' he retorted, though a thread of colour ran up under his fair skin.

'Oh, why? Because *you're* different? One rule for you but another one for me?'

'I certainly wasn't out with the sort of people Lisa runs

with. It's different,' he repeated, flushing harder, 'having a quiet evening with—with friends—'

'Oh, for goodness' sake, you'd think I'd been painting the hospital scarlet! And I certainly haven't! It's no use talking to you, I'm going back on duty,' snapped Cherry, getting to her feet abruptly. She stalked away, carefully not looking in the direction of Ashley and Sister Lamb; and was halfway back towards IC before she remembered that she'd actually got the afternoon off. That somehow made her crosser than ever.

She mooched into the Nurses' Home and went to look at the notice board, knowing that she ought to do something constructive like writing up a case history or putting her notes on theatre work into a proper order.

Someone was advertising for a babysitter. Well, *that* was something she could do, to get herself out of the Nurses' Home for the occasional evening . . . and even Buzz could scarcely criticise *that*!

She rang the number that night, and found herself talking to Charge Nurse Bairstow. It was somehow comforting to find him amiably pleased that it was her, and she arranged to babysit the following day when she had an early evening. Going round there, it seemed odd at first to see him in his ordinary clothes, but he was as large and placid as ever in contrast to his thin, dark, pretty wife to whom he was obviously devoted. Her name was Melanie and she worked as a hairdresser—and offered Cherry a free haircut any time, when Cherry flatly refused to be paid for babysitting. Charge Nurse Bairstow instructed her to stand no nonsense from the kids, and told her to call him by his first name now that she wasn't working for him any more.

The children were ten and four and Cherry found them easy enough to deal with. It made a nice change to spend the evening in a comfortable suburban semi, while the Bairstow parents went to the cinema. It reminded her a little of sitting down to do her homework in her foster-parents' home, as she sat down to write up her notes on drug dosages after the children had gone to sleep, and kept the television purring gently in the background to keep her company.

Pat Bairstow insisted on driving her back, even though the evening's drizzle had stopped by now. He pulled his battered Escort up beside the porter's lodge at the hospital gate.

'Is this all right, or do you want me to take you right round to the Nurses' Home?'

'This is fine,' Cherry told him with a smile, jumping out. 'Good night, Pat, and thanks—next week, if you like?' she called through the open car window as he leaned over to pull the door shut behind her and prepared to drive away.

'We'll see. Depends if I can get away. Good night, lass—and thank *you*!'

Cherry waved cheerfully, turned—and just saved herself from walking slap into a tall dark figure approaching from the other direction. Ashley. He wasn't alone. The slender feminine form of Annis Lamb, looking dashingly smart even in a cape-shouldered raincoat, was close beside him. Cherry gulped, and managed, 'Good evening, Mr Treneager,' since the fact that she was virtually standing on his feet seemed to require some acknowledgment, then made to bolt past the pair of them.

'Wait,' his voice said curtly, and his hand catching her arm jerked her back abruptly. Before Cherry could do more than gasp in surprise, he had turned to his companion. 'Annis, would you mind . . . ?'

'No, Ashley, I'll go on in,' Sister Lamb's soft Scottish voice said huskily. 'Good night to the pair of you!' She gave Cherry one curious glance and walked gracefully away, her elegant figure making Cherry all too conscious that her own rainwear was a well-worn anorak, which wouldn't look at all dashing even if she wasn't wearing it over jeans. Ashley was still holding her elbow as tightly as if he had taken her prisoner—though even as she was thinking so, he let it go with a gesture which was almost one of distaste.

'I suppose you didn't get my note?' he asked curtly. He was frowning at her as heavily as if she had committed some crime, so that her swift jerk of pleasure seemed out of place.

'Did you leave me one? I forgot to look in my pigeonhole today—'

'Simply asking you to ring me. Though you don't have to, of course.' His tone suggested he didn't believe she hadn't had it, Cherry realised disbelievingly. 'I can see you've been particularly busy. I can also see—now—why you were quarrelling with your boy-friend yesterday. Since you obviously don't plan to get in touch with me, I—'

'W-wait a minute!' Cherry gazed up at him—and managed to forget, temporarily, that the night porter was casting them curious glances from his box. 'I didn't—I mean, I haven't—'

'I decided to stop you, to point out that if that's what you meant by "living on an intense level", you ought to be ashamed of yourself!'

'*What?*' she gasped.

'You'll hardly pretend you don't know that particular charge nurse is married—even if he doesn't mind sharing your favours with the other half-dozen! After all, he's quite open about it, isn't he—"Depends if I can get away," isn't that what he said to you?'

Cherry's jaw had dropped, and she felt as if someone had hit her hard in the stomach. She gasped, gulped—then rallied, staring up at the man who stood so tall and dark and accusing over her, and with her temper suddenly going into overdrive. 'Do you mean,' she said on a choke, 'that you stopped me to give me a public telling off? Well, fancy! Have they just put you in charge of nurses' morals, or something? Because if they haven't, do you mind telling me just what right you've got—to—to go round making assumptions about people? Oh, and in case you think I'm going to start making any explanations, to *you*, you're dead wrong! I'm not one of your nieces, though you always seem to forget it! I'm not any relative of yours at all, thank goodness, and heaven help anyone who is! So get out of my life, and—and don't ever speak to me again!'

She didn't know what the porter must be making of that—though her voice had been low with fury, and with the fact that she didn't have enough breath to shout. She didn't wait to see what Ashley had made of it either. She couldn't. She was past him and running, with the choking need to get as far away from him as possible. Tears of anger and hurt were clogging her throat. Well, that was that. Finish. The end. She wouldn't even think of him as Ashley any more. She'd put him away, permanently, and see him as nobody but a hostile stranger.

She hoped he *wouldn't* ever speak to her again—except professionally, if he had to, when he could always address the top of her cap. She hoped—prayed—that she wouldn't find herself working for him, though at least that was ruled out for the next two months. Maybe, she thought wildly, they'd manage to forget to send her to Eyes at all . . . or maybe before she got there he'd be up and off to a better consultancy in London, because surely Northborough wasn't high-powered enough to hold him for long. Just as long as she didn't have to *see* him . . .

There wasn't any logic in crying herself to sleep when she hated his guts. Or in feeling that all the joy had gone out of life—after all, there hadn't been much there in the first place, had there?

One thing she was sure of: even if he found out the truth about Pat Bairstow and made one of his apologies, she wouldn't accept it.

In fact, they didn't exchange another word with each other for almost three months.

CHAPTER NINE

REMEMBERING the grapevine, Cherry took care that everyone knew she was friendly with Melanie Bairstow as well as Pat, and that she babysat for them. It became a regular thing, and she was even invited round to supper with them when they weren't going out. Melanie did do her hair for her, giving her a very short cut again because she said it suited her bone structure, and Pat took to grumbling at her goodhumouredly almost as if she was one of the kids.

Cherry hoped Ashley would hear just what her relationship with the Bairstows was, then decided rigidly that she didn't care whether he did or not.

He did pause once when he met her in a temporarily empty corridor, and looked as if he might speak. Cherry turned her head away, stuck her chin in the air, and swept on past him. After that she never saw him, except in the distance.

She found herself going to parties again, though not through any desire to seek them out, and not with what Buzz called 'Lisa's rackety crowd'. It started when one of the housemen on IC invited her out, to one of the casual 'do's' in the Junior Doctors' Common Room again. Because several people recognised her as having been before, she found herself unexpectedly adopted and drawn into a kind of 'in-group' where nobody seemed to belong to anybody particularly, but everyone talked a lot of nonsense mixed with a lot of shop, and the evening often seemed to end with Cherry making a load of extra coffee to sober one or two of the young doctors up.

Cherry guessed that most of the young doctors secretly preferred a sympathetic sister-figure than anything more romantic, for most of the time, anyway, and her unexpected popularity came from the fact that she behaved accordingly. It was how she felt, so that was the way she was. She knew she'd got herself a reputation for being non-touch except for the odd brotherly hug and some occasional close dancing, and she certainly wasn't inclined to fall romantically in love with anybody. She didn't even think of it, or admit to herself that she still carried a secret and persistent ache around with her. She didn't—and wouldn't.

Lisa had suddenly paired up with Cliff Hamel. Cherry delivered a mild warning, had her head snapped off, and left it—thinking wryly that she, of all people, ought to know better than to interfere in other people's lives. She wasn't seeing much of Buzz these days either, which seemed sad, though they did run into each other now and again across canteen tables or in the Nurses' Home sitting room. He seemed to be flourishing, anyway.

IC was suddenly over, gone as if in a fast-moving dream. After a moment's dread, because she knew which ward she *didn't* want even for night duty, Cherry let herself look at the list and found she was down for the Accident Unit. Another fast-moving one . . . though with sudden empty acres of time between the rushes, she found out as the accident routine swallowed her up. She had been there a week, then three weeks . . . At least she didn't seem to get so tired this night duty, so she must be getting her second wind.

She was just starting her fourth Night Casualty week when she ran into the Peace brothers.

The unit was having a quiet spell and one of the staff nurses had gone for coffee, timing herself to be back when the pubs closed because that might make them busier. The other staff nurse seemed to have vanished too, temporarily, and Cherry was sorting through the splint cupboard while a third-year was desultorily tidying up the reception area.

The sound of sudden loud male voices made her prick up her ears—then prick them up further when someone jeered loudly, 'Oh, come on, sweet'eart, we're only looking for a bit of entertainment, so where are all the pretty nurses, then? I mean, *you* can bandage Darren's 'and up, but *we* want someone to 'old our 'ands too, see?'

Cherry shot out of the splint room without a second's thought, prepared to give back-up. She recognised the new arrivals instantly—they hadn't changed that much since schooldays, though they *were* less spotty—and she hesitated, because the other girl was senior to her. On the other hand, she plainly wasn't sure how to cope, and the Peaces looked at least half drunk. They were all looking very tall and solid and adopting their usual swagger, but knowing them made it easier to wade in without pausing to consider further. Besides, experience reminded her that they were better if you didn't let them get going.

'Shut up, Wayne Peace, and stop making such a noise! This is a hospital, and can't you read the Quiet signs? Dave, you can either hand that bottle over or go and wait outside—preferably the latter. Take Keith with you, unless he's going to faint from the sight of blood, in which case we'll have to treat him as well. How did you cut yourself, Darren? Goodness, didn't you have enough trouble with your eye last year, not to want to come back for *more* treatment?'

Her intervention had the desired effect, and left them gaping. Dave even shuffled his feet, which made Cherry want to giggle—except that she couldn't risk it. 'Well?' she asked sternly. 'How many of you need to stay, and how many are going to wait outside? Darren, you'd better sit down if you're going to look so green—though I don't know why, that gash doesn't look all *that* bad, it's barely dripping!'

She didn't know that a staff nurse had materialised behind her, because she hadn't heard the office door open. She didn't know that the SSO, Mr O'Neill, was there with her, because she couldn't turn round and take her eyes off the Peace brothers when staring them out seemed as effective as lion-taming. She only knew that all three, Wayne, Dave and Keith, had turned exceedingly shifty-eyed and were backing out; while Darren, who always *had* been fairly stupid, was sitting down because she had told him to. Then the SSO's Irish voice broke through her consciousness and almost made her jump.

'Well now, since everyone else has gone we can see to this

laddie, can't we? Nurse, take him into Treatment Room One—no, not you, Nurse Langton, I think we'll let Nurse Maylem do it.' As Darren was led away, and Cherry turned round, she saw amusement dancing in Mr O'Neill's blue eyes, but before anything else he lowered his voice to add, 'And I think we'll just press the "Ware Drunks" buzzer to the Porters, in case those three outside decide to cut up and try breaking some windows. Though I rather think they won't dare . . . Where *did* you learn your technique for dealing with the unruly, Nurse Langton?'

Just then the corner of her eye caught another figure, coming in through the side Casualty door. She turned her head—and froze. Ashley, in full evening dress. He must be coming back from some formal function and had decided to wander in here, for some reason of his own . . . but why *now*? Cherry thought wildly, trying *not* to think, 'Enter the Demon King' as Mr O'Neill glanced across and saw him too.

'Ah, now, you've just missed all the fun,' he said cheerfully, and with an obvious relish. Cherry could willingly have killed him. 'Nurse here may be small, but she's surely got fighting spirit. I've just caught her chasing off three large drunks single-handed and making the fourth sit down. They're an unpleasant lot we've had in here before, too, though not recently. I think the one we've still got is the same one you sewed together before, Ashley, that Peace boy. So do tell, Nurse, so that we can use your technique again. How *did* you do it?'

Cherry decided to address him entirely, and ignore Ashley standing by with one eyebrow politely raised. 'I just happen to know the Peaces,' she told Mr O'Neill. 'I was at school with all of them. So—'

'Ah, that explains the names! But *not* how you got them to shuffle away like that just by glaring at them! I've had more trouble than that with them myself!'

'Well—um—if you *know* the Peaces, you know how to handle them. They're all terrified of their mother, as a matter of fact, and—um—if you've ever heard her ordering them about, it makes it easier to—to—'

'Ah, I see! Well, I'd better go and see what this one has

done to himself this time, I suppose—but I'll call you in if he gives me any trouble,' Mr O'Neill told her with a broad grin.

'I'll come in with you if I may,' said Ashley, speaking for the first time. Why had Cherry ever imagined she'd forgotten that deep drawl . . . ? She turned her head without thinking and immediately met the gaze of a pair of unfathomable dark eyes. He said politely, 'Good evening, Nurse Langton.'

She had to answer, of course, with Mr O'Neill and the staff nurse standing there. 'Good evening, Mr Treneager,' she said with equal politeness—then the splint cupboard seemed to require her urgent attention, so she swished away, trying not to be aware of a certain tall dark figure following Mr O'Neill into the treatment room.

She kept her head firmly in the splint cupboard until there had been time for them to patch Darren up and send him on his way, more than half wishing that some other emergency would come up to make her busy, but of course they never happened when you wanted them. She heard Mr O'Neill's voice obviously drifting out of the department and decided it was safe to emerge. Besides, she ought to be setting up a new stitch trolley to replace the one used on Darren. Treatment Room One was empty. Then it wasn't: Ashley apparently hadn't gone. She looked round at a sound, and there he was in the doorway.

The black and white of the formal clothes suited him beautifully. Cherry looked away again quickly, biting her lip, allowing herself only to wonder coldly what on earth he was doing hanging about Casualty dressed like that. She decided to ignore him. If he required something, he could say so.

'It's almost Christmas,' he said, in a mildly conversational tone.

The season of goodwill? The time when you forgave people for their immoral lives? 'Is it?' she asked indifferently, with an edge of ice in her voice. 'I've been too busy to notice!'

'The Accident Unit does seem to be the one place where no one puts up Christmas decorations.'

'We haven't the space for them, they might get in the way, and Sister doesn't believe in anything which might harbour infection.' That was a longer sentence than she need have given him. Cherry looked up, coldly. 'Is there something you want, Mr Treneager?'

'Not something I'm likely to get, I think,' he said, in the same mild tone as before. And this time he did go. She heard him call out a quiet good night to the staff nurse.

Half an hour later there were ambulance bells, and a road accident to deal with, so that there was no time for private thought. Later on there was a cardiac arrest and a drug overdose and enough to do to see them through until morning, since even when there were no patients everything had to be scrubbed and re-set and tidied.

It might have been coincidence—or Christmas, because everyone did a lot of coming and going—but she seemed to find herself walking past Ashley several times after that. He always gave her a formal hallo: there were always other people around so that she had to answer. He stood in for the SSO in the unit one night, too—but then the two men were friends, and the Eye Department was probably half empty during the Christmas period. He didn't hang around when he wasn't called in, which was something, but they had to get him up twice and the second time Cherry found herself working with him on another batch of road casualties, caused by ice on the roads and over-celebrating. She tried to pretend he was just anyone—and not to admire his deft efficiency, or listen to the deep honey tones in his voice as he soothed a frightened woman.

An early-morning patient came in just as they'd dispatched the last of their previous lot, a radio shift-worker who had skidded off his motorbike and landed heavily on one wrist. It was a minor break but took time to plaster. Cherry was used to seeing accident doctors dark-eyed and stubble-chinned and used to making coffee for them when a rush was over. She didn't know how it happened that she found herself alone in a treatment room with Ashley as they both drank the dark steaming brew; but still, it *had* been a long night . . . She felt a sudden stretch in the silence—and a sudden remembered twinge, an ache which was still there however forcibly she crushed it down. That wouldn't do at all.

'You work well,' he commented, out of the quiet.

'Thank you, Mr Treneager.'

'Hm. That's one of the penalties of seniority, is it? This constant "Mister"—as compared with "Bob" and "Georgc"—?'

Some of the junior doctors Cherry knew had been in helping with the road casualties. 'Are you sure I've reformed enough to be spoken to?' she asked on a sudden snap, and then could have bitten her tongue out. Something impersonal would have been much, much better.

'Don't nag a tired man. Do you have to go on bearing a grudge?'

'I thought you might be making another reference to my reputation,' she said sweetly, since he had raised the subject so openly. He *did* looked tired, though. She wished it wouldn't make her heart turn over, because that made her feel miserably cross and snappy.

'I do know what kind of a reputation you have.' He said it tranquilly instead of angrily, which made her feel worse. 'How about forgetting past quarrels? It's—' he looked at his watch, then looked round in surprise, 'it's Christmas Day.'

'Is it? I suppose it is. I'll probably sleep through all of it. Oh, I'll miss the carol singers!' she said involuntarily. 'And I sang, last year . . .'

'Yes, I remember.' There was a stir somewhere out in the department, and Ashley glanced round. It wasn't another casualty, though, just the first of the day staff coming on. 'Time you were going off,' Ashley said briefly, and began to get up. Then he paused, looked at her, and held out his right hand as if offering a formal handshake. 'Forgiven?' he asked.

It *was* Christmas Day. And he *was* smiling at her, in a remembered fashion which made hating him impossible. Cherry found herself putting a hand into his, and shaking it, in a fashion which really was ridiculous in the middle of Casualty. 'All right,' she said, taking her hand back quickly, 'but don't—'

'I promise not to criticise your friends again. Or leap to any wild conclusions. That is, as long as you promise not to criticise mine,' he said, with a sudden glint of familiar mockery, and did get to his feet this time. 'Oh, by the way, I suppose you and your group will be going to the New Year Dance?'

'I shouldn't think so,' Cherry said repressively, against a longing to be there and see him looking tall and elegant and—just maybe—even dancing with him. 'I'll probably be working, somebody has to. Are—are you going?'

'It's expected, so presumably I shall. Mm—well, Happy Christmas, everyone, it's time those of us who need to sleep went away and slept!'

This last was addressed generally to Cherry and the two day nurses who had just appeared in the treatment-room doorway. They all chorussed 'Happy Christmas' obediently. It was the only answer to make. And Cherry snapped to attention to begin her hand-over to the day staff, while Ashley walked out and away. If she had let herself—which she didn't—she could have imagined she still felt the remembered touch of his hand in that unexpected handshake . . .

She *wouldn't* go to the New Year Dance, though. She'd already said she wasn't going to, claiming that night duty was too much like living in a long dark tunnel for her to crawl out of it and be jolly. Besides, almost all the other Accident Unit night staff were anxious to swop duties so as to be free to go, so it wouldn't be fair to change her mind. Cherry hadn't analysed why she was unwilling to go in the first place. It certainly hadn't been because she didn't want to see Ashley and Annis Lamb together—still not formally engaged, but still known to be a pair by everyone on the circuit.

It was impossible to know what impulse had made him want to be friends again. An innate sense of justice, perhaps—or a fit of boredom. Or a bit of both. Cherry found she was walking off duty with a stupid grin on her face. Then the grin vanished as she realised that he *hadn't* actually apologised. Now why did she let him get away with that? Still, it didn't really matter . . .

She began her nights off on Boxing Day and went round to the Bairstows' with toys for the children and small presents for Pat and Mel, and had a jolly family day until she was too sleepy to last out any longer. Because she dozed off in the middle of supper they plonked her in the spare room and insisted she stayed over: in the end she stayed two nights so that they could go out and celebrate their wedding anniversary leaving her with the children. Pretty soon it was back to work again and car crashes, cardiacs, emergency stomach pains, and whatever else Northborough could throw at its hospital. New Year's Eve and drunks—a broken-bottle fight outside a pub the other side of town bringing ambulances full of the sheepish and the aggressive dripping gore, and accompanying policemen tramping all over and the Accident Unit. A young Pakistani came in having been beaten up by yobs and wouldn't do anything but shake his head mutely when that set of police wanted him to make a statement.

On into January, and the mundane settling-down of the after-Christmas period. In between whiles there was the occasional fit of socialising, though Cherry was too night-duty orientated to want to go out much. In between whiles too there was Ashley to smile at and say hallo whenever they happened to pass each other. No one made anything of it because everyone who had worked on the Accident Unit said friendly hallos, regardless of rank.

She didn't see him much because she was getting her head down to work. The end-of-second-year block and exams were coming up. Then night duty was over in a rush, study block was full of lectures and essays, the exams came and went. Cherry, to her intense surprise, came top.

She went away on holiday, though early March was hardly an ideal time for it. She went to Cornwall and walked, trying not to admit to herself that she had chosen it because it was Ashley's county. The scenery was beautiful, even in cold pre-spring weather. It reminded her too that she hadn't been out to the moors for a long time.

Tramping about alone, sometimes thinking and sometimes not, was salutary. Cherry decided wryly that since she was obviously incurable, she'd probably become a dedicated spinster nurse. Oh well, there were worse things. Walking, of course, inevitably reminded her of Sue, and that other holiday they had spent together. Yes, there were certainly worse things than being alive and healthy . . . so she might as well be grateful for that.

She went back to the hospital to move back into the Day Nurses' Home and consult the list to see where she was posted for the next three months of training, where they were moved around to give them practical experience of almost everything. The printed words seemed to leap out at her: 'C. Langton—Eye Department—' Then she could almost have cried because she wasn't down to follow it up with Eye Theatre: she was to spend the second six weeks on General Theatre instead. Oh, but that *was* an unfair chance . . . She'd probably never see Ashley operate now!

There was a certain wariness in thinking about nursing in his own department. She didn't suppose, wryly, that it would cure her: during her solitary holiday she had finally come to the conclusion that she was stuck with a hopeless attraction and might as well live with it. She still loved him—she supposed it was love, not just habit. If it made her day to see him, then so be it. He was difficult, complex, temperamental, and sometimes thoroughly horrible; but he only had to smile at her and her heart dropped straight through her stomach. Physiologically impossible, she reminded herself mockingly—and went on duty reminding herself warningly that she wouldn't only see *him* at close quarters every day, she'd see Annis Lamb as well . . .

She walked through the glass door into the Eye Department with a carefully blank face, wondering with a sudden quiver of uncertainty whether Sister Lamb would recognise her as the nurse Ashley had stopped to tell off all those months ago.

Apparently not. Sister Lamb greeted her pleasantly in a friendly manner and told her sweetly that she had heard good reports of her. Then she sat down to give a ward report in her soft Scottish voice—and Cherry discovered that the department was in the care of the registrar, John Bland, for the next two weeks, because Ashley had gone off yesterday to attend a surgical symposium.

She could only accept it philosophically, and tell herself that at least it gave her time to learn the ropes. She had better. As a third-year she would be expected to take quite a lot of responsibility.

The Eye Department was quite small: just two wards, though it had a large and flourishing outpatients department. Sister Lamb ran things in a deceptively gentle manner, was invariably sweet to all her nurses—and had an absolute mania for organisation. There were lists for everything. There were numbers for everything too. The nurses were divided into teams and each team was responsible for certain beds no matter who was in them. Senior nurses were supposed to set aside regular times to give teaching sessions to the junior members of their team—'Such good practice,' Sister Lamb said gently, and flashing her beautiful green eyes angelically, 'for when you want to become Nursing Officers!'

'She's a management freak,' Cherry told Pat Bairstow humorously when she ran into him in a corridor and he paused to ask her how she was getting on, and how she'd enjoyed her holiday. 'I even get the feeling that she'd like to *organise* the patients back into good health—not that she isn't thoroughly nice to them, though!'

'All done by kindness? Yes, that sounds like our Annis. She'd have all the Sisters out for team training given half a chance,' Pat said with a twinkle. 'They do say that the only reason she hasn't married that boss of hers is that she can't bear to leave the job, and she might be expected to leave if she'd wed him. Maybe she'll keep him hanging on until she's reached Chief Nursing Officer. Come round one evening, lass,' he added, apparently not noticing Cherry's suddenly blank expression.

'Thanks, I will,' Cherry told him, and escaped—losing her smile as soon as she'd left him. Somehow she'd never really thought . . . of Ashley wanting to marry Annis Lamb and being refused. Well, that was just one more thing, to put away and not think about.

Suddenly it seemed a very long time since the early days—of gossiping and stumbling through work trying not to be clumsy and spending all her free time with Lisa and

Buzz and Suzanne. The three-out-of-four of them left seemed to have drifted apart, and taken up with other friends. All at once it seemed a pity not to be able to set the clock back . . .

Cherry ran into Lisa not ten minutes later on the stairs of the Nurses' Home, and with her thoughts still with her said brightly, 'Hallo, where are you working nowadays? Come and have a coffee?' Then she looked again and saw that Lisa was in tears.

'Lisa? Hey, love, what is it? Come on—where's your room, let's go and talk about it!'

'S-sorry,' gulped Lisa, but she came with her; and when they were inside grabbed a handkerchief and stifled a sob. 'I'm n-not really crying,' she said defiantly, and cast Cherry a watery glance. 'Well, all right, I am, then!'

'I haven't seen you much—'

'You've been busy. So've I—'

'And you were avoiding me during block,' Cherry said neutrally, because she had been well aware of it. She guessed it was because of Cliff Hamel as much as anything. That affair seemed to have lasted beyond anyone's expectation, and Lisa had never forgiven her for disapproving of him.

'Oh, well . . . I really do love him, you know,' said Lisa, bearing out her guess, and looking at Cherry with wide woebegone eyes. 'We're engaged—not with a ring or anything, we can't afford one at the moment, but we *are* engaged!'

'Good for you. So, you're crying for happiness?'

'Yes! And we haven't quarrelled, either! Look, I know you don't like Cliff, but you've got him all wrong, as it happens. I know he puts on an act, but he's really rather shy, and—Cherry, I love him so much, it's not like the other times!'

'So, great! I'm glad for you. Why are you unhappy?' Cherry asked gently.

'I'm n-not really. It's just that—Cliff's got another job, down in London, which is great, a good chance for him. They're hard to get, you know, even for doctors. And I'm—*don't* disapprove—it's the only thing to do: I'm going to quit and go with him. I've just been down to post in my notice.'

'Lisa! Oh, you can't! Look, we're into our third year—'

'It's no use saying we can wait, and be engaged, and get married when I finish. He wants me to marry him now and go with him. He *needs* me! And I want to go! And not because I don't trust him, either,' Lisa added with quick anger, as if countering an argument Cherry hadn't produced. 'I do, it's just that he needs me to be with him. We'll get married and find a flat and—I'm really very happy about it!'

'If you were, why cry?'

'Oh, stupid reasons—thinking of saying goodbye to this place! And—and I suddenly started thinking of Sue. But I don't need to be a nurse,' Lisa said defiantly, 'I can work as an auxiliary, can't I? So it won't all be wasted. One thing about London, there are lots of hospitals!'

'You don't want to work as an auxiliary, and it *would* be a waste! After we've got this far! Lisa, think! And—and you said just now you were thinking of Sue. I wanted—'

'Oh yes, so did I, I know what you're going to say and I thought of that too! If *she* couldn't, at least *we* would. But Cliff matters more. I've never felt like this about anyone, ever. It's no use trying to talk me out of it. Oh lord, is that the phone? It'll probably be him, and I don't want him to guess I've been crying!'

She was scrubbing her face rapidly. 'Don't wait,' she said quickly, 'because if it is him we'll probably talk for ages. And *please* don't try any of your arguments, because my mind really is made up. I'm going with him, and that's the important thing! Let yourself out!'

She was gone in a flash of red curls and flying skirts. Cherry tried to assimilate the shock of it—and her anger against Cliff Hamel. Unfair, perhaps, but he *was* being selfish, to expect Lisa to throw up everything to go with him . . . And whatever Lisa said, she did *not* believe he was shy!

Only two left out of four, then. She stifled a rapid inclination to go and check up on Buzz, deciding wryly that she was showing all the instincts of a mother hen.

She was haunted by Lisa's decision, and was thinking about that as she walked off duty with her mind on that instead of on Sister Lamb's Thought for Today—that her team leaders should work out their own duty-rotas, and get together on them so that everything in the ward was properly covered. Then, all at once, a deep voice penetrated through her consciousness.

'Looking sad and forlorn—why?'

She had almost walked past Ashley without seeing him. They were on one of the outside paths between wards and she looked up with a sharp gladness—he was back! Because he was part of it all, she found herself saying, as if it was perfectly natural to confide in him,

'It's Lisa, my friend, in my set. She's decided to give up. I—she was one of the original four of us—'

'Why is she giving up?'

'To get married. It isn't a question of can't wait,' she added hastily, in case he thought so, 'it's *won't*. Well . . . the doctor she's marrying is going to a job in London, so she's quitting to go with him. She says she'll work as an auxiliary, but it's such a waste!'

'Can't she get into a hospital to train down there?' asked Ashley.

'She'd have to start all over again, wouldn't she?'

'No, she could transfer. Hasn't she thought of that? She might have to repeat a bit to start at the beginning of a year—but then you've only just begun your third year anyway, haven't you?'

'No, she *hasn't* thought of that!' said Cherry, on a sudden hope. 'Do they really let you? Oh thanks, I must *tell* her!'

'I'm surprised the Nursing Officer hasn't told her. I know it's done, because my old hospital had several transferees. For all I know it may be the only one that does, but I shouldn't think so.'

'I don't think the Nursing Officer *did* tell her. Actually I think she just resigned flatly without asking anything. Oh, thanks, you *are* a help!'

Cherry beamed up at him—and only then realised that she was standing here chatting to him as if he was an old friend. She didn't have time to turn defensive, or start blushing, or do anything but feel a kind of dizzy pleasure at seeing him, because he was speaking again.

'If you like, I can find you the right address so that she can write to the Tutorial Department at St Joseph's,' he offered amiably. 'It usually helps if you pick a particular hospital. Want me to?'

'Oh yes, could you? If—if it wouldn't be too much trouble!'

'No trouble. In fact—' he glanced at his watch, 'if you like to come round to the flat now I'll look it out for you straight away. I've just arrived back, and I was going to look in at the department before going home—but I might as well not, at this time of night, when I'm not officially here until tomorrow. I've been away.'

'Yes, I know. I'm working in your department,' Cherry told him decorously.

'Are you, now? Then don't tell me if there've been any crises that Annis and John Bland couldn't deal with between them, though I can't imagine there will have been. Coming?'

Cherry hesitated, and saw his left eyebrow go up in its familiar slant. The old glint of mocking amusement slid into his eyes, reminding her strongly of the past. 'I think you *can* be seen talking to me now,' he drawled, his eyes going over her and lingering pointedly on her cap and belt, 'don't you, Third-Year-Nurse Langton? Even you couldn't claim that anyone's going to make anything out of it . . .'

When he was known to be a pair with Annis Lamb, and Cherry had a firm reputation as everyone's-little-sister. And when, besides, she was working for him. 'No, I don't imagine so,' she said calmly, 'and thank you, I *will* come and get that address. Are you driving or walking? And did you have a nice symposium—whatever that is?'

He proceeded to tell her—and if she was tempted to listen more to his voice than to his words, that couldn't matter since he wouldn't be able to guess it. She knew she was flirting with her own emotions, and that it was a dangerous indulgence to feel a tingling of happiness travelling all round her bloodstream. She might as well feel it while it lasted—and after all, there was no *harm* in being on friendly terms with him again. Until the next storm blew up . . .

CHAPTER TEN

ASHLEY had his stormy moments on the ward, that she had to admit. Unlike most consultants who only came in for rounds, he had a habit of swooping in at any time, in theatre clothes or out of them, so that one couldn't know whether to keep a sharp eye out for green cotton and rubber boots, or for a long white coat.

Unfailingly good with the patients, he didn't otherwise suffer fools gladly. Cherry could see why an earlier female houseman of his had always looked so terrified, and even this one tended to jump unhappily whenever his voice was heard in the distance. It couldn't help to have him mutter scathingly, '*Would* you care to do that corneal graft all over again, Miss Browne? Because you'll have to if you're going to jiggle instead of keeping the patient's head immobilised when I want to inspect the dressing!'

The patients, particularly the elderly female ones, adored him; those nurses who hadn't just suffered a fit of his bad temper exchanged surreptitious grins over him; and Sister Lamb went on being sweet and gentle and organising, with him as much as with anyone else. Cherry had the unholy suspicion that it annoyed him considerably to be reminded gently about 'team nursing' when he'd grabbed the nearest nurse to do something for him.

He could be extraordinarily charming, though—on his better days. When he was, the whole department seemed to brighten up as if in receipt of a bout of sunshine. John Bland, his calm-natured registrar, used to come into the ward after an operating list and make finger signals to the staff nurse, to whom he was engaged, and after a few days Cherry discovered they meant, 'It was a good day,' or 'It was a bad day so watch out,' or sometimes an in-between sign which simply meant 'Be careful'. Cherry bit back a grin when she was given the information, and wondered if

Ashley knew how he was regarded.

She certainly wasn't in a position to tell him, even if she would have wanted to. She didn't see him off the ward, and on it simply kept her head down, like everyone else. She seemed to be doing quite well. Experience on IC had taught her to be quick and careful. She even found herself comforting a first-year in tears in the sluice, and being told dolefully, 'It's all right for seniors like you, you don't bump into things!'

'Whenever you think you might, take a deep breath and count to ten,' Cherry advised her. Then she was suddenly chuckling as she remembered who had given *her* that advice. She made her face quickly grave, and added, 'You *can't* risk bumping into post-op beds, anyway, because after an iridectomy or any sort of repair it's very important to keep the patient's head immobilised—you do know that! And you mustn't drop things with a loud crash either, because if someone's under eye bandages they're bound to jump, aren't they?'

Two years ago she couldn't have imagined sounding so efficient and knowledgeable. Now it came out almost as second nature.

She had the 'It's all right for you' line from one of the other third-years on one occasion: 'It's all right for you, Langton, you're one of Sir's favoured ones! I could have slaughtered you when he growled, "Oh, let Nurse Langton do it, *she* probably knows how," in that scathing way of his, just because I hesitated!'

'That was only because I was standing there,' Cherry protested.

'No, it's because you've taken to it like a duck to water. You even asked Sister if you could go in and watch an op, didn't you? *That* went down well, I should think!'

'Sir didn't know I was there, thank goodness,' Cherry told her lightly. She remembered standing in the background well out of the way; the theatre full of the dancing strains of Vivaldi from a concealed tape-recorder; and the fascination of watching Ashley with a magnifier pulled down over his eyes operating meticulously with tiny tools. 'I just wanted to see what micro-surgery looked like, that's all. It was nice of Sister to let me. But I've had my share of sarcasm too, you know!'

She had also had one of the latest books on eye surgery left in her pigeonhole for her, quite unexpectedly, with a note saying, 'This may help you write up your ward reports —return it when you've finished. A.T.' But she certainly wasn't going to mention that.

Sister Lamb was kind enough to tell her she'd done well, though she *could* cultivate a little more of the team spirit and remember to delegate. Otherwise she'd shown promise and would she please remember to go on teaching her juniors (so as to be good Nursing Officer material, presumably) and would she like to get up a committee amongst her fellow third-years to agitate for more in-service lectures? Cherry kept a careful blank face and said, 'Thank you, Sister, I'll think about it, but I can't do anything until after I've finished Theatre—because of the hours, you know!' *More* in-service lectures—no way!

She returned Ashley's book. She tried not to think how much nicer it would have been to be left an orchid in her pigeonhole—as had happened to a staff nurse last week —and knew wryly that she wasn't the orchid type. The book had been very useful, anyway. And it ill behoved her to think romantic thoughts . . .

She moved to General Theatre which was hot, tiring, and a strain on the leg muscles because there was so much standing still. It also had very unsocial hours because of late lists and early lists and emergency lists, but for the latter she was often working with Mr O'Neill again, which was pleasant because he was invariably cheerful. An inveterate flirt, too, in spite of having married a casualty staff nurse last year. He wasn't unpleasant with it like Cliff Hamel, but he did flirt. Thinking of Cliff Hamel reminded Cherry of Lisa—gone now, but on a promise to see if she *could* get into St Joseph's, and looking the more cheerful for the information, too. Buzz, whom Cherry had started to run into again because he was on General Theatre too, said disapprovingly that he didn't think Lisa *would* try, and she should have waited to get married too. Cherry shrugged, smiled, and was proved right when she had a letter saying that Lisa was restarting next month. At least she sounded happy . . .

After a tiring six weeks (during which Cherry had once threatened to sew a sampler out of swabs and sutures saying 'Happiness is Work', a sentiment she was sure she ought to hold) General Theatre was over. 'Now, Nurse,' Luke O'Neill was saying coaxingly, 'are you sure you won't come and hold my hand while I change, just to celebrate the fact that that's the last time you'll dirty-nurse for me?' He turned his head as someone else came into the sterilising room, obviously not a whit dismayed by being overheard, and said cheerfully, 'Ah, hallo, Ashley, what are *you* doing over here?'

'Just looking into the Recovery Room to see how that accident case progressed. There'll be some eye work to be done there later.' Ashley wasn't in theatre clothes, and he had shed his white coat, too, leaving him looking spruce in shirt-sleeves and dark trousers. Cherry was immediately conscious that her face was shiny and hot and that she was still bundled-up in a smeared theatre gown. His eyes rested on her mildly, but he went on talking to Luke O'Neill. 'Have you finished up in here? Jane will be glad to see you home early for once—your deputy's taken over in Cas, hasn't he?'

'Do you know, I think he's telling me off?' said Luke O'Neill, to the air, but with his blue eyes casting a wicked glance at Cherry. 'Don't you worry, this one can take care of herself. It's our Nurse Langton, the drunk-chaser!'

'Oh yes, I'm sure she can. I'd back her to stop your Irish charm dead in its tracks at ten paces,' Ashley said tranquilly, 'so I should go away and get changed before another emergency comes in and catches you before you can get off duty!'

His sally made Luke O'Neill chuckle, but he did start moving. Cherry wasn't laughing; she was eyeing Ashley with a smouldering look which she was too tired to turn into anything more polite. She opened her mouth as the other surgeon went safely out of earshot, but Ashley got in first, with a smile and a defensive lift of his hand.

'No, don't—I *wasn't* going to say it, I promise you! I was

just going to say, so this is where you've disappeared to!'

'It's no secret,' Cherry said snappishly, wishing her pulse didn't have to jerk at the thought that he had missed her.

'It's hard to keep track. One minute I was congratulating myself that I'd got a good ward nurse; next you were gone. Thanks for sending the book back. Come round and leaf through my library some time to see if I've got any more useful ones!'

Books for her use, and not orchids for her pleasure. And a spot of casual protection for her morals . . . 'Thanks,' Cherry said lightly, swallowing a sudden lump in her throat which was only there because she was tired after a day's threatre work, 'I'll do that. Though I don't suppose you've got any on gynaecology, which is where I'm going next!'

'Come round anyway. You're looking overtired and as if you could do with a square meal. I won't keep you now—I can see you've still got a lot of clearing up to do!'

He went away with one of those charming smiles of his which could be guaranteed to melt the heart, and left Cherry just as lost as ever in her own private morass of love and longing. It was just as well he didn't know, or he'd never cast out these casual invitations. She was perfectly well aware of that. Little Cherry, the waif and stray—a suitable, and undangerous, friends and protégée. She really ought to be used to that thought by now . . . and not let it hurt so much.

Half a loaf was better than no bread. If he asked her she'd go—and she did. Summer, and visiting Ashley's flat: it held a host of reminders. This year, though, since she was by now almost halfway through her third year, he was more inclined to help her with her work than to offer chess and conversation. She knew she could learn a great deal from him, so she set herself to do so. He could turn his intelligence to just about every subject and was nothing if not useful. He also offered his flat as a studying place—in that same casual friendly manner which he interspersed with teasing and the occasional grouch when she turned stupid on some subject or other.

It came up when she grumbled about the new Nurses' Home extension being built right outside her window. 'I know they say they need more space, but I could do without pneumatic drills when I'm stuck in my room trying to write essays on this damned management unit they've landed us with!' Cherry stopped abruptly, suddenly aware that his beloved Annis was a devotee of management, and presumably he approved of it too, since he let his department be run on such organisational lines.

'You're probably objecting to the pneumatic drills due to having a thick head,' he said drily—and unsympathetically. 'I presume your birthday party went well?'

The Bairstows had given the party for her. She had appreciated that, but it wasn't the sort of party Ashley could have been invited to, even casually. 'It *was* my twenty-first,' Cherry said without looking at him. 'Not, of course, that I didn't come of age at eighteen!'

'You're growing positively ancient. I actually did buy you a present: I only haven't given it to you yet due to the fear of having it thrown back at me.' While she looked up at him in swift and defensive surprise, he walked over and opened the desk drawer, coming back with a small box in his hand. 'They merely reminded me of the first time I saw you, in the market. You needn't wear them, if you don't like them!'

He had given her something that wasn't a book, or anything else useful, but . . . earrings. Cherry looked at the pretty little flowered circles with a sudden incredible desire to burst into tears, swallowed, and stammered, 'Th-thank you, they're lovely—'

'No thanks required. No, don't try them on now, you'd need a mirror. To go back to the drills—If you can't ask to change your room, and I suppose you can't —'

'They can't move everybody over to the far side.' Cherry was still staring at the earrings, though she knew she mustn't, and made herself close the box. She told herself staunchly that he had probably bought an identical pair for one of his nieces. 'Sorry—what did you say?'

'I said, why don't you come and study here? I'm out all day, so when you have free mornings or afternoons the place is empty. I can give you a key so that you can let yourself in and out.'

'You can't—I mean I couldn't do that!'

'I really can't see why not. If anyone sees you,' he said drily, 'you could just as easily be visiting the family downstairs. All right, that's fixed, then, and remind me to give you a spare key before you go!'

It seemed really strange to be in the flat without Ashley. She rigorously didn't allow herself to poke about, because that would have been dishonest. Once she got used to it and made herself concentrate, it really was a good place to work, too, near enough to the hospital to get to and fro quickly, and with all his books to look things up in.

No one seemed to wonder where she went, either. She wasn't really close enough to anyone to have questions asked, except for Pat's occasional probing because he and Mel seemed to think she ought to be paired off.

'I'm a world's worker,' she told him virtuously, pulling a face at him to stop him nagging her. 'Now when do I have *time* for a wild love affair in between babysitting for you and writing up on total patient care and organisational techniques?'

'Now look, lass, there's no need to come babysitting if you're cutting down on your freedom!'

'Don't be silly, that *wasn't* what I meant!'

'Well *don't* turn into a younger version of Our Annis! "Organisational techniques" my eye,' he grumbled gloomily, 'I've run my ward without *them* for years!'

'She's very beautiful, though, you must admit.'

'She can't hold a candle to you in my book,' Pat retorted, out of the nonsensical affection he and his wife seemed to hold for her, 'she'd drive any sane man mad with her ways, besides. All sugar and steel underneath, and I'd rather have good honest prettiness any day!'

Why couldn't it be Ashley who thought Annis 'couldn't hold a candle to her' . . . but it was no use thinking that way.

She was used to making sure she got out of the flat before he would want to come in it, if she had a free afternoon *and* evening. Sometimes she didn't manage it. She hadn't managed it one evening when, by taking a surreptitious look at the theatre lists, she had thought he would be operating late and she had some heavy notes on drug management to finish. She heard his key in the door and jumped guiltily—and then a grouchy mutter which sounded very much as if he was in one of his bad tempers. Cherry began to gather her papers into a hasty pile, but he was already in the room.

'Oh, you're still here, are you? And scattering things about fairly thoroughly,' he added as some of her papers slid to the ground. Cherry found herself thinking instantly of John Bland's signal, 'Not a good day, so beware,' and hastily bent down to collect everything.

'Sorry, I'm just going. You're early . . .' It would be better *not* to dare to ask how his operating list had gone, when he was wearing that expression, so she didn't. 'I'll be out of here in no time,' she said breathlessly, aware of the frown, the very dark eyes, the way his face looked thinner when he was in a bad mood. He did look very much as if he was reining himself in.

'You needn't overdo it, and I'll be better when I've had some coffee—*not* that vile brew they have on the hob around theatre,' he said malevolently, and looking through her. Cherry wondered whether to offer to make it for him. No, perhaps not, better to let him have peace. *Man-management*, she thought drily, with a sudden slightly hysterical bubble of unamused laughter inside her. Now wasn't that funny—that she knew Ashley's ways better than most people did?

'I've just said you needn't go, so why are you scuttling about? I offered you the place to do your work in . . . *Sit* there, and finish whatever it was you were doing!'

He stamped off into the kitchen. Cherry glanced uncertainly after him, sat down again, and wrote a few hasty sentences just to show obedience. He came back with a large mug of coffee just as she had finished them and was starting to gather her things together again. He looked slightly more human, and was obviously feeling it, as he said with only half a grouch, 'Take no notice: I had a repair which isn't going to work as well as I wanted it to, too much damage to the optic nerve. *And* the tape-recorder broke down, so I've left John Bland to deal with the glaucoma, he's perfectly capable!'

Cherry didn't feel it would be wise to say 'Sorry' or 'What

bad luck' or any of the placebo phrases which would undoubtedly he simply annoying. She simply smiled at him sympathetically and got up quietly. 'I'll go now, and thanks for the space—'

'Want any supper?'

'No, thank you, I'm going to meet up with a friend in the canteen.' It was a third-year with some notes for her on ear, nose and throat work. Cherry smiled at Ashley again —soothingly, she hoped—and walked across to the door. She could feel him watching her, and as she got there he said casually,

'Oh, by the way . . . just in case you hear it and start an entirely wrong rumour going round, my Ward Sister's engaged, and not to me. A local property developer, in his forties. Quite a suitable match.'

'Oh, I'm sorry!'

She probably shouldn't have come out with it quite like that, nor turned to stare at him with a look of instinctive sympathy. But that was the obvious reason for his bad temper, and however Cherry herself felt, knowing him to be hurt was still a pain. He didn't look hurt. He looked quite sardonically surprised at her expression.

'Sorry? Why? She isn't leaving, so I haven't got to cope with a new Ward Sister. A dedicated lady, Annis, and I doubt if she'd have accepted him if it meant leaving nursing. As it happens I advised her to marry him and stop being so damned difficult; she can't have everything, and it was about time she made up her mind.'

'But—you—'

'Try to restrain your vivid imagination,' he said drily, 'or I'll probably grow evil-tempered again. I've told you before —I'm not husband material, and I don't go round pretending to be!'

'You were *very* inseparable . . .'

'We were convenient company for each other. You needn't look at me like that! She's always known where she was with me: that's what made it convenient.'

Cherry gulped. His attitude seemed bewildering, but certainly not brokenhearted. She couldn't quite take it in. 'I work much too hard for any woman and I'm totally unliveable-with,' Ashley's voice said while she was still gazing at him glassy-eyed. There was almost a touch of satisfaction in his voice, if there hadn't been that underlying bitterness there too. 'So you can put paid to any ideas you may have of suggesting someone for me to court next! And didn't you say you were going out?'

'Um—yes—I'm just going!'

She took away an odd mixture of impressions—his tall dark form leaning languidly in the kitchen doorway; his scowl which seemed to have more than an edge of returning anger in it; and a definite air of suddenly being glad to get rid of her. But no more regret over Annis Lamb than there had been in his voice when he had said, 'I advised her to marry him . . .'

It was a nine days' wonder on the grapevine, but nobody made any suggestion that Mr Ashley Treneager might be brokenhearted. It didn't seem to make any difference to Cherry anyway. She was still using Ashley's flat; he was still being there sometimes to peer over her shoulder and make helpful comments on whatever she was doing. Perhaps less often, because he wasn't actually inviting her in for an evening any more. Fair enough, he was giving her his space instead of his time. He seemed busy and quite good-humoured—and Cherry got busy again too, because there was another spate of parties in the Junior Doctors' Common Room. Since Cherry had done so much studying lately she decided it was time she gave herself time off, anyway, or she'd become thoroughly dull.

She actually enjoyed parties now and again anyway —even if she was insulated from their more romantic moments by her foolish, stubborn, helpless addiction to someone who wasn't present.

Senior doctors didn't usually come into the Junior Doctors' Common Room. Very occasionally they did. Ashley looked in one night with John Bland and his fiancée. The lights were low and Cherry was dancing cheek-to-cheek with a new anæsthetist. Actually it was the result of some goodhumoured joshing because he was very tall and someone had challenged that he wouldn't find it possible to dance that way with a girl of Cherry's height. He was very dark-haired and dark-eyed and she could almost imagine for a moment that he was like a younger version of Ashley . . . and then she looked up and saw him.

He was standing near the door looking round languidly. Then he was hidden from view. Moments later when she could look again he was gone. She was suddenly sore-hearted because she would have liked to go up to him in a friendly but suitably respectful fashion and say something light and amusing and see him give his flashing smile to her. But it was too late now and she couldn't show how much she minded.

Cherry was off duty for the next two days. On the second she decided ruefully that she'd better do some work, third-year commitments being correspondingly heavy to seniority, and after a wry look out at the rising skeleton of the Nurses' Home extension, where they were now banging in rivets, she collected up her books and found Ashley's key.

She had been working for about half an hour when she heard a key in the door, and—against the usual tremor of pleasure which ran along her nerves at the thought of seeing him—she felt a touch of exasperation because he would probably want her to go away and she'd only just got started. Or perhaps he wouldn't mind. He might just be looking in for something, in the middle of a Monday afternoon. As she looked round he came into the room, and his expression promptly changed to one of sardonic dislike. She felt a pang of hurt before she reminded herself swiftly that it was his flat, and he had a right to feel bad-tempered in it if he wanted to.

'So you've decided to take up work again, have you?' he enquired, in that nasty silky tone which was one Cherry particularly disliked. 'No, don't move, I've no doubt it's time you caught up, and I'm glad you still find the place useful! Though incidentally—' he glanced round elaborately before bringing his eyes back to bore darkly into her face—'I hope you *don't* imagine you can also bring your friends here!'

'I wouldn't! It's unfair of you to suggest—' It was no use, he was obviously in one of his worst moods. Someone must have annoyed him, badly. 'I'll go,' Cherry said placatingly, though it didn't seem to placate him because he came across the room to loom over her.

'You needn't—in fact I think you shouldn't. You could probably do with a little concentration, or you won't get far with your next assessment, will you?' he enquired, scathingly. 'You probably think you've got the energy to dance all night and work just as well as ever, but I doubt it. You *should* have more sense, though I'm well aware you haven't!'

'Goodness, you sound like—' Cherry was scrabbling her books together and trying to look lighthearted about it instead of feeling a zoom into depression, so she didn't finish on 'like Buzz', which was what had come immediately to mind. Her pen cap seemed to be missing and she began to hunt for it. His next words brought her head up.

'Like whom? Not my anaesthetist, I presume, since he now seems to fancy his chances with you!'

Cherry turned cold. *That* again? 'Are you having another fit of Moral Rearmament?' she asked icily. It was rude, but her temper had snapped as it suddenly came to her what he had meant to imply by 'bringing your friends here'. Grief and pain and irony and the sheer total unfairness of his view of her warred inside her. She was up on her feet seizing her books off the desk and then dropping half of them because her hands were shaking. 'Are you sure you wouldn't like to accuse me of having an affair with Pat Bairstow again?' she enquired with a sarcasm as bitter as his. 'My *real* friends don't go round believing—'

'I said, sit down and do some work, because it's obviously time you did!' His hand slammed down on the books she was trying to collect, and he held them down so that she couldn't reach them. 'Your love affairs are really no business of mine, as I'm well aware—you're obviously too young and stubborn to listen to advice, so I don't know why I bother with you! Just because you've got the makings of a good nurse, I suppose! Well, get your work done and we won't argue!'

'No, because you're so evil-tempered and—and evil-minded that you're not worth arguing with! Just give me a minute to find your key and you can have it back—' Cherry was near to tears, but she wasn't going to let them come. 'And kindly let me have my books, *Mister* Treneager, and I'll get out of your way for good and all!'

'Don't be so hysterical,' he said coldly, 'and don't be so rude either. I'll try to ignore it, this time, and collect what I came for and leave you to work. *When* you're ready to get settled. As I said—'

'As *I* said, I want my books, and I'm going! To lead the most immoral life I can find!'

It wasn't either wise or dignified to struggle with him, when he was quite inflexibly strong and seemed determined to keep her books out of her reach. And then suddenly it wasn't a struggle, because his arms came round her to pinion her firmly and then—unbelievably—he was holding her so tightly against him that she could scarcely breathe. His head came down and his lips found hers and he was kissing her very hard and bruisingly on the mouth so that she really *couldn't* breathe . . . and didn't care whether she could or not, because her blood seemed to liquefy into a passionate acceptance of his angry embrace. It seemed to go on for a long time. And then he raised his head and stared at her, and looked almost as bemused as she felt. And then, much more gently but still with a suppressed passion which went coursing through her entire body, he was kissing her again . . .

He let her go very gently, after a timeless moment. Cherry could feel his fingers sliding away from her curls, where they seemed to have been tangled. Ashley said nothing at all for a long, long second, but simply looked at her, with something very startled in the black depths of his eyes.

'Damn. How did that happen . . . ?' His voice was deep and rough. 'How . . .'

'Ashley?'

It came out very small and breathless, and sounded pleading. She might just as well have said out loud, 'Don't go away,' and her heart must certainly have been there in her eyes. She saw him see it, and a rueful look crept in to join the shock that still lingered on his face.

'I *don't* do all the things you think I do—'

The plea was still there: she couldn't help it. She saw him swallow. Then he said, 'No, I don't suppose you do. I didn't mean . . .'

'I've loved you for ever.' There didn't seem any point in not saying it. 'I *love* you—are you listening? It doesn't matter that you don't. I mean, you wouldn't, after all—'

'Wouldn't I?' He was still holding her, loosely enough now for her to have moved out of his arms, if she had wanted to. 'When I raked you down, that other time . . . Annis told me I was jealous. I virtually took her to pieces for saying so. You were just a small child I was taking an interest in—'

'I'm *not* a child. I never was, you know.' Cherry put up a tentative hand to touch his cheek. '*Were* you jealous? I—I certainly never thought of that.'

'I have a damnably jealous and possessive nature. It goes with the bad temper.' He said it wryly, and as if acknowledging that it was so; and for her. 'If today wasn't jealousy . . . well, it obviously was, wasn't it? I must be very bad at recognising my own emotions. Particularly when they creep up on me.' His hand came up to touch her hair again, wonderingly. 'You're an insidious little creature, my dear —my very dear Nurse Cherry Langton . . .' There was the whole world of tenderness in the honey of his deep voice. 'But . . . It won't do, you know.'

'What—won't?'

The happiness beyond all belief which had been seeping through her couldn't take his denial. It *was* a denial. She could read it in his face, and then feel it in the way he put her away from him with firm gentleness. He steadied her when she swayed, then moved very firmly away to set a space of several feet between them. He cleared his throat, but spoke quickly before she could say anything more. 'This won't,' he told her, with a kind of harshness in his voice even though the tenderness was still there too. 'You—and me. I've told you, I'm not husband material. And you're worth nothing less. Besides, you need a man in your own age group, not—'

'Ashley, you can't say that! I don't want anyone but you. I never have! Oh, how can you be so *blind*?'

'I was, but I'm not now.' He said it steadily and without moving, his eyes dark pools. There might have been regret in them. There was certainly decision. 'No, Cherry. Not a man with failure already behind him. Not for you. I'm not—'

'For goodness' sake, I don't expect you to m-marry me. I just—I just *love* you!'

'Loving has very little to do with it—and I *don't* go round corrupting the innocent! It would be marriage or nothing for you and me. I seem to have done enough harm.' There was bitterness in his voice and in the twist of his mouth, and a self-blame that brought Cherry's mouth open with the words ready to tumble out, if he had let her say them. 'You'll forget me quite quickly,' he said firmly, 'particularly if I'm not here. And I'm not going to be, which is just as well. I'm going away—'

'When? Where? Take me with you!' she pleaded.

'No, child, don't be silly. I've got a six-month sabbatical coming up. As to where—America first, probably, to study some of the new techniques over there. Then—I don't know, back to London, I expect. I think I'll speed things up,' he added, his eyes now apparently looking inward on a frown, 'It would be better if—'

'Ashley!'

It seemed stupid just to go on saying his name. Cherry couldn't believe it . . . couldn't believe that he would put her away from him, because of past bitterness, and on a principle. Not if he loved her. Not if the way he had been looking and sounding were, could possibly be, true . . .

'Please stop looking at me like that.' He spoke wearily, but with gentleness. 'And go away now, please. You mustn't come here again. I mean it—and since I'll be leaving very soon, there won't be any point. You're very young, and you *will* forget me, except perhaps as a friend you once had.'

'I wish you'd stop saying I'm *young*! Age just isn't relevant! And do you really think I stay young—nursing the crippled and the dying and seeing people torn half to pieces after accidents or—or ripping each other up in drunken brawls? You've seen me work!' Cherry felt as if she was fighting for her life. 'Do you think a child could do what I have to do? I'm a nurse—'

'And you'll be a good one. You must go ahead and do well at it, and then settle down and get married some time later to some young man who'll love and treasure you and give you his time.' There was the world of bitterness in the straight line of his mouth, and if she wasn't imagining it, a touch of unwilling distaste in his eyes as if the idea didn't really please him as much as he was trying to make out. Cherry felt a stab of hope. Then despair, because he was going on. 'No, it *won't* be me. I'm neither young enough nor, as you ought to be able to imagine, capable of change. At least I know myself that well! A workaholic with a failed marriage behind him is no fit mate for anyone. So it's just as well I'm going away.'

'In six months' time I'll be qualified. Less than six months!'

'Don't nurse illusions, my dear. I'm not coming back for you. And in six months' time everything will look quite different—you'll see. Now, will you please go?'

He was looking more inflexible than she had ever seen him. And she couldn't go on throwing herself at a man who didn't want her. Cherry gathered up her books with numb fingers. His key, which she had scrabbled for before, lay on the desk, but she knew she couldn't pick that up. He would only ask for it back in that same quiet, polite voice he had just used on her. She walked past him. He even moved out of her way so that she shouldn't come close. She felt as if she was bleeding to death inside, so that her nursing training started whispering mockingly inside her head with a list of symptoms of haemorrhage. At the door she had to turn and look back at him.

'You don't love me. It's all right—I never expected you to—'

'Go away, Cherry. Now!'

She went.

CHAPTER ELEVEN

ASHLEY vanished so quickly from the hospital scene that it caused ripples. The mutterings soon died as other things came up to talk about. John Bland took over the Eye Department. He married his staff nurse in celebration of his new status. Sister Lamb went on being engaged: probably she was waiting until she could get her wedding thoroughly organised, and her fiancé appeared to be the patient type.

Cherry worked. What else was there to do?

She had schooled herself as an actress for two years so that no one should know she loved Ashley. So it wasn't really any different. Except that he wasn't there to look out for.

Sometimes, in fantasy, she imagined him coming back—appearing suddenly in front of her, tall and dark and noticeable with the eagle face and the white flash in his hair—and giving her his heartbreakingly beautiful smile and saying, 'I was wrong—forgiven?'

She knew it wouldn't happen, of course . . . miracles like that didn't. Not to her.

There was the usual rash of third-year engagements because time was passing and qualification was only a matter of months away. All sorts of people started appearing with engagement rings pinned into their top pockets, looking shiny-eyed and pleased.

It was lucky that Cherry was sent on night duty, because that made an excuse for looking peaky. It was easy enough to give a wan smile and say, 'You *know* what I'm like on nights!'

Time went past steadily, sometimes fast, sometimes at a crawl. Sometimes it was unbearable not to get out—*away*!—and Cherry took a bus out to the moors to gulp in deep draughts of fresh air. The scenery was heartbreakingly beautiful, but it didn't matter what she showed in her face, alone out there. If she had tears running down her cheeks it could have been because of the wind in her eyes.

Back on to day duty, she had General Medical for what would be her last ward before Finals. It was an unrushed ward, in general, so it was quite a good one to have drawn when there was an enormous volume of revision to be worked through, during the next two and a half months.

Christmas. Cherry tried to let it go by without thinking too much about it because there were sharp memories, of last year. She didn't go to any parties, except a small one at the Bairstows', because she had dropped right out of that scene, stubbornly concentrating on nothing but work. She certainly didn't go to the New Year Dance—nobody actually asked her because she'd developed a reputation for being unsociable. She just wasn't seeing anyone, and if her friends liked to assume she was working herself into a fret over Finals they were perfectly entitled to. After all, lots of people *were*, at this time in the year, and the Nurses' Home Supervisor even had a supply of tranquillisers.

And then suddenly there was Buzz.

Cherry had once come upon Lisa crying; she would never have thought the same would happen with Buzz. She put her head round his door to see if he would go through some revision with her. He was standing over by the window staring out and she had begun, 'It's only me, how about a question-and-answer session—Buzz? You might at least turn round when I speak to you!'

She had come further into the room, feeling a little cross because he didn't have to be so stiff with her, even if they'd scarcely met recently. Then she saw with horror that his fair skin was all blotchy and his shoulders were stiff and there was something very like despair in his reddened eyes. She gulped and moved closer to him.

'Hey, I'm sorry . . . Do—do you want me to go away?'

'No,' he said bleakly, and simply looked at her.

'Well then . . . Do you want to talk about it? Buzz? What *is* it, love—exams? Oh, come on now, you'll do all right!'

'I probably shan't even take them. My head's all in pieces—'

'Oh, of course it isn't, or it'll soon go back together again! Why, anyway?' The terrible despair in his face was something new, and she began to be really worried. 'Come on, lovey, it's only me, and you really *had* better talk about it! Sit down—you can't go on standing there and—'

'And wishing I wasn't alive? You can stand looking out of windows and feel that—'

'Buzz, you wouldn't!' Cherry exclaimed fiercely. They were on the second floor and she glanced sharply towards the window. At least it was shut.

'Guess not. You can't here, can you? Not with the job we do . . . It isn't bloody high enough anyway,' he said bleakly, frightening her so that she spoke to him quite sternly.

'No, you *can't* with the job we do! Haven't you seen enough people dying who don't want to? Please, Buzz love, do sit down and talk to me about it! You *can't* be in such a panic over the exams! I know it's RGN quite soon, and then the hospital finals a couple of weeks after that, but you'll manage—you *know* you will!'

'Like I said, I probably shan't even take them. I don't care any more. I just want to go right away!' He glanced at her very bleakly, but he did move away from the window and sat down slowly on one corner of his bed. 'It isn't exam nerves,' he said bitterly, 'and all right, I will tell you about it . . . I love someone. I love her. Oh, she *can't* . . .'

'Buzz—honey.' Cherry had to wake him up from the despair he was falling back into. 'Tell me. It might help.'

'Her name's Jarmila—Jarmila Singh. She's—my friend Kedi's sister. I used to meet her going round there. She was only just a kid in the beginning. Then . . . she grew up kind of suddenly. She used to come out with Kedi and me. They're very strict, you know, she wasn't allowed out on her own. Only then . . . Well, I fell in love with her. And she with me.' His hands twisted together suddenly. 'I wanted to tell her father, but she always said no, or she couldn't meet me at all . . . We used to meet secretly when she could pretend she was going round to a girl friend after school. Cherry, she's so sweet and bright and intelligent! She's eighteen now—'

'Go on, love. What happened?'

'Oh, Kedi found out we were meeting, and followed her.

We had a terrible row about it. He was my friend, too—I thought,' Buzz said bitterly. 'It wasn't as if I didn't want to marry her—I did! Just as soon as I qualified! And she wanted it too—although she'd never say she *would*, only that she loved me and wanted to. But then after Kedi saw us, she was forbidden to see me at all. *He* forbade her; though that was effective enough because he only agreed not to tell their father if she promised never to see me again. And then he told me that she's been promised in marriage to someone ever since she was fourteen . . . and she can't go against it.'

'Can't she?'

Buzz shook his head. 'I tried that,' he said grimly. 'I wanted to go to their father and ask if she couldn't marry me instead. Or—or just run off with her, for that matter. But it was pointed out to me,' he drew a shuddering breath, 'that if she did that she'd lose her culture and her parents and everything—that I wouldn't be being fair to her. And no way would the family let her marry a non-Sikh, not ever. Oh, it's not all one-way, you know,' he said bitterly, 'we're just as *out* to them as people like my father think they are to us. We couldn't even talk about it! Kedi watched her all the time so that she wouldn't break her promise and see me. Except just once, to say goodbye . . . with him standing three feet away.'

'Couldn't it *possibly* come right in the end?' Cherry asked hesitantly, but he shook his head.

'No.' And suddenly, heartbreakingly, there were tears rolling down his cheeks again, openly. 'Do you know what today is? It's her *wedding* day—and so I was just standing there and . . .'

Cherry's arms went round him and she held him very tightly as his head went down on her shoulder. 'Oh, poor Buzz,' she said gently, rocking him a little for instinctive comfort. 'Oh, I'm so sorry . . . Poor love, it's awful . . .'

Poor Buzz—him, of all people. Buzz who had said so snootily that no one was going to distract him before he got his RGN. 'There are still the exams,' Cherry said steadily over his head, 'your *job*, my lad, and while it may seem small comfort, work's an—an anodyne, is that the word? I should know. It may not be what you want most in the world, but it sure takes your mind off things.' She was talking as much for the soothing sound of her voice as expecting her words to get through to him—talking half to herself, too. He did seem to have heard her, though, because he said with muffled despair,

'I don't think I *can* go on. I've told you, my head's all to pieces. I've tried—I just can't concentrate—'

'You will. And I'm going to help you—yes, I am! We'll go through everything together. You know—like we did early on?'

'I can't, Cherry. I'll never make it. I'm all in bits! I might as well quit now, I'll only fail. Besides, what's the use of any of it?'

'Lots of use, and don't you dare argue with me! Besides—Buzz? After all the fighting you did to get the career you wanted—are you going to let your father think he was *right*?'

It was the key: his head came up. 'I wish I could,' he said, with less of a shake in his voice. 'I meant to show him. Oh God, though, I'm not sure if I *can*—'

'Oh yes. You'll do it for me—and with me. And you'll do it to show your father how right you were. You'll even do it for your Jarmila, because I'm sure she wouldn't want you to fail. Come on, Buzz my dear, we can do it! I need your help as well as you needing mine. We'll get through and shine, by a team effort!'

Oh help, she was sounding like Annis Lamb—but it worked. And it went on working.

After that she was with Buzz all the time. She was almost policing him, making sure that he wasn't going to fall into despair again. She even changed some duties to make her off duty fit in with his, and they were always together—so much so that one or two people started to look knowing. Cherry didn't care what anyone thought, because she was stubbornly determined to get Buzz through the exams whatever else she did. She nagged him. He even got cross with her, though she could feel underneath that he was still clinging to her like a lifeline. They revised, talked, made future plans. He even started thinking about afterwards, and *when* they qualified, not *if*. And then the official RGN papers hit them.

Cherry came out saying, 'There you are, you see, we did get diseases of the liver—wasn't that lucky we looked them up?'

Then there were the hospital finals. They didn't seem nearly as bad, though ward assessments right through training counted in with those, too.

'We'll have to do our six months' staffing.' Buzz was making plans again. He had started going on about them quite obsessionally. Everyone hoped to get their six months' staff nursing within Northborough Royal itself, and there was a certain amount of sudden willingness to do extra duties and being intensely polite to Sisters and Nursing Officers. '*Then* I don't see why we shouldn't set up this convalescent home idea. Look, there's a hole in the market, and I'm sure my grandmother would guarantee us a loan. We'd both be qualified nurses with experience—'

He was including Cherry in his plans. He seemed to be taking it for granted that she'd come into partnership with him. He had a streak of his father in him after all, she thought, wanting to set up in business on his own.

'It's an idea . . . I haven't any money to put in, though, and I'm sure you ought to find a partner who has. Anyway, let's—let's wait until the results are out, shall we?'

She didn't know what she wanted to do, and that was the truth. At least exams had taken her mind off her dull ache. Now they were over she felt quite lost. Emptiness seemed to stretch ahead of her.

She ran into Annis Lamb and the Sister stopped to press her to join a committee and also mentioned sweetly that there just *might* be a staff nurse job in the Eye Department. Cherry was such a good team nurse . . . She even called her Cherry rather than Nurse Langton. Cherry didn't mean to ask—and then found herself asking, very politely, 'Have you heard anything of Mr Treneager, Sister?'

'Oh, yes, we're in touch! He's not coming back, you know. I rather thought he wouldn't. It's rather a small department here, and he's talented enough for better things. Mr Bland will get the permanent job, I'm quite sure.' Annis smiled her sweet smile. 'And you, Cherry —I'm not going to tell you, of course, but the RGN lists *have* arrived and they'll be posted up tomorrow—the hospital finals list too! And I think you'll be pleased!'

Cherry wasn't so much pleased as stunned. She had passed her RGN with distinction. She had also won the Hospital Silver Medal.

Buzz had passed—less well than her, but passed. She took care to let him think he would have done better than her if he hadn't been upset, because she could feel that he needed to think so. She felt almost numb about her silver medal anyway. It didn't seem to mean anything compared with that confirmation of her thoughts—'He isn't coming back, you know—'

'Don't nurse illusions, my dear—I'm not coming back for you . . .'

'Well, who's the bright girl, then?' Pat Bairstow asked her teasingly, adding, 'I'm right proud of you! And what's all this about a convalescent home, you and your lad? You'll do your staffing first, of course . . .' He looked deadpan for a moment. 'I've a staff nurse vacancy coming up myself. Of course you may not want it—'

'Pat, I can't think of anything I'd rather do! Can I really?'

So that was fixed. Buzz got a job on General Surgical, which he had been angling for because he thought it would be good for later and post-operative convalescents. He was still deep in his plans—for himself and Cherry. Cherry was still stalling, and saying he ought to find a partner with money to put in. She just didn't know . . .

Then she suddenly got a letter from her bank manager, saying that five thousand pounds had been paid into her account.

It had to be a mistake. She went to see him. It wasn't. The money had been paid in anonymously, but definitely for her. The donor had given her full name, her profession, even her age—just in case there might be more than one Cherry Langton. 'A grateful patient?' the bank manager asked with a smile.

'Could you at least tell me *where* it was paid in?'

'I'll look it up, Miss Langton.' He went away; came back.

'London—I'm afraid that's all the information I have!'

It was a thoroughgoing mystery. Cherry puzzled over it. She went to bed trying to think *who* she knew who was rich—and generous—and in London . . .

She woke up in the morning with a sudden sharp suspicion. Who did she know who was rich . . . ?

She sought out Annis Lamb, and managed to insert a very casual query. 'Is Mr Treneager in London . . . ?'

'Yes, he is. He's been back from America a little while and doing some locum consultant work and private practice while he looks round. We're in touch quite often. I believe Mr O'Neill hears from him too. You know, I was *so* sorry you decided to go to Orthopaedics instead of coming to me!'

'Would you happen to have Mr Treneager's present address, Sister?'

'Do call me Annis, you're a senior now. Yes, I think I do. It must be on my address list.' She had her list on her, too, organised lady that she was. 'I'm not sure where he's actually living, because I think he's been staying with friends and moving around. He has the use of some consulting rooms, though, just round the corner from St Joseph's. Here's the address, do write it down!'

Cherry organised her off duty to give her two clear days, looked up the trains, and caught the fast to London. She was angry—burningly, furiously angry. So it *was* him . . . and how *dared* he give her five thousand pounds? How dared he imagine she'd take it? What was she—someone to be *paid off*—?

She found the consulting rooms quite easily, in a quiet street full of tall gracious houses. It was only when she got there that she hesitated. He might not be there today. Still, she'd got two whole days to find him in—and throw his money back in his face. In a sack, if necessary!

She went in. A pleasant middle-aged secretary told her that Mr Treneager *was* in. 'But do you have an appointment?' she asked dubiously.

'No, I'm a personal friend, and I just happened to be passing. Would you ask him if he'd see me, please? And tell him I'll wait, if he's busy?'

The woman went to an inner door, tapped, and opened it. 'Mr Treneager, there's a Miss Langton here to see you,' Cherry heard her saying, and then a deep murmur. Then the woman came back saying, 'Would you please go in?'

Cherry drew a deep breath and marched in. It was a pleasant room, nicely if anonymously furnished. She didn't look round it. Ashley was sitting behind a large desk and he didn't get up as she came in. He was looking just the same . . . thin and dark and distinguished; eyes so dark they were almost black; lined; almost lazy-looking in the way he sat with his legs stretched out; very tidy. And watchful.

A silence stretched between them as they looked at each other. Then he said, 'This is a surprise. Will you sit down?'

'No, I won't. And it isn't a surprise, or it shouldn't be. You know damned well why I've come, don't you? You gave me five thousand pounds—didn't you?'

'Did I? Now, what's become of banking confidentiality?'

'Oh, don't give me that! You knew I'd guess! And you can have it back!'

'I don't want it back. All this fuss about a little money? You can call it a wedding present,' he said coolly, unmovingly.

'A w –' Cherry broke off, staring at him, her mouth a thin line of anger. 'Don't you mean a pay-off?' she asked scathingly. 'And how *could* you? You know perfectly well I won't take it—and if you don't know, you're just plain stupid, and no one would call you that! How *could* you—'

'It's what I said it was, a wedding present. Surely that's allowed, between friends?' She wasn't even managing to make him angry—or perhaps she was. A muscle jumped in his cheek. 'I put it there anonymously because of your hang-ups, yes. To avoid the necessity of your coming screaming in here—'

'I'm not screaming.' Cherry kept her voice deliberately in its normal range. She even sat down, on the chair in front of his desk, elaborately—and grimly. She was actually sitting down because her legs didn't seem to want to hold her up any more. They were turning to cotton wool just from looking at him. All her misery came surging back through every vein and bone and muscle, and she fought it down.

'Do tell me,' she asked, 'who I'm supposed to be marrying?'

'You and young Bascombe are back together again, aren't you? And quite openly inseparable. I like to keep in touch,' Ashley said drily—and meeting her accusing eyes without a flicker in his own. 'It sounds very suitable. You've known each other a long time. He's a good-looking boy and quite able—'

'Dear me, the grapevine does have a long arm!' She was mixing metaphors, but she didn't care. 'Annis, I suppose?'

'I also have other sources—'

'Oh yes, Luke O'Neill! And he's quite a gossip. Thank you so much for your interest, Mr Treneager. But—'

'You have some plans for—a convalescent home, isn't it? Well, the money could be useful to put into that. It'll give you a proper stake—a partnership.' That muscle was jumping in his cheek again, though there was no other sign of emotion. 'Grapevines,' he said, as if anticipating her comment, 'would have tendrils, I think, don't you?'

If only he would come out from behind the desk, she could hit him. It seemed to stretch like a barrier between them. If only he would come out from behind the desk . . . Cherry didn't know what she would have done, only that she didn't seem to stand a chance with him sitting there immobile. 'Thank you for your interest,' she said again, 'and you're *very* well informed, I can see—except for a few minor points! One, I don't intend to marry Buzz, he's a friend, that's all, which is all he's ever been! Two, yes I suppose I *might* go into partnership with him, but I haven't actually decided yet . . . and if I do it'll be on my *own* terms! And—and certainly not on any pay-off money from *you*!'

She had got through to him this time. She could see the glow of anger beginning in his eyes. 'Will you stop saying that?' he said roughly. 'You know perfectly well it wasn't intended to be—'

'Oh? What else did you think I'd think it was? Let's look at the facts. I'm a—a sort of unwanted extra you've happened to pick up along the way. You didn't mean to, you made that quite clear! You told me I'd get over you: I haven't. Not that it matters. It's *my* business if I have to go round being heartsick about the most impossible man ever!

You've—you've tormented me and accused me of being immoral and God knows what else! And now you're trying to marry me off to salve your conscience! Oh yes, you are, Ashley!' She wished he'd move, instead of sitting there so still letting her angry words hit him. 'And—and if you want me to forget you, which I can't anyway, how the *bloody hell* do you think I can forget someone who suddenly puts large sums of money into my bank account? Because you knew I'd guess—you *must* have known!'

'Maybe I did know.' There was a great deal of that rough anger in his voice now, and his eyes had narrowed. 'As for the "unwanted extra . . ." don't put yourself so low! And I doubt if you know as much as I do, about *wanting* . . .' As her pulse began to beat extra fast he was going on. 'Maybe—just maybe—I fell prey to temptation—and jealousy—and put that money in your bank account because it was the surest way I could think of to bring you down here like a bat out of hell to throw it back in my face!'

'Did you? *Did* you, Ashley?'

'I may have done. We know I'm very bad at recognising my own motives, don't we?' But he still hadn't moved.

There was one last desperate chance. Cherry was willing to try anything. Besides, it would show whether he really cared. Or not.

'Actually I probably will marry Buzz in the end,' she told him, with her chin up and a touch of scorn in her voice. She kept her eyes steadily on Ashley's face. 'He'll never love me, of course. He's in love with a Sikh girl, Jarmila, but she had to go into an arranged marriage and it almost broke him up. That's why I was around with him all the time, to keep him going. But yes, Buzz may well decide one of these days that I'd make a reasonable wife for him. He won't expect me to have other chances because he sees me as plain and ordinary and—and sensible—and of course since I know about Jarmila, he can count on my not expecting too much from him! It's pretty well bound to happen, really. Particularly if I go into partnership with him. We'll get married—and he'll never pretend to love me—and I'll never love him, though I probably won't let him know it—'

'That's emotional blackmail!' grated Ashley. 'And you

needn't think I'm taken in by it!' But there was the flicker of something in his eyes.

'No, it's not, it's truth. That's what *will* happen.' Because Cherry could suddenly see that it very well might, she found herself caught up in grief. Ashley's outline turned misty, and she got to her feet, wearily. 'I got the Silver Medal,' she found herself saying irrelevantly, and with a tiny break in her voice, 'because of all you taught me. Only I can't think of anything at all that I want to do with it . . .'

It was as if something snapped and released him. Ashley came round the desk and scooped her into his arms, holding her roughly but very very tightly. 'Oh, come *here*,' he growled, and then, 'You certainly will *not* marry some idiot boy who thinks you're plain and sensible—good God, he wouldn't last five minutes! How could you be fool enough—but I suppose you would, wouldn't you, just to spite me?' He drew in a ragged breath, and seemed to be between anger and exasperation, and—love? The look in his eyes said so. 'You can't say I didn't warn you, my darling—I'm very bad husband material! I'm a workaholic and I lose my temper—'

'I know. Oh, I do know! But *I love you*!'

'Marry me and it's for life—no way out, ever. I'm not—'

'No way out ever is fine by me.' Cherry looked up at him with tenderness, out of her stubbornly enduring love, and suddenly she was smiling radiantly at him from a bubble of happiness. 'Oh, Ashley, I have *missed* you!'

'About a fraction of the amount I've missed you, I should imagine,' he said drily; but the hand that moved round to stroke her hair was gentle, and there was a touch of disbelieving wonder in his eyes. 'You're a stubborn child—young woman!—but I love you very, very much. And you're beautiful. You were such a funny little round thing when I first saw you, but now—'

'Oh, you beast—and it was being such a lovely compliment!' Cherry wanted to look outraged, but her smile kept breaking through. Then her face became serious, and she reached up to touch his cheek as she stood in the circle of his arms. 'I'm not beautiful,' she said gravely, 'but I'll love you for ever.'

His arms tightened and he turned his face briefly against her hand. 'Yes, you are beautiful,' he told her, his voice a deep honeyed rumble. 'To me. You can be no more than an ordinary very pretty girl to everyone else if you want to be—and I think you'd better, don't you? Knowing my jealous streak! But to me, you're . . . Cherry sweetheart, are you—absolutely sure? My track record really isn't very good.' There was that bitterness on his mouth again, and a haunt from the past in his eyes. 'You're so young, you deserve better than—'

'Stop it, Ashley!'

'Ordering me about?' he asked with the ghost of his old mockery.

'Yes.' Cherry put a finger against his lips to stop him saying anything more. 'Someone has to. Someone has to make you see—that *now*'s the only important time. Now and the future. The past is over, Ashley.'

'Yes,' he said, smiling down at her in a way that made her heart flip, and do a complete somersault. 'Yes, it is.'

Doctor Nurse Romances

Amongst the intense emotional pressures of modern medical life, doctors and nurses often find romance. Read about their lives and loves in the other two Doctor Nurse titles available this month.

NURSE ISOBEL'S DREAM
by Hazel Fisher

'A dream of a doctor' — that was what all the nursing staff of Highcastle Hospital in Northumbria called Adam Sheridan. All, that is, except Staff Nurse Isobel Ford, who resented the coldly handsome Dr Sheridan's jibes about her Southern origins.

LOVE'S CURE
by Margaret Barker

Six years after completing her training, Staff Nurse Sarah Williams finds herself back on the wards. She's the new nurse — for the second time around — but this time there's the added complication of her widowhood, her two children and hostile Dr John Simmonds!

Mills & Boon
the rose of romance

Mills & Boon

4 Doctor Nurse Romances FREE

Coping with the daily tragedies and ordeals of a busy hospital, and sharing the satisfaction of a difficult job well done, people find themselves unexpectedly drawn together. Mills & Boon Doctor Nurse Romances capture perfectly the excitement, the intrigue and the emotions of modern medicine, that so often lead to overwhelming and blissful love. By becoming a regular reader of Mills & Boon Doctor Nurse Romances you can enjoy SIX superb new titles every two months plus a whole range of special benefits: your very own personal membership card, a free newsletter packed with recipes, competitions, bargain book offers, plus big cash savings.

AND an Introductory FREE GIFT for YOU.
Turn over the page for details.

Fill in and send this coupon back today and we'll send you

4 Introductory Doctor Nurse Romances yours to keep FREE

At the same time we will reserve a subscription to Mills & Boon Doctor Nurse Romances for you. Every two months you will receive the latest 6 new titles, delivered direct to your door. You don't pay extra for delivery. Postage and packing is always completely Free. There is no obligation or commitment – you receive books only for as long as you want to.

It's easy! Fill in the coupon below and return it to MILLS & BOON READER SERVICE, FREEPOST, P.O. BOX 236, CROYDON, SURREY CR9 9EL.

Please note: READERS IN SOUTH AFRICA write to Mills & Boon Ltd., Postbag X3010, Randburg 2125, S. Africa.

FREE BOOKS CERTIFICATE

To: Mills & Boon Reader Service, FREEPOST, P.O. Box 236, Croydon, Surrey CR9 9EL.

Please send me, free and without obligation, four Dr. Nurse Romances, and reserve a Reade Service Subscription for me. If I decide to subscribe I shall receive, following my free parcel c books, six new Dr. Nurse Romances every two months for £6.00*, post and packing free. If decide not to subscribe, I shall write to you within 10 days. The free books are mine to keep i any case. I understand that I may cancel my subscription at any time simply by writing to you. am over 18 years of age.
Please write in BLOCK CAPITALS.

Name ______________________________

Address ______________________________

____

______________________________ Postcode ______________________________

SEND NO MONEY — TAKE NO RISKS

Remember, postcodes speed delivery. Offer applies in UK only and is not valid to present subscribers. Mills & Boon reserve the right to exercise discretion in granting membership. If price changes are changes are necessary you will be notified. Offer expires 31st March 1986.

8DN

EP1

*Subject to possible V.A.T.